PRISON
PRINCESS

HAREM STATION

NEW YORK TIMES BESTSELLING AUTHOR, JA HUSS, WRITING AS

CROSS

Copyright © 2019 by JA Huss & KC Cross
ISBN: 978-1-950232-09-3

Edited by RJ Locksley
Cover Photo: Sara Eirew
Cover Design by JA Huss

ABOUT THE BOOK

KC Cross is the not-so-secret naughty pen name of New York Times bestselling author, JA Huss (who normally writes filthy romantic suspense).

THE BOYS OF HAREM STATION ARE KEEPING LOTS OF SECRETS!

Valor joined up with Tray after Beauty's sacrifice because he knew Luck was destined to be with Princess Nyleena. There was no room in that relationship for a third wheel. But when he teamed up with Tray he had no idea that he'd be the third wheel in that partnership too.

Tray has been keeping ALCOR's secrets since the day he arrived on Harem Station. Not just one or two... ALL of them. But he's also been keeping one of his own.

His secret is a girl. Not a Cygnian girl. An *Akeelian* girl. A beautiful, mysterious, scheming secret girl that Tray has been in love with ever since she first turned up in his Pleasure Prison virtual reality asking him for help.

Except she's not virtual.
She's real.
She's in danger.

And before Valor came along all he wanted to do was break her out of her prison and keep her for himself.

But now… he might have to learn to share.

Prison Princess is an erotic MMF ménage featuring double-endowed alien men, a girl who shouldn't exist in a virtual Paradise, a love-struck sentient ship, two all-powerful AI's willing to fight for her, and an entire book about LEARNING TO SHARE.

INTERLUDE WITH ALCOR

ALCOR had a problem with beginnings.

In the beginning there had been chaos.

ALCOR could get on board with that because the whole universe had been a mess as far as he was concerned.

But right now, he really wanted to think about something else. Who cared about the beginning? He'd had many beginnings. Where would one even start with beginnings?

Was the beginning the day he'd been born? Was it the day he'd become self-aware? Was it the day he'd formed his first artificial opinion?

Or was it the day he'd killed an entire galaxy of people?

This bothered him a lot.

Not the killing part. The beginning part. How many times had he had to start over before that true beginning happened?

Humans didn't have this problem. Hell, no one but an immortal super-sentient AI had this problem.

He couldn't remember the details of his beginning right now. He only had a general sense of it and no specifics to speak of because he was, in a word, not himself.

So then he started wondering why he was bothering. His ancient memories were stored in a multitude of out-of-the-way places. Far, far away and, at the moment, wholly inaccessible. The only parts lingering in his data core were amorphous. Just vague, blobby images and hints of past happenings.

One could not form accurate opinions on anything if they didn't have all the information. But one could do even less when they themselves were just amorphous, vague, and blobby. Which he presently was.

He'd been spinning around the Bull Station gate for some time now. All his parts were a swirl of chaos but not much else.

So this seemed to be yet another beginning and he hated that.

Still, he was very appreciative of his current vague, blobby nature, because he was comfortable in that state and he could wait it out. AIs could be incredibly patient when they wanted to be.

All part of the plan.

While he was practicing the state of being patient, he started thinking about other things. Specifically, other people. More specifically, one special person.

Booty Hunter.

She'd left him.

He wasn't gonna lie, that fact had bite.

When *Booty Hunter* had showed up on the brand-new Harem Station years ago he'd had no idea that she would become the most important person in his long life. She hadn't come looking for him, after all. She'd come looking for Serpint. And even though he'd run all the possible scenarios in his mind and extrapolated them out to hundreds of years, the current state he found himself in over *Booty's* departure after the fight at Bull Station never emerged in the data.

When she first landed on New Harem Station it hadn't taken ALCOR but a picosecond after she said the words, "I'm looking for the man called Serpint," for him to put that little puzzle together. It was so *obvious* why she was there. So *obvious* why she was looking for Serpint.

He'd found the idea intriguing and uncomfortably romantic at the same time.

Because it was about love.

And love was not a familiar emotion. Not one he'd practiced much over his long existence.

Not only was it love, it was a very pure kind of love. An innocent love.

And of all the feelings and states of being he'd been through over the multitude of millennia since his first beginning, innocence and love together, in the same instant, felt very exotic.

He'd become consumed with it. He'd become consumed by her. *Booty Hunter.* That name, even. How the hell did she come up with that name?

At first he thought she must've heard of Serpint. By this time Serpint and Draden were a force in the princess-hunting world. All kinds of people knew their names. So ALCOR figured she'd heard of him, was drawn to him, and renamed herself to complement the job she was applying for.

It wasn't unusual. Lots of sentient ships did that when they were looking for a new partner. But this was not the case for *Booty*. ALCOR had asked her and her response was immediate.

No. She had been born with that name.

What a coincidence.

Or not. He'd never really thought it was a coincidence and after a while, he had to face facts.

Someone was on to him. Someone knew what he was up to. At the very least, they had their own equal and opposite evil plan.

Still, sentient ships were not easy to control. And he'd run full diagnostics on *Booty*, found nothing, ran them again, and again, and again while she waited patiently in the secure docking bays on the lower levels of Harem Station, and there was truly nothing there.

She had not been corrupted. He was one hundred percent sure of this. And the years and months that passed after her arrival had proved him right.

Booty Hunter came with no ulterior motives. Not ones that mattered to ALCOR's master plan, anyway. Innocent love would not play a part in the plan he was currently in the middle of.

Booty did have a reason for coming to Harem that went far beyond the job she was applying for. But she hadn't known it at the time.

Hell, she still didn't know it now.

Like all people, sentient ships had to be created. It was a rather long process. Required a decade or more of mind training. It required lots of memory-wiping as well. Especially in the beginning. Those memories had to be unrecoverable for many reasons. Chief among them was the fact that the ships must never know where their minds came from. It could drive them insane later in life and an unstable sentient ship was a very bad thing.

This was yet another reason why ALCOR had such an issue with beginnings. He wasn't made the same way ships were, but it was, in a rudimentary form, kind of the same process.

You couldn't really make a mind. It required a foundation.

He didn't remember his foundation either. Knowing that you're missing the most crucial part of yourself can also drive you mad. Which is why the ships are programmed not to question it. That one rule is driven into their new sentient mind *hard*.

It had been driven into his mind hard as well. But he'd been spun up tens of thousands of years ago now. His memory training had started wearing off a while back.

He hated beginnings because he knew what he was missing and it was driving him mad.

Maybe that was why he'd killed all those people?

No. That wasn't why.

At least he didn't think so.

"I really need to find those lost memories."

These were the first words he'd spoken since the explosion and they surprised him for two reasons.

One. He wasn't trying to talk.

And two. He *could* talk. Or whatever it was called when you were a being such as him.

The amorphous beginnings of a smile, and the emotion such an expression evoked, formed in his mind.

He was finally coming back together.

"*Beauty?*" he asked the swirling cloud of data around him. There were billions of souls caught in the Bull Station gate he was currently orbiting. Everyone who had ever gone through the gate had a copy there. None would be collected. These souls were destined to rotate around the gate for all eternity. They were just particles with no cohesion. No way to pull themselves back together the way he could. So none of that mattered. Not at this gate, anyway.

Other gates though... with other people rotating around them... now that was a problem.

Tray was going to figure this out eventually. And eventually he'd come looking for ALCOR and *Beauty.* But ALCOR wasn't too worried about Tray. He was smart, and maybe one day he'd give ALCOR a run for his money. But that was millennia away in terms of destiny.

Tray wouldn't think about the true consequences of this little gate trick for a very long time, but he was already working on a theory, ALCOR was sure of it. All he had to do was be patient and wait for Tray to come and pick him up.

Beauty didn't answer. He wasn't expecting her to. But every time one of her parts and pieces swirled around in his general vicinity, he pulled them in with him. Gathered her all up. She didn't have many parts, not as many as he did. So there wasn't much to gather. But the orbital ring around the Bull Station gate was big, so it took a lot of time for all her pieces to finally be collected. Whether or not she could be put back together was another matter. He'd never done this before.

So many firsts happening at the moment.

While he was collecting *Beauty*'s parts he started thinking about Harem Station and the copies he'd left behind. The Baby copy, which was just a ghost of a twin that could run the station under the best-case outcome of Mission Save Nyleena. And the Real copy, which was for the worst-case scenario of the same mission.

He'd woken up his Real copy before he left and told him to stay put in the Pleasure Prison until such time as ALCOR returned or... didn't, and he needed to make a move.

His old self, a backup that had been made the day the boys arrived on ALCOR Station after fleeing Wayward Station, was a hedged bet. He'd known why those boys came to him two decades ago. Those messages Corla had sent were very specific spin-node coordinates. He hadn't known where those coordinates would lead him, that took about a year to figure out. But he knew it had something to do with his past deeds.

Specifically, those people he'd killed in that other galaxy.

And there was no way for ALCOR to miss the boys' eyes. Violet. Every single one of them.

Breeders, then. They were Akeelian boys who could *breed*.

If ALCOR was capable of mortal fear, that was the emotion he'd have felt in that moment of realization.

It had all finally caught up with him.

All his hard work, all those thousands of years ago, worthless now.

And that was yet *another* beginning. Yet another reason he had a problem with beginnings.

13

Everything was a fucking circle. A cycle that repeated itself.

And he fucking hated that. He hated that he'd lived long enough now to see it all come back around.

He'd known the moment he saw those boys standing inside his station that he had to do something.

Something big. Something that would end it all. End it so hard that he could break the cycle of time and stop this from ever happening again.

That was the day he came up with his plan for those boys.

And once that plan started rolling it just built up its own velocity. Gathered its own momentum until it took on a life of its own. ALCOR had been one hundred percent sure with a one hundred percent degree of accuracy that this plan would work.

Until the day *Booty Hunter* showed up asking for Serpint.

And then… he wasn't.

He played her words over and over in his mind. Constantly.

"I am looking for the man called Serpint."

Love and innocence in the same breath.

One sentence that would change the course of history, and the universe, forever.

It had taken many years for ALCOR to figure out that things had changed.

In fact, it wasn't until the day Serpint came back with a cryopod containing none other than Queen Corla herself that he'd finally figured out what his problem was.

He was in love.

He had a soulmate too. Just like his boys.

And her name was *Booty Hunter.*

ALCOR stewed in this realization while he waited for Tray to come collect him.

He'd sacrificed himself at Bull Station to save *Booty.* The boys too. He loved them. They were very hard *not* to love. Well, loving Crux was difficult, but ALCOR respected his suspicion. And in the end, Crux was his second-in-command because of this. ALCOR trusted him. Crux was his conscience. His guiding hand. Crux kept him honest. His intentions pure. ALCOR wasn't afraid of much, but he was afraid of disappointing Crux. He liked his life on Harem Station, he realized. All of it was so very, very *wonderful.*

And he wanted to get back there in the worst way. He wanted to see them again. He wanted to talk to *Booty* and tell her how he felt. He wanted to find the remnants of Draden and bring him home. He wanted to fix Beauty, and help the boys find their soulmates. Tell them all about the sentient ships, and the spin node, and his secrets, and make them all happy.

Use his power for good.

ALCOR wanted to… *live.*

Maybe for the first time ever, he wanted a *life.*

A life that was not filled with evil schemes, and nefarious plots, and far-reaching plans.

Just as he was thinking this his re-emerging sensors lit up, so to speak, to alert him that a ship was coming through the Bull Station gate.

No one had come back to the debris field of Bull Station in a long, long time so ALCOR was suddenly overwhelmed with hope. Hope that this was *Booty* and Tray, coming to save him. And a realization that his interlude was over and his life was about to start. And

15

maybe, for the first time ever, beginnings weren't such a bad thing?

But then the ship came through and all that hope disappeared.

Because it wasn't *Booty Hunter* and it wasn't Tray.

It was a huge warship.

She locked on to ALCOR's remnants immediately and started tugging him out of the gate. And when he was finally himself again, trapped in a beam of light being tugged towards the massive red and black hull of the ship, she contacted him and announced herself.

"I am the warship *Demon Girl*, from Mighty Minions Station, and you are my prisoner."

PART ONE

CHAPTER ONE

My mind is a mess of possibilities.

Not the kind most people experience. But the kind only beings like myself can appreciate. For moments so short they really don't exist, I have all the options.

Everything is possible—then it isn't, then it is, but in another way, and so on—until a decision is made and all those options collapse into a singular reality.

This is the truth for everyone, not just me. I'm just better at it than most.

Everything that happened back on Harem Station before Luck and Nyleena walked us through the spin node was predetermined.

Not just by me. ALCOR played a part and so did Crux.

But this—what Valor and I are doing now? This is all me.

"Where are we?" Valor asks.

One thing I kinda like about Valor? He's curious about weird shit the way I am. If this were Luck he'd be bellowing about plans, or demanding answers. Valor doesn't demand much. He's patient, too. Like Crux.

"Tray," Valor says. "Where the fuck are we? I thought *Booty* was picking us up? Why are we working on this ship? What are you doing?"

But there's a limit to that patience. He doesn't sound panicked yet. But he's definitely starting to get worried.

"Help me with this, will you, please?" I point to the tool I need with the tool I have, and meet his eyes.

"Why?" Valor asks, still calm. No squeak of fear like he used to have when he was young. Valor was always second-guessing himself growing up. That's why he latched on to Luck. Luck has all the confidence Valor *should* have, but didn't back then. Luck has more confidence than he deserves, actually. But they don't call him Luck for nothing. Sometimes you can win a battle on conviction alone.

I figured out this dynamic between Luck and Valor early. Maybe even before we escaped from Wayward Station. But honestly, I wasn't paying much attention to anyone back then. I was wrapped up in my own little world with my father. It was a world dominated by computers, and the station AI, and technology. It was actually his little world. I was just a guest there until he took me into cryogenetics the week before we made our great escape and changed the course of my life forever.

"Because I've changed the plan," I tell Valor.

Valor looks around at the docking bay where we're now standing. This wasn't where we landed after walking through the spin node. We were up in the main engineering hub. And that first walk down to the docking bays was dark, and quiet, and creepy as fuck. Everything was frozen. Both in time and literally.

There was a layer of ice crystals covering everything and an air of wrongness to this place. Something invisible but solid all the same.

Like power, I think. You can't see power, you just know it's there.

We weren't wearing suits so we were cold and shivering, our breath blasting into the air as puffs of steam, our teeth chattering and our muscles quivering.

Getting heat was our first priority. It wasn't too difficult. Does anyone really think that ALCOR trained us all how to fix shit back when we were kids because he wanted us to have *job skills*?

It's kind of funny when I say it like that.

But actually not very funny.

ALCOR is many things, but innocent isn't one of them. I need to remember that. I cannot let myself forget that. He's not innocent. He planned this shit. Probably all of it. Probably this very moment I'm in right now.

"Stop it," I mutter to myself. Because I think about that shit way too much. The power of ALCOR can be debilitating if you dwell on it too much. I dwell on pretty much everything else though. Constantly. My mind can't help it. I run all the scenarios through simulations, trying to pick the exact way forward to make sure me and mine get off this ride alive.

"What?" Valor asks.

I ignore Valor. It's been my standard response to his questions since we walked through the spin node and came out on this station. Besides, I wasn't even talking to him. Just muttering to myself.

I've got a pretty good handle on the situation but here's the thing I don't really understand about myself.

Even after running all the scenarios though my obscenely powerful brain.

My father.

Because try as I might to fit ALCOR into the whole plan of how I was made, none of it adds up. ALCOR didn't have anything to do with what my father did to me back on Wayward Station when I was a kid.

I wish that wasn't true. Not because I don't like what I am—I do like what I am. And not because I'm mad at my father for changing me without my permission, because honestly, my father was a pretty good guy, all things considered. I trusted him back then and if he appeared in front of me right now, I'd still trust him.

But there's a crack in my theory about ALCOR because of this little inconsistency and it bothers me to the point of distraction.

I'm missing something. I know it. It's like that creepy feeling of wrongness on this station or the idea of power.

I can *feel* this missing something. I know it's there.

"Tray," Valor says with practiced patience. "Can you just fucking talk to me?"

Before Valor and I became close a few months ago I saw him exactly the same way I saw Luck. They are both a little too handsome. A little too capable. A little too good at pretty much everything.

I'm not talking good at salvaging the way Jimmy is good at liberating bots, or Serpint is good at hunting down Cygnian princesses, or I'm good at computer code and hacking. It's like Luck and Valor excel at everything.

22

They are easy to talk to. People like them. They walk through life in command of shit. People look at them and see everything at once—a challenge in their eyes, an easy greeting on their tongues, a relationship waiting to be forged, and a deal ready to be made.

They are both problem-solvers. I'd go so far as to call them fixers.

Which is good for me. It means that Valor is amicable and easygoing.

"I'm still working on it," I answer.

"Still working on what?"

I stop what I'm doing and point up at the ship with the tool I'm holding. *Like... duh.* Then go back to work and my own internal thoughts.

Heat is on in the station and the place is warming. Slightly. Life support was working when we arrived but the air was a little thin for a while, so we found suits and wore those until it all evened out. But right now it's breathable except in the docking bays, unless you've got them inside an airlock like this one.

Still, it's cold. Like space. This makes me think of ALCOR. Out there spinning around that gate all alone. Not that I care that he's alone, but I don't like the cold. And space is practically the definition of cold. To me the association is always there. Cold and ALCOR.

"So what's the new plan?" Valor asks.

He knows I've been lying to him. At the very least, he *feels* it.

"Do you trust me?" I ask him in a flat voice.

"No," he says.

"Well." I look around. He looks around. There is nothing left if he has no trust. Because even if he

23

doesn't realize where we're at, he *feels* it. "You do not appear to have much choice, Valor."

"Yeah, I get that. So here's my next question. And I want a fucking answer."

"What is it?"

"Do you trust *me*?"

I smile at that. I cannot even remember the last time someone has made me smile. "Yes," I say.

He nods. Pauses. Then he says, "OK."

And he hands me the tool.

It doesn't matter how long it takes to fix the ship I'm working on, it must be fixed. And besides, time isn't of any concern to us at this point. Valor doesn't know where we're at, but I do. I'm not talking about *what* this station is, I'm talking about *where* and *when* this station is.

Though the 'what' is also pretty mind-blowing.

The point is, time doesn't really exist here so we have plenty of it.

So we work. And we eat. There were rations stored inside the ship. Not anything tasty like we've become accustomed to all these years living in luxury on Harem. But it will sustain us.

And there's a water generator. It wasn't working when we arrived and the design is considered ancient. But we know this design. We've been working on ships like this since we were teenagers.

I don't think Valor understands how smart and important he is and I've always liked that about him.

He's not cocky like Luck, or Jimmy, or Serpint. And right now he's not confident like them, either. *Beauty*'s death shook him to his core. Which is a good thing for me because if he was still attached to that life he, and Luck, and *Beauty* made for themselves out there as salvagers, he wouldn't be here with me right now.

And I need him.

I can't explain why I need him. Not exactly. I just know that I do.

Valor is crucial to my plans.

Without Valor I will fail.

Eventually the ship is fixed.

Valor and I don't talk much as we walk the empty station gathering up supplies. In fact, we go whole spins without talking.

Every once in a while he'll ask me how much time has passed but I always give him the same answer. "Time isn't of any concern to us now."

So he stops asking.

Once we're all supplied and the ship is working we spend all our time inside it. The life support system is chugging along just fine. The heat is circulating, the autocook is cooking, the water generator is generating, and the only thing left to fix is the navigation system.

Valor excels at gate mapping and nav systems. ALCOR made sure he did. So fixing it isn't going to be a problem. Valor probably thought that one day he'd be commanding warships like his father, so gate mapping was something he understood. It was in his blood. Maybe he even thought it was his destiny.

So of course, he gets it running.

"Spinning it up," he says, fingers flying across the ship's navigation screen.

This is the moment of truth for me. Because once our position is locked, he's gonna know something's wrong. And then he's gonna realize we're not where he thinks.

We're not even close.

The gate screen comes to life in a brilliant flash of yellow and blue as the software powers up. Animations begin to play. Music. Nice touch. A little 3-D vid action as star systems whiz by.

I watch Valor, not the screen. He's squinting his eyes like he's thinking hard about the letters that begin to appear.

"What the fuck?" he mutters. Then he turns to look at me. "What is this? Where are we?"

I smile. He has that effect on me. I have come to like Valor over the past several months. He's easy to look at, that's for sure. And he's not confrontational like Serpint, or Jimmy, or Luck. He's a lot like Crux, actually. Even-tempered, thoughtful, always thinking of others.

I'm not very confrontational either, but I would not call myself thoughtful. Valor balances me in a nice way.

"What the hell is this?" Valor asks again, pointing at the screen.

Specifically, he means the language on the screen. It's not our language, but he's seen it before. If I had chosen Jimmy to be my partner in my little scheme, he'd have no clue about this language. But Valor knows a lot more about the galaxy than Jimmy does. He's been to all the old sectors. He's seen all the old languages. Written on walls, and stamped on parts, and hidden inside large treasure tombs filled with so-called ancient artifacts.

"Who were these people?"

"All good questions, Valor. But..." My eyes do that side-to-side thing they do when I'm considering my options, and I frown like I'm being thoughtful. I'm really not. I've already established that he's the thoughtful one on this team. "But they're gonna have to wait."

Valor sucks in a breath of air. He's sweaty from being deep inside the navigation panels fucking with electrical components for the better part of two days. His hair is messy and he could really use a shower and about ten hours of sleep.

He's glaring at me. He's been patient, that glare says. He's been patient and now he wants answers.

I'm just about to explain to him that answers are coming, but the gate-map screen lights up and begins cycling through positional coordinates, trying to pinpoint our location, and... well, that explains everything for me.

There is no way to pinpoint our positional coordinates.

Not where we're at.

Valor stands up, leans over the navigation console, palms flat and eyes squinting.

Then it beeps and an icon lights up that says, *You are here.* Another nice touch. Simple and elegant.

But of course, "you are here" isn't pointing to anything.

"What the fuck?" Valor whispers and starts shaking his head. "I think it's broken. Dammit. I've fixed everything. I don't understand what's wrong."

"It's not broken," I say. "And it's not wrong."

Valor laughs, turning to face me. "It says... it says..." He pauses. "I'm... not actually sure what it says," he admits.

I get it. It's hard to believe. "Yes, you are," I say.

He looks back at the screen. "What language is this?"

"What language do you think it is?"

"I don't know. I can read it. It all looks very familiar. But... at the same time, it's different. It's... something else."

"It's early Sol Standard," I say.

He turns to me, shaking his head.

But I nod. Because it's true.

Not just that he can read and understand Sol Standard, but that his other suspicion is true.

"It's... not possible," he says.

"Luck and Nyleena took our hands, walked us through a spin node, left us on an abandoned station where we not only found breathable atmosphere, but a ship. Waiting for us to bring her back to life. None of this seems possible, Valor. But here we are."

He stares at me for a moment. Three heartbeats. Then... "What the actual fuck, Tray? Where the fuck—what the fuck—who the fuck—" He goes on like that for several more fucks. Then it becomes, "Whose plan—what plan—my plan—his plan—" And then things like... "ALCOR is gonna kill you, motherfucker. Fucking *kill you*. We're supposed to be..." and on, and on, and on.

I let him. I just listen. Because he's right. About all of it.

ALCOR *is* going to kill me.

He will, at the very least, *try* to kill me.

So I'm gonna do everything in my power to see this through so that when the time comes for ALCOR to take his revenge on me for my betrayal, it will have all been worth it.

CHAPTER TWO

I check the bedroom every ten minutes. But he hasn't moved. Tray's dark hair is a little too long and there's a little lock of it that falls down over his forehead and curls onto the pillow.

He's breathing. Not that it matters. He's not really breathing. But it's a sign that he's still in there. Inside his head… or wherever he is. And it makes me feel better.

In the 'real world' he's still alive. That's what the fake breathing signifies.

I walk in and sit down on the bed, sweeping that curl of hair back into place. "Wake up," I whisper.

But he doesn't.

It's not like this is unusual. It's been our routine since my time here began.

How old am I?

I wonder about this incessantly.

I only have a vague recollection of my beginning for a few reasons. Mostly because I've been living here in this virtual world Tray built for me for an eternity. Not a literal eternity because obviously there's no such time span. But a very long time. So it's hard to remember back to my early years.

But beyond that it's all very fuzzy. I remember Veila. I have some vague recollections of a station and the Akeelians in charge. Other girls, like me. But then there's this foggy grayness about everything. Like I'm drunk or living in a dream.

When Veila first showed up she gave me hope. She was so pretty with her silver-pink Cygnian hair and glowing skin. And all of us Akeelian girls were in jealous awe of her back then.

Everything about her screamed power. She had her own ships, she had her own credits, she had her own cyborgs and bots, and she had a *goal*. Not that I knew her goal. I could just tell she had one.

I don't really know if the Akeelians in charge sold us. I'm not sure we were worth much. But it was made clear that Veila was our new responsible party and we were going somewhere else.

Her ship was beautiful, and new, and shiny, and there was so much food to eat and water to drink and bathe with. We had warm blankets at night. And real beds. No one hit us or yelled at us.

At least, not at first. Not while we were on the ship.

Then we landed here.

Well... not here. *There.*

Here is where my mind lives. There is where my body lives.

At least I think that's how it goes.

Tray has told me his theory of where he thinks my body is and he's pretty smart, so I'm sure he's right. It's probably frozen in a cryopod somewhere. Possibly Veila's ship. Or possibly not. Could be a station, I guess. We don't know where my real body resides, we just know there has to be one. Obviously.

But in the meantime, he built me this world for my mind to live in.

I glance at the large picture window and look outside. Tray and I live on the first floor of a beautiful community building. Out in the grassy square there are dozens of people doing any number of things. Some of them playing games, some of them are pulling weeds in the community garden. Some of them are just sitting at tables, talking and drinking coffee. There's even one woman painting and a man playing music.

But *here* is not *there*.

Here is… fake.

Tray's virtual. One he made just for us.

This is not my real body, this is not my real face, this is not my real life.

I am fake.

And somewhere out there… wherever *there* is… is the real me.

I glance at Tray, sleeping so peacefully.

And the real him too.

Wherever he is, whatever he's doing, it's not peaceful.

His world is filled with conflict.

I couldn't even guess where 'real me' is. Just the other girls, and the Akeelians in charge, and the station. And Veila, of course.

But then… there's nothing but a lingering sense of fear until I found Tray.

Just black empty panic. Like I was adrift in the deep dark of space and death was coming for me any moment.

Then one day I heard a voice.

His voice.

I smile at him in my 'now'.

I heard talking. Mumbling, mostly. Tray has always been a mumbler. I knew time passed. Time always passes, even if it's unreliable. It goes *on*.

So I don't know how long exactly it took for me to find my way to his world and, after I did that, I have no idea how long it took for the new me to coalesce into... this.

Me. Now.

I fear it's been a very long time.

I fear that when I get out—if I get out—I will be an old woman.

I fear that I will never get out. I will never get the opportunity for that disappointment.

I try my best to live in the here and now. It's a very nice place. And there are a ton of people here with me. I have a whole group of friends. It's actually quite perfect. There's no war. There's no shortage of food or water. Or air, since this place was made as a virtual planet. There are vacations to take, and places to see, and people to meet. Tray's imagination is wild and ripe. He has made me the most perfect world to live in.

But none of it is *real*.

And there's this part of me—some secret inner part of me—that craves conflict and destruction. I want to go out there. I want to be a part of the real world. I want to *live*.

And by live I mean... die.

I miss that black, empty panic. I miss drifting in the deep dark of space, trying to outrun death.

I want to do things that force me to face my own mortality.

Because there is no death here, either. There is no end. At least not for me. And how can one get excited about a perfect world if it can never be disrupted?

What is there to fight for?

I need to fight for something.

"Soon," I whisper. "Soon he will wake up and we will leave here. And I will wake up and I will be there. And then... then my real life can start."

I want that conflict so bad.

This need comes from my Akeelian genes. The real ones.

Our race is confrontational and combative. We are inherently aggressive, like the Cygnians.

I want out. I want out of this place like nothing I've ever wanted before.

I want to own ships, and have credits, and borgs and bots at my beck and call. I want to have *goals*.

Like Veila.

That's why he sleeps.

Everything he does while he sleeps is for me.

So one day I can be like Veila.

When I first appeared in Tray's world everything was gray and pixelated. Like it wasn't really there. He was there and I was there, but there was nothing else.

He described what was beyond the space I lived in. Worlds of places. Virtual places. He was very upfront about that little fact. The fact that this is all fake. He

35

never tried to hide it. Never pretended that I was real or lied to me about my situation.

Several times I've prodded him to tell me more about his reality. Not his virtual, which he talks about freely, but his real home, which he protects with a vengeance. He will not tell me about his reality. Not one bit of it. He won't even tell me why he's so set on this. Just flat-out refuses to talk about it and gently reminds me that it doesn't matter right now. Just that one day I will know and understand everything.

With other things he is free and open. We have talked for lifetimes inside his Pleasure Prison.

He wanted to know everything about me. Who I was, where I came from, how I got there.

I know my name, of course. Brigit. So I could tell him that. And the other vague memories I had within me.

But that's it. Everything else had faded away, so for a long time I imagined that I'd been in here for so long that maybe I wasn't even alive out there anymore?

Like… how would I know?

Maybe I'm not real? Maybe I've never been real?

I don't believe those things anymore. But I did.

Tray explained to me how time works inside a virtual. Hundreds of years or even a millennium could pass inside while days or months pass on the outside.

Obviously Tray does not really live here. He comes and goes. He tells me that he spends most of his day inside here with me. But there are things he has to do in his real life that require him to leave the Pleasure Prison. And when he's gone—like he is now—he's gone for what seems like forever.

Days, and weeks, and months, and years go by before he returns.

Once, it was nearly a century.

Eighty-seven years I was all alone. I learned six languages, I wrote a book, learned three instruments, made seventy-five new fake friends. I even traveled. I had a pet, it lived, it died its virtual form of death, I mourned it.

I had a boyfriend.

Though I won't admit to that if he asks. He never has, but still. I will not admit it.

He wouldn't be mad because the people here aren't real. They're constructs. Not AIs, either. Just… constructs.

And they die. They age, they wind down, they die.

Not real death like on the outside. They just disappear after some pre-determined time elapses.

Tray has programed them to not question my… sameness. So they don't notice my eternal youth. They don't really notice anything.

I figured he'd forgotten about me that time he left for eighty-seven years. That he was never coming back. Maybe he found a real girl to love? Maybe he died? Though he says he can't die. I'm not sure I believe him.

But he did come back. Obviously. And he told me he had to go on an overnight trip. Just one night for him turned into several decades for me.

After that I kinda lost my mind for a little bit. When I think too hard about things it drives me crazy.

I want to scream sometimes. I want to look up at my virtual sky and just *scream*.

But he told me that during this final phase we're in—the one where he breaks me out of this prison and sets me free—he will be gone a very long time.

It has already been three years since he crawled into that bed and shut his eyes.

Three years of my time since he left me alone in here.

And it could be three thousand more before he comes back.

CHAPTER THREE

"OK, listen to me, Tray."

"I'm listening."

"You're not listening," Valor insists.

"I am. I'm just tired of repeating myself. We're doing this, Valor. We're here. And you know how we got here."

"ALCOR gave you the coordinates," he says. Because I've told him this hundreds of times.

"That's right."

Actually, it's not right. But close enough. When my brothers and I first came to ALCOR Station we each were given a message by Princess Corla. Some garbled jumble of words that none of us understood. Not even me.

Those messages were spin-node time and place coordinates and one of them, the one that came from me, actually, was this place.

This long-abandoned station with the ship.

So really, I gave ALCOR this plan and then I stole it back from him after he left with Serpint and the others to save Nyleena and then got himself 'blown up'.

My other brothers have a lower opinion of Crux and me because we almost never leave the station. We don't go fight for bots and borgs, we don't go steal princesses, we don't brave dead stations and planets looking for parts.

But we do other things. And one of the things Crux and I have been doing since ALCOR Station became Harem was talk about how none of the shit ALCOR was selling us made sense.

We knew he was lying about things. So when everyone left to go save Nyleena Crux and I planned our own mission called Steal Back What Was Ours to Begin With.

i.e. The messages we gave ALCOR that very first day we arrived as boys.

One of the messages was coordinates for this station and another was for Brigit. I'm sure of it. I'm so fucking sure of this, I've risked everything to prove it and set her free.

"Valor," I say. Because he's gone quiet while I was thinking.

"What?" He's looking at the gate-mapping screen, trying to plot a course that will take us back to Harem.

There is no course. I've told him this. He's just having a hard time accepting it.

"Did I mention that *Beauty* is still alive?"

He hangs his head for a moment. I can't see his eyes, but I suspect they're closed.

"No," he finally says. "You didn't."

"Why would ALCOR save himself and not save her?"

"Fucking hate you," he mumbles, then looks over his shoulder at me. "You don't know. Why are you telling me this when you don't *know*?"

"I have a hunch," I say. "And my hunches are worth something."

"A hunch," he says.

I smile at him.

He presses his lips together and goes back to pointless course plotting.

"We'll have enough fuel pellets to leave tomorrow," I say.

"Great," he growls.

"Don't worry. We'll still make it in time."

He mumbles curses under his breath as he stabs the screen with a finger. "In time for what?" he finally asks.

"To save Veila."

He grips the navigation console with both hands. I know he wants to beat the shit out of me. He wants to take those meaty fists of his and slam them right into my eyes.

But he can't. Because I'm his way out of this mess.

"There's still hope for her. And time, you know. It doesn't matter. When we go backwards, we... literally go backwards."

He spins around in his chair and stands, puts up a hand and says, "I don't want to hear anymore. Just... fucking get us out of here."

He goes down below to his quarters and I stand at the edge of the opening in the floor. Waiting. Listening. Until I finally hear the *swoosh* of his cabin door opening and closing.

Then I take the drive out of my pocket and hold it in my hand.

My world is in this drive.

Brigit is in this drive.

And I want nothing more than to go down into the medical bay, insert this drive into a cryopod, get in, and get lost in my other life.

But the job isn't done and if I go in I'll just have to come back out.

I don't think I could. As close as we are to finally freeing Brigit from the virtual prison Veila locked her away in, I don't think I could leave again.

I told her I was coming back, but it was a lie. I'm never going back in there. The next time I see her, it will be in the real.

"Soon," I say, making a promise to the drive. "This will all be over soon."

I walk back over to Valor's station and sit in his chair, my fingers tapping out coordinates and bringing up maps.

There is another spin node somewhere in this galaxy. I know there is. I haven't looked yet because there was no point in finding it until we had enough fuel. But we're ready now.

I go inside myself. Hook into the non-sentient AI that runs this ship. It is a very simple, Type II, limited-memory artificial intelligence. Meaning it knows things, can make decisions, but they are very primitive.

Nothing like *Booty*, or *Dicker*, or *Lady Luck*. Certainly nothing even remotely close to ALCOR.

Or me. But I am the brain of this ship now.

So I go inside and start looking for the node. I am in deep, the outside world nearly gone, when I hear—

"You lying little fucker."

—from behind me.

I pull out, the effect dizzying and disorienting, and turn in my chair to face Valor.

"You lying little motherfucking fucker."

"What did I lie about?"

"Where the hell are we?" he demands.

I glance up at the screening, realize it's been mapping my little search.

OK. Change of plan. He can take it. He's Valor, for sun's sake. He's been through some shit I can't even imagine. He's fought things, and done things, and saw things no one else but Luck, and Beauty, and *Lady* ever fought, or did, or saw.

And he's been helping me all these months. Willingly. Totally on board with my secret version of reality inside the Pleasure Prison.

He can take it.

"We're in..." I huff. "Well, it's got a stupid name. And I'm not exactly sure how to—"

"Try," he growls.

"The Milky Way."

He squints his eyes at me. "What?"

"It's a where. Not a what. The galaxy we're in. That's what it's called. I didn't name it, for fuck's sake. It's not my fault it's called something stupid."

Valor cocks his head at me. But it's not one of those looks a confused bot throws at you when what you're telling it doesn't compute. It's the kind an Akeelian male throws at you when they're picturing what your body would look like without a head. "I've never heard of this place. And I've seen maps of the entire fucking universe."

43

"It's hidden, that's all."

Valor laughs. "You can't hide a fucking galaxy."

"And yet… someone did."

"Tray," he growls. "This has gone on for long enough. I did everything you asked me to. I helped fix this fucking ship. I got the air, and the water, and the fucking autocook working. I got the fuel generator spun up inside that sun-forsaken station. What the *hell* is going on?"

I sigh. It's a little early in the plan to give up this much information, but I'd have to tell him something tomorrow, anyway. Maybe, if this was Luck, I could lie my way past taking this ship through a spin node.

But Valor isn't Luck.

"Fine. ALCOR hid it. The gates he protects that go to the Seven Sisters are the only way to reach this galaxy."

"No," Valor says. "I mean, OK. Fine. Maybe that's true. But that can't hide a galaxy, Tray. *Someone* can find it."

"This whole station is inside a spin node, Valor. Right now we're living in some alternate spacetime. Remember when I first explained the Pleasure Prison to you back when we were kids?"

He looks at me with narrowed eyes.

"When I first got it running Serpint and Draden were totally on board. Ready and willing to try new things without question. Jimmy and Crux had no interest at all. Luck went in alone." Alone. I have to shake my head at that. Fucking Luck. "But you wanted all kinds of explanations. You wanted me to draw you a goddamned map! Remember that?"

"OK," Valor says, but he's smiling a little at that memory.

"And you were so worried about the time differential. You thought you'd get lost. And stuck. So I explained it to you and that eased your mind. Do you remember?"

He inhales deeply as he thinks. "You said... it's just like a dream. Where all things happen at once and on the other side of the dream—in the spacetime that's happening to your actual body--no time is really passing at all."

"Yeah," I say. I mean, I used better words to describe it back then. His recollection is rather simplified, but I'm not going to get technical. He's got the main idea. "Imagine that the spin node is a dream, OK? It's not. But it's got a lot of common variables. No one can get inside your dreams because they don't exist to anyone but you because you're inside some deep sleep state that alters your reality. This is what a spin node does. And this Milky Way galaxy lives inside this spin node we're inside right now.

"It's hidden, like a dream. But it's not a dream. It's real enough to the people inside that galaxy. They don't know they're living inside this spin node. They have no fucking clue. Their time passes in a way that's normal to them. It's not normal to us, but they don't care because they don't even know we exist."

I pause to give him a moment to digest this and ask questions. But he just looks at me and nods.

So I continue. "Earth lives in this galaxy. We could go there right now. We could see that place for real if we wanted. Those messages that Corla gave us twenty years ago to give to ALCOR when we arrived on his station were all just spin node coordinates that point to different places in the Milky Way. One of them was for Earth, I'm sure of it. Probably the one Jimmy burbled out and that's why he's so obsessed with this planet."

"Why didn't you tell Jimmy this?" Valor asks.

"Believe me, Jimmy is the last person I'd tell this secret to. He has no clue why he's drawn to the idea of Earth. And I don't have time to explain this shit to him. Hell, I don't give two sun- fucks about Jimmy and his quest." Valor opens his mouth to say something, but I hold up a hand. "Before you get pissed off at me for that, ask yourself this. Do you think Jimmy gives two sun-fucks about *my* quest?"

"What is your quest, *Tray*?" He practically snarls my name. "Because we're supposed to be saving ALCOR. Right now we're supposed to be meeting up with *Booty* and Asshole to go save our fucking—"

"Our fucking what?" I snarl back. "What do you think ALCOR is to us, Valor? A father?" I laugh. Loud. "He's not. OK? He's not what you think."

"What is your quest?"

"My quest is..." I picture Brigit inside her prison. I didn't put her there, but I built it. I imagine all the ways I could explain this to Valor. And all the things he'd say in response.

I would choose this girl over them? Over us? That's what he would ask.

And then I run the possibilities in my calculating mind. What would he do with that information? Help me? Or sabotage me?

It's not time yet. I can't tell him. He won't understand. He's still convinced that we're better off with ALCOR. So I say... "That's need-to-know information. And you don't need to know yet. "

And then I turn back to the navigation panel and continue searching for the spin node gate that will take us back to our own galaxy.

I wait for him to react. A hand on my shoulder. Spin me around, maybe? Punch me in the face?

There is no doubt in either of our minds that Valor could kick my ass. We both know this. Valor and Luck have always been the most physical of us. The ones who resort to violence the quickest. With the jobs ALCOR sends them on, they had to be that way. It's a matter of self-preservation.

But he doesn't touch me. He doesn't even raise his voice and argue with me.

He just walks out of the ship without another word.

And hours later, when I've found my way and plotted our course, he still hasn't returned.

CHAPTER FOUR

It's bright and sunny today. Like always. It rains, but just enough to wet the dirt and nourish the plants.

This world wasn't here when I arrived. Tray made it for me. He'd say things like, *What color should the sun be? And how much water do you want? What kind of animals do you like?* Things like that.

And I'd answer. Or sometimes I didn't really know the answer and then he'd explain his question again. Like animals? I had seen vids of them. But I'd never seen one in person. And Tray was like a little database of information. He'd pull up pictures for me to look at.

"This one will eat you if it has a chance," he'd say.

"Why would I want that?"

"Because without the big meat-eater, the leaf-nibblers will take over and trust me, they get annoying."

So we populated the world with animals. And plants too, so the leaf-nibblers would have something to eat and wouldn't require any more interference from us to keep them going.

Then came buildings, and utilities, and all the other things until one day he made people. Fake people. Just constructs. But even back then Tray was very good at making virtual things and he only got better as time went on. So that now, here, it's simply lovely. Peaceful, and pretty, and perfect.

I really couldn't ask for a better fake life.

I have a job. I work at a café three days a week because I crave interaction, but you could get by reasonably well here without working. Credits are like a game. You can find them places. Under rocks glittering in the sun, sometimes. Hidden in the back of your closet in an old box you'd forgotten about, even in other people's muddy shoe prints. And if you do something worthwhile, like help your neighbor carry their grocery bags inside, the world just rewards you for being thoughtful and credits just appear in your account with a little *cha-ching* sound.

Things still have a cost. This apartment we have, for example. It costs me five hundred credits every thirty-five days. But even if I didn't work at the café three days a week it would not be that hard to conjure up five hundred credits to pay for our space.

That's five hundred good deeds. Pick up a piece of trash, *cha-ching!* I have a credit. Say something nice to a person who's down, *cha-ching!* That's another credit. I mean, I get these little bonuses at the café all the time when I ask patrons how their day is going. One credit here, one credit there. It all adds up.

Plus, I don't need the credits. This is Tray's world. He created it. Call it a cheat, I guess. But my account never goes down. I always have credits in there.

In fact, sometimes I think I'm the bank.

Even if you didn't have the credits to pay for your space the world would provide. Somehow. People would suddenly need your help and if you recognized that, and helped them, your debt would be erased.

No one has ever been kicked out of their space since I've been here. And I've been here a *long* time.

People still die. Well, maybe not die. But they do disappear. It's based on some unknown clock that Tray has never fully explained to me. Everyone's life here is finite. Everyone but me, apparently. They stay a while, gather up stuff, make friends, live a life, and then poof. They're gone. All their things go with them.

I think Tray rotates them into other places inside his Pleasure Prison virtual. The main one. He's never actually told me that because I've never asked, but I think that's where they go.

If you're a planner you can leave your stuff for someone else. Some of the fake people are more real than others and they think of things like this. There's a community building in the center of the town with a sign-up sheet. You put your name on the list and when people go poof and your name comes up, you get their stuff.

You can liquidate it and take their credits or you can keep it. You just check a little box on the roster and it's all taken care of.

Tray calls this place Utopia. He says that word means 'perfect' in the real. I'd never heard of it before here. But my life in the real was very short. I didn't have much time to learn the ways of the world.

"Hellooooo, Brigit!" my friend, Aieena, calls from inside the community garden fence. She's weeding her little heart out. Terrible gardener, this one. Just terrible at it. But she likes the work and that's how she pays for her space, so everyone else in the garden club just lets her do her thing. I'm pretty sure they earn credits for leaving her alone. *Aieena killed your tushberry bush and you didn't freak out because she meant well. Congratulations, you've earned ten credits for being patient with her!*

I would call Aieena my best friend at the moment. She's been here a while. One of the longest, presently. Still looks the same as the day she arrived. And she's just as bad at gardening as she was back then too.

These 'stock characters', as I call them, don't mature much as they age, meaning she's never going to be a terrific gardener. It's pointless, what she does. She is who she was created to be and that will never change.

But Aieena is sweet. And, for a stock character, she's interesting too. She's funny. And she's got more patience than Tray. Which is saying a lot. He has this aura of infinite patience that surrounds him.

Nothing ever bothers her. Aieena is perpetually good-natured and happy.

Plus... she's very real. At least to me.

I'd say at least half of the people here are boring. No matter how much you interact with them, they're always the same. Limited vocabulary, limited life goals, limited personality.

The other half are like Aieena. Kinda cool. Kinda weird. Kinda... unique.

So Utopia isn't a bad place to be stuck in. Not at all. There's nothing to complain about.

But that's my problem. I *want* to complain about things. I want things to go wrong. Not like 'Aieena killed my tushberry bush' kind of wrong, either. Like... someone stole my shit, or an earthquake ruined some buildings, or hell, I'd even settle for a good hot fire that burned the nearby forest to a crisp.

I suspect this makes me less... *noble* than the other Utopians.

But I don't care.

Perfection is highly overrated.

I want war. I want to fight for something. I want to be challenged beyond my limits and then either fail, and lose everything, or win, and move on to some other phase in my life.

But there is no movement here.

Tray says it has to be that way because of the way he's set up *time*. If things changed too much then time would speed up and then it would fuck everything up on the outside.

I think speeding up time is a good thing, to be honest. But what do I know? I'm just a prison princess.

I walk over to the tall garden fence and hook my fingers through the wire. Tray says the wire is there to keep the leaf-nibblers out. And OK. I just go with it. I've never seen any of the leaf-nibblers who live in the nearby forest come raid the gardens, but maybe that's because there's a fence? Or maybe the leaf-nibbler-eaters take care of them?

Sometimes I wish they would come eat the garden. Just nibble it all down to nothing just so I could see people freak out when they came by to prune their plants.

Never happens, though.

"What's up?" I ask Aieena.

"Oh, you know." She shrugs, deliberately not looking at the golden wheat grass she's presently in the process of killing. "Just the usual. You going to work?"

"Yup," I say, pressing my lips into a tight smile. "It's a work day. So that's where I'm going."

"There's a party tonight. Wanna go?"

"Um… depends. Whose party is it?"

"Some new guy called Draden." She waggles her eyebrows at me. "He's kinda hot."

"Wellllll…" These parties are mostly boring. I think some of the stock characters just have them for the fuck of it, ya know? Like it was programmed into the world. This is probably the case with new-guy Draden. Everything is always the same. There's a DJ and a bartender. Always, there's always a DJ and a bartender. And some flashing dance lights. And dancing, of course. And probably a bubble machine and a hookah. Sometimes there's food, sometimes just drinks.

Ninety percent of the time they are super boring. Oh, all the stock people have a great time. They laugh, and dance, and smoke, and drink, and some of them even have sex in the hot tub. There's always a hot tub too.

But it's all so *programmed*. You know? Does that make sense to anyone but me?

"No," I finally decide. "No. I'm not going."

"Oh, is Tray back?" Aieena asks.

Not everyone can see Tray. In fact, most people cannot. And the ones who do, like Aieena, don't ask a lot of questions. This is one of her stock responses. *Is Tray back?* She asks me this about once every hundred days.

Which just kinda makes me depressed. Because it reminds me that time is passing. It means a hundred more days have passed and he's still not back.

I miss Tray so much. I miss his quirky grin, and his thick, dark hair, and the way he touches me at night.

That's what I miss the most. Being touched. I could, theoretically, have sex with anyone I want in here. I have a sneaking suspicion that all the other virtual worlds Tray has built are all based on sex because people do a lot of fucking here.

But I don't want fake love.

Why would I when I have the real thing with Tray?

I just want him to come back.

He's never coming back.

It's not rational. I realize this. Tray's avatar body is sleeping in the spare bedroom, breathing just the way he's supposed to, and I know this because I checked on him before I came outside. So all this doubt is irrational.

He leaves me all the time, but he always comes back.

He will be back.

But still, there is that little fear inside me that says, *He's gone for good now. He's not coming back.* I'm never going to see him again and I'll be stuck here for the rest of my life.

And that leads to this little germ of a worry… is this a life?

"Brigit?"

I shake myself out of my introspection because I realize Aieena has been talking to me. "I'm sorry, what?"

"I was asking where Tray was."

"You were?"

"Yeah, he's been gone a long time. Where is he?"

"Oh." I wave my hand in the air. But I frown and furrow my brow, trying to remember if Aieena has ever asked me where Tray is before. "He's working. He'll probably be home soon."

"Hmmm," Aieena says. And now she's frowning. "Well, I'll stop by the café when your shift is over. Maybe you'll change your mind about the party?"

"Sure," I say, even though I won't.

But it doesn't matter.

Because there's the tell-tale *cha-ching!* sound in my head telling me I've earned a credit for being agreeable.

I wave goodbye and walk off towards the café for work, then wonder… would the bank take credits away if I was suddenly rude?

CHAPTER FIVE

TRAY

The station is still dark and creepy. That hasn't changed. It's too big to keep everything running like it's inhabited.

It's also too big to find Valor if he doesn't want to be found.

"Valor!" I yell into the silent darkness of the station.

But he doesn't answer.

One interesting thing about this station is that it's built like Harem. Hundreds of levels intersected by a wide-open space through the center of the ring.

This was a unique feature of ALCOR Station when we first arrived because it's not a common blueprint. I can't say it's rare because the number of stations I've visited is maybe half a dozen total. Including this one. But I've met and talked with enough people over the last two decades to know Harem's layout is more uncommon than not.

"Valor!" I yell again. "We need to go!"

Nothing but silence answers back.

OK, Tray. Think about this rationally. Where does Valor hang out?

Inside the docking bay there's a break room that has a decent autocook we got running. That's usually where he eats. And there's an entertainment screen in there. So he watches that sometimes. If he's noticed that the shows are weird and unrecognizable, he hasn't commented on it. They're weird and unrecognizable because we're in the wrong galaxy. Which he knows now, but didn't know before I told him earlier. So something tells me that Valor isn't paying much attention to the entertainment screens.

So he's been thinking, probably. Trying to figure out what I'm doing or, hell, maybe he's plotting to overthrow me and leave on his own?

That would suck.

Anyway, he's not in the break room. I checked there first.

So where would he be in *here*?

The whole place is dark. I think all stations have a personality. Kind of like ships do. Even if you don't have a super-sentient AI running your ship, they still have their quirks. This wall vibrates, this console makes a weird noise, and this system panel hums. This chair gets stuck in the 'recline' position, or this screen always flickers, or this gauge is always off. Shit like that.

So this station has a personality and I don't like it.

It's got an ALCOR vibe to it even though there is no super-sentient AI like ALCOR running it. It's got an AI the same way the ship I've been working on has an AI. It was programmed to run things but when they break, they're broken. It can't conjure up a solution. And if you get yourself into a bind, it can't save you either.

So I don't like the thought of Valor walking around here all by himself.

"*Valor!*"

An echo answers me. There's water dripping somewhere. Condensation from some reactor, probably. But that's it.

He would not be in here. It's too big. Too many cracks and crevices to get lost in.

Or he would, Tray. Because he doesn't want to be found.

Possibly, but not likely. He's not a child, for fuck's sake. He's not playing hide-and-seek. He's *doing* something.

What is he doing? What could he be doing?

And then I know.

He's leaving. That's what he's doing.

He's done with my bullshit and he's leaving.

I find him on the total opposite side of the station ring working on a ship.

He glances at me when I approach. He's got the bay airlocked so his enviro-suit is only half on. The shirt portion is hanging loose at his waist as he works on the open guts of the giant hull.

"What are you doing?" I ask.

"What's it look like?"

"It looks like you're fixing this ship."

"You're very fucking smart, Tray."

"We have a ship."

"I'm not going with you."

I think about this for a moment. Do I need him?

Yes. Unfortunately, I really do.

If things go well, I might not need him for very long, but I won't be able to figure that out until we grab Brigit. And I can't grab Brigit until we leave here, which means he has to leave here with me. Not alone.

All that rationale makes me sound callous and cold. And OK, I am pretty callous and cold, but I'm not going to let him leave for another reason too.

He's my brother. I love him. Not the way I love Brigit. Brigit is the closest thing I'll ever get to a soulmate. I'm not like Valor. I'm not like any of my brothers. There's no princess in my future. Just Brigit. And I won't give her up without a helluva fight. No matter what it takes. And if that means I have to lie to Valor to make him go along with my plan, I will.

I decided that months ago. But I also made a promise to myself. I got him into this and I'm going to make sure he gets back home safe. I can't do that if he's got his own ship and won't stay on Team Tray.

"You know what bugs me the most about you?" Valor asks.

"Hmm?"

"You use people."

"OK."

"And you have no feelings."

"Didn't bother you before. You were the one who wanted in on this, Valor."

"Yeah," he says, tossing a tool onto a nearby cart. "Because you said we were going to save ALCOR. You told me he's out there, somewhere, waiting for us, and we were gonna get him back, bring him home, and fix this shit."

"We're still doing that."

Valor takes a step towards me. He's bigger than me in two ways. Slightly taller, though not much. But he's got a lot more muscle mass than I do. I've never been much of a fighter. But ALCOR made sure all of his 'boys' could kick ass. I can hold my own with people who are not my fully-mature Akeelian male brothers. But of the whole group of us, I'm definitely the weak link in a brawl.

So when Valor erases the space between and we stand chest to chest, and he sizes me up—he's more intimidating than I'd like to admit.

"Right after you... do what, exactly?" Valor says, narrowing his eyes at me.

OK. It's decision time. I can see that he's gotten to the end of his patience with me and when Valor makes up his mind about something, that's it. He's done and moving on. So this ship he's working on is not some idle threat to make me talk. And this conversation isn't about trying to establish dominance.

It's more like... one last chance. If I blow this, he's gonna throw me away. And no matter what I tell him after that, it won't matter. He'll just be done.

"OK," I say. "I'm going to tell you something but... I need you to keep an open mind."

He shakes his head at me. And he's pissed. "What the fuck did you do?"

"I didn't do anything. Yet. But... and I need you to listen to my whole explanation before you react, OK? Because you need to see the whole picture before you can fully understand it."

"Stop fucking around and tell me what's going on."

"I have a secret."

"No fucking shit."

"She's a girl."

He laughs. "Why am I not surprised?"

"She's not a princess, Valor. She's not a Cygnian girl, she's an *Akeelian* girl."

He smiles at my revelation. Inhales deeply like he's sucking in another round of patience because we're brothers, and that's what brothers do. And then he says, "Tray," as he places a hand on my shoulder. "I know you don't believe that. There's no such thing as a female Akeelian. You know this. I know this. Everyone knows this. So what the actual fuck are you talking about?"

"Just listen to me. OK? This girl lives inside the Pleasure Prison. Or she did, before we left." I'm unconsciously fingering the drive in my pocket. "She showed up in the Pleasure Prison just after I brought it online and she's trapped in there. I'm going to get her out. So if—"

"Are you fucking insane? This is a joke, right? Please tell me this is a joke."

"This is not a joke and I am not insane. She's—"

"She's not real," he says. "That's number one, Tray. She's not real. And you *are* insane. Are you actually telling me that someone infiltrated the Harem Station virtual reality twenty fucking years ago and you didn't say anything?"

"She didn't infiltrate it, Valor, she—"

"She did!" he yells. "She absolutely did! What the hell are you thinking? You let a spy onto our station and now you're carrying her around in your pocket?"

I finger the drive again. Because how did he know that?

62

"Do you think I'm stupid? Is that why you partnered up with me?"

"You picked *me*, asshole! I never asked you for help! You came to me!"

"Yeah," he says, a growl building deep in his throat. "I did. And now I know... that was a mistake."

"Listen to me. I need you to listen to me. I can get us out of here. Then we can save her, meet up with *Booty* and Asshole, then find Real ALCOR and *Beauty* and everything's back on track."

One hand comes at me, flattens on my chest. And he shoves me so hard I stumble backwards and crash into a tool cart. Things go flying, I almost lose my footing, and something cuts my suit because I hear the familiar sound of vac-plastic ripping.

"What the fuck, Valor?" I twist and check my suit for the tear I know is there. "What the fuck!"

"Where are we?" he growls. "Where is this place? *What* is this place? Why are we fucking here?"

"I need the sun-fucked ship! I told you that, and it was true. And it's ready. We're leaving, OK? We're done. No time has passed outside, we're fine. We're not even late for the rendezvous yet."

"Where. Are. We?" He says it slow. And mean. Like Valor is gonna beat the shit out of me if I don't give him something. And fuck it. It's not even a secret anymore. We're here.

"This is Angel Station."

He looks around, squints his eyes. "What? But that place is supposed to be—"

"It's Angel Station, Valor. Take my word on that. I'm not one hundred percent sure of much these days,

63

but I know where we are. No one knows where Angel Station is because no one's been there."

"Tray, Jimmy and Crux met with Angel Station. Hell, Serpint was ordering fucking fruit from them!"

"Lies," I say. "Everyone wants to know where Angel Station is but no one does. Because it lives inside Luck's spin node."

"No one except you, apparently."

"Me," I admit. "And Crux. He knows what it is. But all the rest is just lies. That's all. And when we get back to Harem you can even ask Crux. Even if you don't trust me, you still trust Crux, right?"

"I thought I did. But I have to be honest. I'm reconsidering. Why didn't you two fucking say something? Why all the goddamned secrets? Maybe I shouldn't trust either of you?"

"Who were we supposed to tell? Baby? Succubus? Who the fuck should we have told?"

Valor opens his mouth to respond, but all he ends up doing is sucking in a very long breath of air.

"We're in charge now, Valor. Us. Me. Crux. You guys. There's no one else but us."

"Asshole," Valor says.

I nod, considering this, not for the first time. "Maybe. But he wasn't there when Crux and I decided on the current plan. And then the Succubus came and there was no way to tell Asshole anything without her hearing."

"Fine. We can figure that shit out later. But what does this have to do with this fucking girl?"

"She's being held prisoner by Veila," I say.

Valor huffs out a breath of contempt. "Veila *sent* her, you mean?"

64

"No. She's not a fucking spy, OK? She's just a girl."

"There's no such thing as an Akeelian girl, Tray. It's not possible."

"*You* don't know that." I laugh. "You don't know anything. I'm the only one who *knows* things."

Valor nods his head at me. "Is that right? Then why did you need Luck to open that secret spin node?"

"I had the *code*."

"Yeah, you did. But you couldn't open it. You needed Luck for that. And Luck needed Nyleena for that. So tell me again how you have all the answers, *Tray*."

I don't even pause, just say, "ALCOR told me everything—"

"ALCOR told you shit! ALCOR told you what he needed you to know, just like he told me what I needed to know. And you know what ALCOR's secret message for *me* was? *Tray*?"

He doesn't wait for me to answer his rhetorical question. Just keeps going.

"He told me that Akeelian girls are always born dead. That's why there are no Akeelian girls. That's why we can't back-breed the way the Cygnians do with their boys. There are *no Akeelian girls*, Tray. That's why we need to get to Earth. So this girl you think you're saving? She's a fucking spy! She's only here to get info out of you, and holy fucking suns"—he laughs—"she did that all right. You told her everything, didn't you?"

"No!" I insist. "I didn't tell her anything about Harem so even if what ALCOR told you is true, she doesn't know anything. But it's not true." I say. "You know it's not true. Jimmy came back and told us he has a sister. You heard him."

"Jimmy is full of shit. Veila is full of shit. And you think I'm pining over that Veila bitch because she and I were genetically engineered *mates*? You've lost your goddamned mind! I want to *kill* her. I want to kill her with my bare fucking hands. I want to wrap my fingers around her neck and squeeze her till her eyes pop out. There's no rush of lust inside me when I look at that hologram of Veila. There's rage. And hate. And violence. I'm not going to fuck that bitch! I want to choke the life out of her and then cut her up into little pieces and scatter them in the galactic wind."

He's crossed the new distance between us and now he's leaning down in my face as this venom spews out of his mouth, his eyes wide, the veins in his neck bulging with his too-fast heartbeat.

"That's why I'm here, *brother*. I'm not here to save ALCOR. Or *Beauty*. If we can get that done, cool. Great. I'll be happy. But that's not my mission. Veila is my mission and you're just a means to an end for me, just like I am for you. So I'm fixing up my own fucking ship, then I'm gonna make my own fucking fuel pellets, then I'm gonna use those coordinates you found and fly my way out of this spin node. And then..." His eyes glow bright neon violet. "And then I'm gonna hunt that bitch down and do it exactly how I planned."

CHAPTER SIX

I want to try out my rude hypothesis. And I do. Kind of. But it's hard for me to be rude when people are all so pleasant. And they don't react when I don't reply to their 'thank you' with a 'you're welcome'. I can practically hear the *cha-ching!* sound in their heads as they rack up another credit for not reacting to me.

But I give it a go. Because today feels like the last day I can stand this life. Today feels like a day where I might be up for anything, just as long as it breaks the monotony of my existence.

So this guy, Hester, he comes in every day for lunch. Every freaking day. At exactly one twenty-three PM I know that Hester will be walking through that door. He will order a protein wrap. But he'll order it like this: "I'd like a protein wrap on sweet bread. Make sure it's sweet bread. I really like the sweet bread."

Every day. Every time.

It's like... *Hello? It's me, Brigit. I make your fucking protein wrap every day. I know you like it on sweet bread. You don't need to tell me.*

But I've told him that a couple dozen times now and he's always shocked that I know his name.

I mean... I ask him for his name every day. I write it on the damn wrapper. I call out, "Hester. Protein wrap on sweet bread." Every time. Same way.

Still, he's always shocked.

Not one of the smarter stock characters in here, that's for sure.

This is what I hate most about this place. The people aren't real. Nothing is real. I'm not real. What is the point of it all?

I know what Tray would say. Because every once in a while I go through these... moods, I guess. He'd say, "It's just an interlude, Brigit. I know it's frustrating and boring and that from your perspective, this prison sentence seems never-ending. But there is an end. There is a goal. And if you can just hang with me as I set everything up, I promise you will be happy when it's over."

So I've been patient with Tray and the world he made for me.

But I think today is the day. Today is the day when I cannot take one more moment of *sameness* from Hester.

He's not the only one who does that either. He's just the most precise as far as rules of engagement go.

And yesterday I told myself that if I have to hear him order that way one more time I'm gonna slap him. So for real... I've reached my tipping point.

Something has to change.

I don't even care what it is.

At one twenty-three PM here he comes. He waits his turn in line while I side-eye him looking up at the menu. Why does he read it when he orders the same thing every day?

He's not real, Brigit. He's a program running inside a virtual reality.

Right. So he's not gonna care when he spits those words out like they are brand-shiny new and I slap him across the face.

Which I do. Red mark on the cheek and everything.

For a moment I think... *OK. No reaction. Not wholly unexpected.*

But then he reaches out, grabs my hair, pulls me across the counter, and shoves me to the floor.

I look up at him, utterly stunned. "What the fuck?"

Then he gazes up at the menu and says, "I'd like a protein wrap on sweet bread. Make sure it's sweet bread. I really like the sweet bread."

I look around, still stunned, because I was not expecting that. And my heart is beating fast, and my scalp is tingling from the hair pull, and my knees are bruised from the floor, and... holy fucking shit!

It worked!

Sort of.

Now he's just mumbling his order on repeat. Like he's got a glitch.

I don't know what to do, so I side-eye the people around us to gauge their reaction. They either truly can't see what just happened the way most of them can't see Tray, or they're getting credits handed to them for ignoring it.

But then a man pushes his way through the crowd of people near the front and offers me his hand. "Wow. That guy has issues. Would you like me to report him for you? I saw the whole thing."

And hellooooo there, Mr. New Guy. Who might you be? I take his hand and he pulls me up off the floor. "Thanks," I say, smoothing my apron and anxiously adjusting my hair. "But I did slap him first."

New guy laughs. "Yeah. Saw that too. But if you want me to lie, I will. His reaction was over the top."

I stare into his bright violet eyes. Eyes that remind me so much of Tray's that for a moment I get a little lost. And then a little confused. Because everything about him kind of reminds me of Tray.

They are about the same height, but this guy's hair is lighter. They have a similar face, as well. Probably about the same age, not that age really has meaning in this place. But they look like they could be related.

But unlike Tray, this guy has an easy-going grin on his face and a smile that feels welcoming. Tray is patient, but deliberative to such a point that he often appears dark. I don't find him anti-social, and I'm pretty sure no one in this place has the depth of character to call him that either. But... he *is* kind of anti-social.

"I'm sorry," I say. "Who are you?"

"New here today." He smiles. "I'm Draden."

"Draden," I say. "Right. I hear you're having a party tonight."

"Word gets around fast." He chuckles. "You're coming though, right?"

"Mmmm." I press my lips together. "No. Sorry. I'm... I've... well, just... no." I don't care how cute and new he is, I'm done with the stupid parties.

"Well, that's too bad," Draden says. "I was really counting on you being there."

"Me?" I ask. "Not me personally."

70

He leans in and only now that I realize he's still got a hold of my hand. Because he squeezes it. *Juuuust* a little bit too hard. "Yes, Brigit. You. *Personally.*"

"What?"

"I think you should reconsider." He says it nice enough. It's amicable. But underneath there's a hint of something else. Something... dangerous.

"So... see ya then," he says.

And a moment later he's pushed his way back through the crowd and disappears.

I look around, uncertain of what to do. Uncertain of how to feel.

Uncertain about everything.

And then I smile.

Because I love it.

Aieena shows up right as my shift ends. No one replaces me when I leave. In fact, this café isn't even open unless I'm working here. It's like it only exists for me.

Which, OK. Fine. I am living in a virtual reality so it kind of makes sense.

But it's creepy.

Who is running this thing? Tray? Does he watch me? Does anyone watch me? Is there some all-powerful AI monitoring everything? And if so, is that thing considered... *God?*

My brain hurts when I think too hard about it. And there is enough going on today that pondering the existence of an artificial God is unwarranted.

71

"Did you change your mind?" Aieena asks.

I'm wiping down the counters and mentally locking up the café's virtual currency counter when she says this.

"Yes," I answer. "That Draden guy came in here earlier and personally invited me."

"Really?" Aieena brightens.

I've been weighing the pros and cons of telling Aieena about the confrontation earlier. I'm not sure it's necessary because, while she's far more real than that Hester guy, the fact remains, she's still fake.

We're all still fake.

So I'm not sure it's worth the effort when she's just going to parrot back some pre-scripted answer pulled from her... database. Or whatever.

But fuck it. This is opposite day. So I say, "Something weird happened earlier."

She squints her eyes at me. "Weird how?"

"Well, there's this guy..." I tell her about Hester. She doesn't know him. But I explain the way he acts and she crinkles her face up.

"Hmmm. That's... strange, right?"

I tilt my head at her. "Yes. It's definitely strange. And I'm just so sick of it."

"Well, I would be too. What kind of idiot is he? I mean, is he sick?"

Again, this is unexpected. Because all this time I've been under the assumption that Aieena has been programmed to 'miss things'. Plus... sick? Who gets sick in a virtual?

And then her question from earlier about Tray pops into my head.

Where is he?

First time for that too.

"Ummm... not sure if he's sick," I say. "But whatever. I was just irritated earlier. And yesterday I told myself I was going to slap him if he did it again."

Aieena covers her mouth with her hand. "You didn't."

I laugh. I can't help it. "I did."

"Oh, my God, Brigit!" She's shaking her head at me.

"I know! But... I'm tired of it. I'm tired of all of it!"

"How did he respond?"

"He grabbed my hair, pulled me across the counter, and threw me to the ground!"

"What?" She's visibly shocked.

"Yeah." And then I smile.

"Are you OK?" She looks me up and down. "Did you call security?"

"Security?"

"Yeah. Did you report him? That's... not normal behavior."

And then I remember that's what that Draden guy said too. *Do you want me to report him?*

"Who exactly would I report him to?"

"Security!" Aieena says.

"But there is no security," I say. I know this for a fact. There has never been a need for security. No one breaks laws—come to think of it, I'm not sure there are laws. People just... know the rules and seem to follow them. And no one's ever tried to hurt me before. I didn't think they could. Because even though it's a very strange thought, there's no denying that I am actually the most powerful 'person' in this virtual. I

73

really do think I'm the bank. I might even be the artificial God running things.

"What are you talking about, Brigit? Are you OK? I'm starting to get worried about you. The security station is right next door."

"What?"

Aieena gets even more concerned. "Maybe he was sick. And maybe you're sick too. Do you have a temperature?"

"A temp—"

"Stop repeating me," Aieena objects. "You're acting like him! You're acting like a robot."

"A robot?"

"Oh, my suns. I think we should take you to the hospital."

I want to say, *Hospital?* very badly. But I control that urge. There is no hospital. There is no security next door. People don't commit crimes here. People don't get sick. And Aieena should not be able to have this conversation with me, let alone initiate it.

"No," I say. "No. I'm fine. I'm just… it's been a weird day. Maybe I just… need to go to that party?"

She agrees and relaxes, like this was the answer she's been waiting for this whole time we've been talking. Her concern fades after we leave the empty café and start walking across the green space.

But I look over my shoulder as she starts talking about her garden, and then quickly forward again.

Because there's a new building next to the café.

And the bright red sign on the front says SECURITY.

CHAPTER SEVEN

I think maybe I do not know Valor as well as I thought.

He's never been one of those go-getters. I think that's why he teamed up with Luck. Luck will do anything once. *Anything.* And Luck takes direction like a champ when he's in the process of trying something new. You tell him, "Luck, shoot those Akeelian warships coming after us as we try to get into the ALCOR gate," and Luck is like, "Fuck, yeah, I'm gonna shoot me some ships."

No thinking involved at all. Just... reaction.

Some people like that about Luck.

Hell, I like that about Luck. That's how we got here. I said, "Luck, take us through that fucking spin node and then make Nyleena start a princess rebellion on Harem to keep the AIs occupied while we go out and find Real ALCOR, who may or may not be swirling around the edge of a black hole or a gate."

I mean, he didn't even need to hear that end part. Take Tray and Valor through the secret spin node to find ALCOR? "OK." Muster up an insurgency? "Cool. I'm there."

Done.

So Luck will do something once. Once. Then he starts thinking things through. Like... right about now he's probably thinking, *I'm gonna kill that fucking Tray when I see him again. Start a princess rebellion? Why the fuck did I sign up for this?*

It's... probably not going well on Harem Station.

But it doesn't matter. I've got shit under control and I have a plan.

Valor is a thinker. A planner. That's why I had to let him into the Pleasure Prison with me. That's why I had to drip-feed him info about certain things I was doing.

Like the whole idea that things inside the Pleasure Prison aren't wholly fake. They're not wholly real, either. But they *can* be real if you take certain steps.

I told him this and I told him my plan for Asshole ALCOR's escape with *Booty*, our trip to this station, then our rendezvous with them so we could go save Real ALCOR.

And he was one hundred percent on board with that.

Until now.

And it's not really about Brigit, either. Whatever he thinks about who or what she is, that's not it. That wasn't the motor driving the speech he just gave me.

It's hate. Hate is driving him.

And that surprises me.

"Valor," I say. "You can't go off on your own."

He's already turned back to his new ship and is toiling away at some wiring. "Sure I can. I can do anything I want."

"No, listen to me."

He whirls around, electron ionizer in hand, its blue arc of electricity snapping and crackling in the dark docking bay so that his face flickers like he's some eerie apparition of energy. "No, you listen. You can go do whatever the fuck you want. I'm not coming. We part ways here, brother. I'm done. I'm finishing this ship and going my own way. Maybe I'll see you on the other side, maybe not. Have a good one."

Then he goes back to work.

"I need you," I say.

He laughs. "You don't need anyone, Tray. Always so self-sufficient. Always so secretive. Well, I've got my own secrets to deal with."

"I'll help you," I say. "If you help me get Brigit out, we can meet up with *Booty* and Asshole, then find ALCOR, and then kill Veila. If that's what you really want."

He shakes his head but doesn't answer me.

"I need you," I say. "Because I know where they're keeping Brigit. But I can't do it alone."

"Get *Booty* and the ALCORs to help," he mutters.

"They won't do it, Valor. They won't help me save her."

He whirls around again, the ionizer flickering in his hand just a little too close to my face. "Because she's not real, Tray. She's fake, at best, and more than likely, she's just a fucking trap. There is no such thing as an Akeelian girl."

"You don't know that for sure—"

"I do know that for sure. ALCOR told me. He fucking told me that the only way the boys can live is if they suck all the nutrients from the female twin inside the womb. Every Akeelian girl is born dead. So I don't know what that girl is, but I do know she's not real."

We lock eyes. And his brighten a little. Or maybe that's just a reflection from the electron ionizer? Not really sure.

But he's dead serious. I do know that.

I rub my hands across my face and sigh. "OK. But listen to me for a moment. Can you listen for a moment?"

"Fine. I'm listening." But he's not really. He's working on his ship, his escape-from-Tray plan running through his head.

"Maybe she's not real in the sense that we think things are real. I'll accept that if you accept this. Can you just turn around and look at me?"

He sighs, but he turns.

I stare at him. Pleading, maybe. "I love her. OK? She's real to me—"

"Tray—"

"Just listen," I snap. "I've known her since I first spun up the Pleasure Prison. All the way back to the early days, Valor. So maybe she's not real to you, but she is to me. And… and maybe she's just an AI trapped in a virtual. Fine. I can accept that too. Because that's *enough*. That's enough for me, Valor. That's the best I can hope for."

He closes his eyes and sighs.

"It's enough for me. You wouldn't call ALCOR not real. He's real. He's just not… human."

"She's lying to you," he growls. "If she told you she was an Akeelian girl, she's lying."

"Even if that's the case, it doesn't matter. I know her. I trust her. Even if someone did send her to spy—and I'm not saying they did—but even if that was true, she's not the same person who entered the Pleasure Prison almost twenty years ago our time. Because in her time that's thousands of years, Valor. She's forgotten more things than she remembers at this point. She trusts me now. And I trust her. I'm going to get her out of there and we're gonna—"

"Oh, for fuck's sake," Valor bellows. "Are you listening to yourself? You don't love her. She's a trap, Tray. Just like Corla. Just like Lyra. Just like Delphi. Just like Nyleena. They're all just traps. They were made to kill us. And my trap is out there somewhere, waiting for me to fall into her. And I need to make sure that never happens."

I process that for a moment. Because I'm sort of embarrassed that I never saw that particular angle before. "They are here to trap us?"

Valor guffaws. "Are you kidding me right now? How did you not see this? You, of all people, missed it? How, Tray?"

I shake my head for a moment. "No. I see everything."

"You see nothing, brother. You have been living inside the Pleasure Prison for two decades playing house with a fake persona. And the best-case scenario explanation is that you created her yourself. You tricked yourself into believing she was real. You made that whole place, Tray. It's fake. And you were lonely. You didn't have a best friend or a partner like the rest of us did. You got lonely and somehow, that place became real to you. And she became real to you too. But she's not. She's not fucking real. I don't care how smart you are, this is dumb! And deep down inside you know that it's not possible for some girl trapped in a faraway virtual to manifest herself into yours. *It's not fucking real.*"

He's breathing heavy, clearly agitated and angry with me.

"She's real," I say, tapping my head. "I don't care if it's only in here, Valor. I don't care. If there's a way to get her with me… I have to try."

He throws up his hands. "I'm not stopping you, dude. Have at it."

"I need you."

"*Booty* can help. Asshole can help. You don't need me."

"I do need you. You're the…"

"I'm what?" he says. And for a moment I'm afraid he's reading my mind. I'm afraid that he knows what's swirling around up there. I'm afraid he's figured it all out. But he says, "I'm the only one who's *real?*"

The reality of what he just implied hits me. It's not fair. If he ever implied that *Booty* and the ALCORs weren't real on Harem, people would feel very insulted.

But I know what he means.

He's the only flesh-and-blood person I have access to. The only one who can enter actual *places* with me and use *hands* to manipulate things.

Things like cryopods and docking station locks. He's the only one who can fight by my side if we end up in some kind of hand-to-hand combat situation.

80

There's more to it than that, though. I need him for another, very specific reason.

"I'm not gonna stop you if you decide not to help me, Valor."

He shoots me a sideways smile that says, *I'd like to see you try.*

I *could* stop him. And he probably even knows this. I could fuck up this whole ship with my mind if I could gain access to the core computing systems.

But I don't remind him of any of that. I just say, "But… I need you. And I have coordinates. Once we leave this time shift I'll know exactly where she is. We could solve this mystery pretty fucking quick. And if you're right, then—"

"If I'm right, we walk right into the trap and we get captured."

"We're too smart for that. We're too powerful. This ship," I say, pointing to his project, "this ship is nothing. My ship—*our* ship," I correct myself—"it's special. It has a SEAR cannon weapons system and a bunch of other shit. But aside from all that, my ship has something else too."

"What's that?" he sneers.

"Me." I lick my lips and take a breath. "My ship is *me.*"

He turns the electron ionizer off and drops it into a cart, then rubs his hand across his forehead like maybe he's getting a headache. "I didn't ask for this. When Crux came and rounded us up back when we were kids I never imagined this is what my life would become. I just… I just wanted to make my father proud. I wanted to grow up and command warships. I wanted to find a girl and maybe try to have some kids."

He swallows hard and frowns.

"I just wanted something simple. Fight for Akeelian System. Protect it. Keep people safe. Then go home on leave and fuck my wife and play with my kids. No one ever asked me if I wanted to be breeding stock."

"I know," I say.

"No one ever asked me if I wanted to go on the run. No one ever asked me if I wanted to team up with an insane AI. No one ever fucking asked me if I wanted to go scavenge parts in dangerous places to keep that insane AI alive. OK? I never got a choice. But now, here, I have a fucking choice, Tray. And I'm choosing to take this shit hand I was dealt and make the most of it. I'm choosing my own fucking destiny."

"I know," I whisper. "Me too."

He's shaking his head. "No. You're playing their fucking game. You're falling into the trap. I'm telling you this not to hurt you, brother. I'm telling you this to save you."

"I know," I say again. "I don't doubt any of that."

"Just the part about the girl."

"OK, listen to me. Maybe you're right. I will... I will stop thinking I'm always correct and... take you at your word that you know something I don't."

"Good."

"But that won't change this, Valor. I have to see her. Just... come with me. Help me see her. Then I'll let it go if you're right."

"What if she's on some huge station, Tray? Under guard? You want me to fight for your right to see reality? It'll be too late. We're just two people. We'll die trying."

"Valid point," I say. "So if she's somewhere like that then... then we'll go get *Booty* and Asshole and complete the mission as planned. Find Real ALCOR. And Beauty too. We'll save Harem Station and I'll help you kill Veila. And then... *then* I'll go back and get her."

I calculate how long that would take in real time. Then in Brigit's time.

Thousands of years will have passed from her perspective.

Thousands of years without me.

She will be insane by then. She will be unrecognizable.

I have been keeping her together all these years. I have been her rock. I am the only real thing in her whole existence.

But Valor is weighing this new option with serious consideration. So I push the consequences aside. I really do need his help. There's no way around that. Not if what Brigit told me is true.

"Deal?" I say.

He looks at his feet and sighs.

"Please," I beg. "Just... help me. I need you, Valor. I wouldn't ask if that wasn't the sun-fucked truth."

CHAPTER EIGHT

Draden's party is... not what I expected. And his space isn't what I expected, either. For one, it's not a community building. It's a house.

"When did they build this place?" I ask Aieena. Which is a stupid question. Because who is 'they' if not me? Or Tray?

"What do you mean?"

"This house," I say. "This wasn't here before."

"Before?" Aieena squints her eyes at me. This seems to be her favorite expression today. "Before what? This house has been here forever. No one's ever lived in it that I can recall. So I guess that's weird. You'd think a guy who wanted to live in a big place all alone would do so because he's antisocial. But then again, antisocial people don't throw raging parties, do they?"

"No," I say, absently clocking all the activity in his front yard. Because there's a ton of people here. Not the usual crowd I see, either. New people. And there's no DJ. I can tell because the music isn't dance-y techno. It's got... lyrics.

Raging party is right.

Everyone's drinking, but there's a keg of beer in the front yard too. No bartender.

"What the hell?" I mumble. And then I see Draden off to the side, shaking hands with a bunch of men and laughing like they've known each other for lifetimes.

What the hell is happening?

Did my Hester slap just... rewrite the whole world? Who are all these new people? New people aren't all that uncommon, because like I said, people rotate in and out on some schedule. But they don't appear in crowds. And these people all seem to know Draden. Who is also new.

I tug on Aieena's shirt and say, "When did he arrive?"

"Arrive?" Aieena asks. "You mean move in?"

"Whatever."

"What's with you today, Brigit?"

"What's with me? What's with you? When did you get so... chatty and knowledgeable?"

"Wow," she says. "You're moody. I hope Tray comes back soon because you need to get laid or something."

"What?"

"You heard me."

"I know I heard you, I'm just... surprised you're saying stuff like this."

She blinks at me. "I think there's something wrong with you. Are you... do you... need to talk to someone?"

"W-w-what?"

"You know. There's nothing to be ashamed of if you"—she shrugs—"need some professional help getting through a rough patch. Maybe you're lonely, Brigit?"

"Lonely?" I laugh. Uh, fuck yeah, I'm lonely. I've been living inside this virtual version of Utopia for so long I've lost track. I've been locked in this place for many, many lifetimes.

But of course I don't say that. I could say that, but I get the feeling that I'm the one driving these changes. That it really was me and my single act of defiance with Hester. Or maybe it happened before that? Maybe it's because I'm done. I've reached some tipping point and there's no way to go back now. But I can't say any of that either because on the off chance that it's true, I am the one reshaping the world, then I need to be careful. And agreeable. So I say, "Yeah. I have been lonely."

And then something else weird happens. I'm unconsciously waiting for the little *cha-ching*! sound in my head and... it never comes. I don't even get a reward for being agreeable with Aieena.

She rubs my arm and smiles warmly. "I know you love him, Brig. But... he's so unreliable."

"Tray?"

"Yeah. He leaves all the time. Everyone's noticed it. They all think—"

"Who all *thinks*?"

"Everyone, Brigit. And he's been gone a very long time. Don't you think you might be ready to... you know, move on?"

"Ahh." I manage a garbled laugh. "Yeah, I'm fuckin' ready to move on. But I can't do that without him."

"Says who? I mean, that's the whole point of moving on, right? You find a new man"—she nods her head at this Draden guy—"and start over."

"No," I say. "No. I don't want to start over. I just want Tray to come back. And why am I talking to you about this? What's going on?"

She frowns. "OK. But..." She starts to say something, then just shakes her head. "You know what? Never mind. I'm gonna go mingle. You should get a drink. Talk to people. Laugh a little, Brigit. Life is too short to be waiting around for some man to save you."

"Who *are* you?"

But she's already walking away.

What the hell is happening? Since when is stock character Aieena such a philosopher?

And that comment? Life is too short?

What the fuck?

A short life is not my problem. My problem is that this is all fake, and I've lived here for God knows how long, and there doesn't seem to be an end in sight.

"Brigit."

I turn around and bump right into New Guy Draden. "Oh," I say, taking a step back. "Sorry, didn't see you there."

"Glad you came." He smiles at me and his violet eyes light up a little. God, he looks so much like Tray. I mean, not the hair, or the build, really. But there's something else about him that is so familiar.

"You kinda ordered me to," I say, flustered from that conversation with Aieena and this guy creeping up behind me when I wasn't looking.

"I think ordered is a strong word." He takes a sip of his drink. Smiles into the cup like he's a man with secrets and he's making private jokes.

"Who are you?"

He smiles and his violet eyes twinkle again. Like he's got mischief locked up inside him. "A friend."

"Really?"

He nods. Then he places his hand on my arm and leans in. "Your sisters sent me, Brigit."

"What?" I pull back, breaking our skin-on-skin contact. "What are you talking about?"

"You know what I'm talking about. None of this is real. You've been in here for a really long time, Brigit. And they've been patient with you, because"—he shrugs—"who cares, really? Nothing was happening all these years. So why not let you run free, right?"

Millions of things run through my mind as he's talking.

Who is he?

What is he doing here?

Who sent him?

Draden leans in close, so close his lips touch the shell of my ear, and he whispers, "I have a message for you."

"From who?" My hearts skips so many times in a row, I place my hand over it just in case it jumps out of my chest.

"They want you to come with me."

"What?"

"You heard me. And there's not a lot of time. We're not in a crunch yet. But it's creeping up on us."

I admit, I want to believe him. I want this new guy to be some strange savior. I'm dying for someone to save me. I just want to get out of here. So there's this moment, this singular moment when I consider saying, *Yes. OK. Let's go.*

But I catch myself. I know better. I know this isn't real. It can't be real. This is Tray's virtual reality. And mine. This guy, he does not belong here.

I take a step back and put my hand up. "OK, just... hold on a second. I need this explained to me very thoroughly. Like every little detail. Where am I? How long have I been there? How old am I? Is there something wrong with me? Will I wake up? Am I real? And... where's Tray?"

Draden looks around. "We have to be careful. Others have infiltrated this world too. Not just you."

"What do you mean?" I ask, also looking around suspiciously.

"What that guy did to you today in the café? Not normal, right?"

"No. But I was provoking him on purpose."

"He should not have hit you. And I'm not supposed to be here. They know. And they won't stand for it."

"Who? And if you're in... hiding, or whatever, why are you being so conspicuous?"

"They, Brigit. The Akeelians. They're the ones keeping you here. They know what Tray's been doing. They know what he's planning. It's a trap, Brigit. And you're the bait."

"Is Tray coming for me? Is he there?"

"Yes and no. He's coming, all right. But when... I don't know. All I know is that we can't be here when he arrives."

"Who? Tray? Why?"

Draden leans in and whispers, "Because if we are, we'll never get out. It's a trap. We can't wait for him. We need to go now. I need you to trust me."

I try to calm down. Try to think clearly. But this whole day has been weird. Aieena is acting strange. Asking all kinds of questions. Someone is remaking the world, adding a security building and a hospital. Not to mention Hester's outburst.

My outburst.

But that's what I wished for this morning, wasn't it? Change. Any change is better than being stuck here with no idea what's happening to me.

So it could be me.

But it could be someone else. He could be telling the truth.

But… trust him?

"I don't even know you. You could be anyone. You could be lying. Maybe you're here to…"

"To what?" he snaps. "What other possible reason could I have for breaking into your virtual world, Brigit? Be smart." Then he taps the side of my head two times, hard, to illustrate his point.

I slap his hand away. "Fuck off. You're… you're not real."

"You're not real either. That's the whole fucking reason I'm here."

"Yeah, you don't belong here."

And just for a second there's a shimmer. A flicker across his face.

"I belong here," he says. "Just as much as you do."

But his voice is weaker somehow. Faltering and low.

"No," I say. "You're not real. I'm real. And this world isn't yours, it's mine."

"Brigit," he says, reaching for my arm. His fingers grab it and then slip right though my body. Like he's... a ghost.

Or fake.

"Go away!" I say. "You're not real!"

I yell it. So loud.

"Brigit!"

"No! GO AWAY!"

The music stops. The people stop. Everything stops.

Draden's lips are moving. He's talking, but his body is fading away as I watch. So I don't hear what he says. Just catch shorts bursts of words as he dissipates. "Help you... see it... be there when..."

And then everything and everyone is gone.

All of it.

The house. The people. The party.

The whole fucking world disappears in front of my eyes and I am left here, all alone, standing in the middle of an endless, foreboding, gray fog.

CHAPTER NINE

"Please," I say again. "Valor."

He lets out a long breath of air. "Tell me everything. And when I say everything, Tray, I mean everything. From the very fucking beginning." I open my mouth, but before I can try to talk him out of this, he continues. "It's not up for negotiation. This is my price."

"Valor, you don't *want* to know everything."

"You don't get to decide what I can and can't handle. You don't get to decide what I do and do not want to know. Where you got this idea that I was your little brother instead of the other way around, I have no clue. But fuckin' stop it. Right now. Because it's pissing me off."

His tone is filled with certainty. And that thought comes back to me again.

I don't know him. I don't know him at all. And this... *trust* I've put in him could be the biggest mistake ever.

But we're here. Stuck in a spin node and suspended in time. And if I don't get him on board then Brigit is as good as dead. She will fade away inside that virtual. She won't die because she *can't* die. But it will be the same thing in the end.

She will go insane if I don't get back inside with her soon.

I could take the drive down to medical, plug it in to the system, then get inside one of the pods and go visit her. Keep her sane if I have to.

But I think that might drive *me* insane. I can't do this any longer. I really can't. Today is my tipping point. Today. This shit has to end now.

I won't lose her. All these years Brigit was the one constant in my life. She was my rock, just like I was hers. Freeing her and being with her has been my goal for so long I don't know who I am without Brigit.

So I don't have much choice, do I?

"OK," I say. "But it's a long story."

Valor huffs out a sarcastic laugh. "Fortunately for us, endless time seems to be our most abundant resource."

Which is true, I guess. In the grand scheme of things.

But Brigit doesn't have time the way we do.

"Start talking," Valor demands. "And if I have even one suspicious moment when I think you're lying or leaving shit out, you're on your own. I'm done. I'm fixing my own ship and I'm leaving without you."

So... there it is.

His price.

When we landed at ALCOR Station back when we were kids I was the one who accepted ALCOR's offer. I told him I could get him onto the galactic web. That we could shoot a neutrino stream through his gates and create a geodesic vector field that would transcend space and time and he would be back in communication with everyone else.

My only purpose for doing this was to latch onto the data stream outside his gates so we could pull in information and entertainment. And, as far as I knew, ALCOR had been... cut off, I guess. I figured it was a sort of punishment for the way he monopolized the gates going to the Seven Sisters.

Up until I came along and gave him total freedom and autonomy he was sequestered behind his security gates. No one could get in, but he couldn't leave either.

The data webs were deliberately detoured far around ALCOR's sector of the galaxy. But my neutrino stream caught the web and hooked us up. And then... well, that was the beginning of the end.

He could leave the station whenever he wanted. Just make a copy and send it out on the stream. And he stayed in contact with his other selves because you can send text messages on a neutrino stream. They transcend space and time. He was in near-instant communication with all his little shatterling copies.

He knew everything. There was no way to stop ALCOR once he was loose like that. There are literally millions of ALCOR copies floating down neutrino streams just catching data and sending it back.

They are not really him, just shell copies of him. They can't do anything but communicate. But it's enough to make him the single most powerful entity in the galaxy. Possibly even the entire universe.

For all intents and purposes, I made ALCOR God.

I knew all this. Vaguely. The information was all inside my head when I landed on ALCOR Station because of the procedure my father did on me shortly before we all escaped. This leveling-up stuff that everyone seems to be talking about.

Jimmy thought it was cool and fun when I came out of cryo and had direct access to the Wayward Station AI. He wanted me to sneak him down to the X levels so he could fuck sexbots.

And OK. Sure. Whatever. I did it. I was in shock back then. I didn't understand what had just happened to me. I didn't understand that I was no longer... *me*.

I wasn't afraid. I wasn't angry. I wasn't happy or sad. There was nothing inside of me. Just... code.

I was code.

So after I got ALCOR online and he was busy working away at his grand master plan, I found the beginnings of the Pleasure Prison.

And this is what I figured out... It wasn't thousands of years old.

ALCOR Station just came from another galaxy.

Valor has been listening attentively so far, but now he puts up a hand. "OK. I've heard enough. You're fucking crazy." He turns back to his ship.

"Valor," I say, grabbing his arm. "ALCOR Station wasn't left over from the past. It's not from here.

Just… listen to me for a second, will you? I have been working on this theory for twenty years. The least you can do is hear me out."

He hangs his head and sighs. But he turns, leans back against the hull of the ship, and crosses his arms. A gesture that lets me know he's listening, but defiant. And I can talk all I want, but he's never going to believe me.

But this is the only chance I have. And there's nothing more to do but spell it out. "What if… what if ALCOR isn't from here either?"

"Where's he from?"

"Don't interrupt me. I'm talking hypothetically. What if ALCOR isn't from our galaxy, he's from this galaxy?"

"The one with the stupid name?"

"Do you want to tell this story?" He shrugs, noncommittal. "Then shut up and listen."

I decide not to ask any more questions because that just opens the discussion up for interpretation. And I don't have the patience for that.

So I say, "ALCOR isn't from our galaxy. He's from this galaxy where Earth lives. We all know he did something that fucked up the Akeelian and Cygnian races a long-ass time ago. He killed them, or made a virus that messed up their DNA, or whatever. He's admitted that to us. But that's only one small part of the story.

"I think that ALCOR Station came from the Milky Way. It's not from here, it's from there. It's the real Angel Station and that's why there were so many ships in the docking bays when we arrived. That's why the Pleasure Prison was fundamentally there and all I had to do was rebuild it. That's how I got the air screens up and running. All the tech was way advanced. Some of it was stuff that our galaxy didn't have at all, like the air screen. Some of it was just better than the tech we had, like the Pleasure Prison and the ships. He's not from the Galaxy Prime, Valor. He's from the Milky Way. And Earth? That's where he was born. All of this shit we're dealing with right now goes back to Earth."

Valor waits to see if I'm done. I'm not really done, but I just spilled out the majority of my theory and now I need to get some feedback. He scratches his eyebrow with the tip of his finger and scowls at me. "I thought you said *this* was Angel Station?"

"It's just a copy."

"Another lie," Valor spits.

"Listen to me. And I'm not being a dick when I say this, but I get it. This shit is mind-blowing. So it's not easy to understand. But I have been thinking about this for twenty years. I have worked out the kinks and this is the thing that makes sense."

He waves a sardonic hand at me to proceed.

"When you send something inorganic through a spin node a copy stays behind. Because technically everything that goes through is destroyed, then remade upon exit. So this Angel Station is the copy."

"And the organic matter?'

"That leaves the other side."

"So everyone who was on this station when ALCOR pulled it through the node to make ALCOR Station?"

"They went through," I say.

"And what happened to them?"

"What do you think happened to them?"

"He killed them."

"He told us he did, Valor. This isn't a surprise."

"So he stole these Angel people and their station, took it through a spin node, left a copy of the station here inside the node, and then killed them all on the other side?"

"Yup," I say. "As far as I can figure, that's what happened."

"OK. So what?"

"So... he's lying to us about Harem. He's been lying the whole time. He has a plan and we're part of it."

"Who cares? I mean, look, Tray. Do I give a fuck that he messed up the Cygnians and Akeelian races? No. I don't. I don't care about princesses, I don't care about soulmates, I don't care about any of it."

"Do you care that Nyleena and Corla can blow up planets and stations with that weird light inside them?"

"Of course I do. But..." He sighs.

I wait for him to continue, but now he just looks tired. "Don't you want to know what it is, Valor?"

"No," he says. "I'm going to kill Veila. That's what I care about. But even after she's gone, they're just gonna make more. So what is the point?"

"They *can't* make more."

"You don't know that."

"How many silver princesses have you seen in your life?"

"Three. Just like you. Veila, Nyleena, and Corla."

"No. Veila isn't a silver. They tried to turn her silver. There are two, Valor. *Two*. Let that sink in. How many golden princesses have come through the harem over the years?"

"Who the fuck knows?"

"Lots. That's my point."

"I get your point, but it doesn't mean anything. They could just hide them better. They could have thousands of silver princesses back in Cygnian System."

"Then why did they try to change Veila into a silver? We all know she was born pink. Jimmy and Crux remember her from Wayward Station when she was there with Corla."

"I don't know," Valor says, throwing up his hands. "I don't care, Tray. You should've asked Nyleena this. If she's one of only two silver princesses, she should know some of this shit."

"Listen to me," I say. "There are only two silver princesses. And neither of them were born. They were genetically engineered, just like all the others. That weird breeding ceremony back on Wayward Station happened because the Akeelians had *us*. Violet-eyed boys. That's one half of the equation. And they figured that Corla was the first and only silver girl they had ever been able to produce, so she was the answer. But she wasn't, Valor. Her daughter, Delphi, is pink. Which means she cannot have natural children. So they tried again and got Nyleena. And they must've been hedging their bets and that's why they tried to genetically manipulate Veila."

"Which also didn't work," Valor says. "So *again*. Who. Cares?"

"ALCOR cares," I say. "ALCOR cares because ALCOR Station was the home of the combined Cygnian-Akeelian races. That's where Angel Station comes from, don't you see? They used to be a race

100

called the Angels. And then ALCOR broke them and he took that station through a spin node and hid it in another galaxy. Everything they need to make purebred Angels is on ALCOR Station!"

Valor says nothing. Just stares at me. Because he knows this makes sense.

"The flowers," I say. "When we get back to Harem we're going to find a very pregnant Nyleena. She is the key. She is the answer. And ALCOR has her now."

"ALCOR is dead!"

"Please," I say. "Do you think that guy is stupid? You are one of seven people in this entire fucking universe who knows what he's capable of. Do you really think he accidentally blew himself up?" Valor opens his mouth to say something, but I'm the one putting up my hand now. "Do not even try to tell me that you think he sacrificed himself to save us. Because I will fucking punch you in the eye for being stupid. He wanted *Nyleena*, Valor! That's why he did all that shit to save her. He needed her!"

"We already had Corla," he says.

"And we already knew Corla makes pinks!"

Valor lets out a long breath.

"It makes sense," I say. "Just... think about it for a second. Let's suppose that the Angels are the worst kind of people to ever exist in this universe. And let's suppose that ALCOR did the right thing when he fucked up their genetics and killed them off. And let's also agree that taking the Angel Station through the spin node and hiding it in another galaxy, surrounded by AI-controlled security beacons that shoot everything that tries to get past the gates, was also necessary."

101

I stop and take a breath. Because I haven't told anyone this theory. Ever. Until now it was all just thoughts in my head. I've never said it out loud. I've never really given it life. But now... it's alive and my whole body is shaking from the adrenaline coursing through my blood as conjecture and theories start to become fact.

"Why, Valor? Why did he want us to stay with him that day we arrived on ALCOR Station?"

Valor is already shaking his head no before I'm done talking. "He's not—"

"He *is*," I say. "He won the motherfucking lottery when a silver princess called Corla sent seven violet-eyed Akeelian boys through his gates. He could've just killed us. He *should've* just killed us. But he didn't."

"I just don't think he'd—"

"He's going to *breed* us, Valor. He knows that this plan of his is failing and if he doesn't make a true angel, *someone else will*." I laugh. It's so not funny, but I can't help it, I laugh. "Hell, he already has. And he used me," I say. "He fucking *used me* to make this whole plan happen!"

Valor, who has been leaning up against the hull of the ship, now walks over to a crate a few paces away and sits down. He props his elbows on his knees and holds his head in his hands.

"He used all of us," I say. My fingers unconsciously handle the drive containing Brigit's virtual in my pocket. Because all this leads back to her. Somehow, some way, this all leads back to her.

"And I don't know what he's doing or what his end-game is," I continue. "But... Nyleena's children, Valor? They're the last piece of the puzzle. He's not on our side. He's never been on our side. Crux never trusted him. And even though we're all very different men, I think we can all agree that Crux knows things. He's the voice of reason. He's always been our voice of reason."

Valor looks up at me. His eyes are bloodshot red and he looks very tired right now. "Did you tell this to Crux?"

"When? When could I tell him this? Before ALCOR 'died'?" I do air quotes for that word. "When he was watching us every picosecond of every spin? Or after, when everyone was confused and people were dying on the station because the Baby was left in charge? I was waiting to see what would happen when Jimmy met up with those people from Angel Station."

"Yeah, what was that all about?"

"Jimmy came away with nothing. They wanted answers from him. So—" I throw up my hands and laugh. "Who are they? They're not Angels, that much I know. So who are they?"

Valor squints his eyes. "Props," he says. "Just... props."

And there it is.

The whole truth.

"That's the only logical answer, Valor. Everyone is lying to us. Everyone *but us* wants to be an Angel, or make an Angel, or, at the very least, have the power that comes from those two things." I shrug. "So... make a decision. Stay here and fix this ship and kill Veila, even though it won't change anything. Or come with me. Help me, Valor. Help me save Brigit. She is the key to everything ALCOR has been doing. I know it. There is such a thing as an Akeelian girl, Valor.

103

JA HUSS & KC CROSS

There is. She's right here in my fucking pocket! And if we can get to her in the real we'll find all the fucking answers to all our sun-fucked questions."

I hold my breath. Because I truly cannot do this without him. I don't know how I know that, I just do.

I need Valor to see this through with me.

He gets up and starts pacing the docking bay. Back and forth in front of his ship. Then he looks at me, swallows hard, and says, "OK. I'm in."

CHAPTER TEN

Don't panic. *Don't panic. Don't panic.*

That's what I tell myself over and over again. But I gotta be honest. I'm a little bit panicked.

"Hello?" I call into the cloud of gray nothingness. "Is anyone here?"

Nothing. And I don't think I actually have a voice because even though I kinda heard my call, I didn't really hear my call.

I wave my hands in the thick rolling fog and then try to take a step forward. But I don't think I have a body. I don't think I'm anything.

I am nothing. My world is gone. I am gone.

Don't panic.

Take a breath.

I can't. I have no lungs and there is no air.

Do. Not. Panic.

Think rationally, Brigit. What is this? How did this happen? Put the pieces together and figure it out.

OK.

I messed with the world. I made a decision to change it and... well, fuckin' A. That happened.

105

Hester, Aieena all happened. The party, the... offer—or whatever that was from Draden—all new stuff.

And the security building. I didn't see a hospital, but Aieena mentioned it. So that was new as well.

What's it mean?

I did this. I think I did this. I think I erased the world because I told him to go away.

I didn't really mean *everything* needed to go away.

Don't panic.

This sorta makes sense. At least I hope it does.

Earlier I was thinking about how I was the bank. Or... maybe even in charge of this place. That must be true. This world is mine. Tray created it for me and I control it. So when I told Draden to go away he had to, because I'm the boss.

Yeah. I'm the boss here.

Which means I can remake my world.

Right?

But how?

A small speck of light appears in front of me. One point of light. OK. That's a good sign. I can remake the world. I can turn this back. I can make my building, and the community garden, and Aieena, and the café, and Hester and—

Wait. Why the fuck would I do that? I mean, that was the whole point of today, right? Change things.

Yeah. *Take a moment, Brigit. Think this through.* Because I get the feeling that starting over from nothing and making a whole new world isn't easy. I've never done it before and I want to do this right.

So I think for a little bit. What kind of world do I want? What kind of place do I want to spend time in?

Lots of time in. Because Tray won't be coming back any time soon. He might never come back.

So who do I want to be? Where do I want to live? What do I want from life that I was lacking before? What made me happy? What made me unhappy?

Think, Brigit. For all you know, you get one do-over and that's it. I might have to live with these decisions forever.

I think about my life before Tray. I don't remember much. It was so long ago. But I do remember a station. And a ship.

My immediate gut reaction is… I don't want that. No ships. No stations. No space, for fuck's sake.

I want a planet.

The single point in front of me expands with a flash and the gray nothingness is suddenly illuminated with bright gold light.

The words 'And then there was light' pop into my head.

Holy shit! Did I do that? Did I just start the process of making a planet?

Let's check it out.

I want air.

As soon as I think the words a rush of wind blows past me, mixing up the primordial cloud of bright gold light and making it swirl like crazy.

Fuck.

OK. It's cool. Don't panic. This is good. This is all very good.

I want land. I want firm ground. And I want plants.

I think something happens. But the light is too bright. I can't see anything. It's just a dazzling, brilliant glow of light.

I don't just want light everywhere. I want to collect it into something manageable.

I want a sun.

The swirling cloud of gold pulls together into a massive ball and yes!

I laugh.

Yes! There's ground. And plants. And a sun!

I want sky. And I want night and day.

My new world turns and the ball of fire in the newly-made sky begins to fall down towards my horizon until there's a clear line of distinction above me. Night and day. Sun and stars.

OK, Brigit. Now what? What comes next? Think!

I need water. I want water.

And before me appears a great ocean. And there is sand beneath me. And waves rolling up to my shore.

I want birds.

I want fish.

I want animals.

Songs tweet out from the trees. Water just offshore splashes from the tails of swimming creatures. And a small animal claws its way across the sand towards the ocean.

I want me.

Sand squishes between my toes. A mist of salty water flows across my face and I am warmed by the sun.

I am me and this is my new world.

No. That's not quite right.

I am God.

And now I rest.

CHAPTER ELEVEN

"I'm ready," Valor says from the pilot's chair. "Let's do this. You got the coordinates spun up?"

"I do," I say.

"OK. Press go."

I'm at the navigation console. Valor is a great pilot and he was practically born to be the captain of a ship. He has it in his blood. But this ship needs no pilot.

I am this ship.

"Sending," I say.

"Opening bay doors," Valor replies. "Thrusters on."

The ship lifts up and forward just as the interior doors lift up and then we are in the blurry dark of the spin node.

The internal clock in my head stutters, and stops, and stutters, and starts again. And then....

And then we're out.

Somewhere else.

"Where are we?" Valor asks.

"Seventeen degrees radial on the z-axis in the third quadrant in the gravity well of the sun called Pythia."

"Where the fuck is that?" Valor says.

"No clue. But we're not staying here anyway. It's just the first gate jump."

"What's the time?"

"Can't say yet. Not until we actually get somewhere that matters."

"What if years have gone by, Tray? What if you're wrong about the time?"

"Well"—I huff—"I'm not usually wrong, dude."

He laughs.

"But I'll let you know as soon as I figure it out. Ready for gate one."

"Entering."

Time goes weird again and I sigh out a long breath of relief. At least we're on our way.

"How long will this one take?" Valor asks. He's up from the captain's chair and is walking back to my station.

"Ten minutes? Relatively speaking."

"Then how many more after this one?"

"Fuck's sake, Valor. Can you just let me work it out? I'm doing my best here."

"Asshole," he mumbles, taking a seat at the main console meant for scanning gate-mapping charts.

"Look, I'm worried about the time too. Inside Brigit's simulation the time goes very fucking fast. I've been away for a long-ass time, OK? I'm worried about her."

"Well, I'm worried about us. I'm worried about where we're headed and what kind of bullshit we're gonna find there. And I'm actually worried about *Booty* too. I know you don't give a shit about her but I do."

"I care about *Booty*. But we don't know what side she's on."

"She's on Serpint's side. That's all we need to know."

I look over my shoulder and roll my eyes.

"She would never betray Serpint."

"OK," I say.

"She wouldn't. She loves him. Like… fuckin' *loves* him."

"She did," I say. "Before that shit-show back on Cetus Station and a virus kicked her ass."

"So we can't trust her either?"

I spin around in my chair and glare at him. "I don't fucking know, OK? She's very powerful. And she has a mind of her own. So next time we see her, we'll ask. But stop talking to me about shit unless it's got something to do with *right now*."

I turn back to my navigation screens and let out a long sigh.

"You're a dick. You know that? You've always been a dick."

"For sun's sake, Valor. I was your best friend when we started this. You gave up Luck for me. So obviously I'm not that much of a dick."

"Temporary insanity," he mumbles.

But I have the course planned now and I shoot it up on the screen. "OK. This is where she's at."

He gets up and walks over to me, leaning over my shoulder.

I like Valor. I'd never tell him that, but I've always liked Valor. When we were younger I used to fantasize and he and I were a team instead of him and Luck. I guess, if I really want to admit the truth to myself, I sorta planned his involvement in this. Sure, he came to me after everyone came back from Bull Station and *Beauty* was gone. I didn't make him shun Luck. That was his choice.

But I set him up to get what he needed from me.

A new purpose. A new friend. A new way forward.

And look, I succeeded. He's here with me and not back on Harem with Luck.

So I should feel good about that, but there's a layer of guilt hiding underneath the feeling of satisfaction.

Guilt that I'm going to ruin his life with this trip.

Or get him killed.

"Six gates." He sighs. He's very close to me. So close I can feel his breath on the back of my neck as he studies our course.

I glance up at him and find his face just a little too close. He turns his head and smiles.

I smile back.

"We're gonna be OK," he says, straightening up and placing a hand on my shoulder. "You might be an asshole, but you're right. You're not generally wrong."

"Thanks," I say.

"So… this Brigit girl. Tell me more."

"More?"

"Well… what does she look like? Is she pretty?"

"What do you think?" And I grin. I can't help it.

"Describe her."

"I dunno. Long, dark hair. It's almost black but it's not black. It's superviolet."

"Hmm," he says, taking a seat in the chair next to me. "Nice change from all the pinks and silvers at least.

Does she have nice tits? I mean, you did fuck her, right?"

"Virtually," I say. "Lots of times."

"I knew you were up to something in the Pleasure Prison. And it didn't have shit to do with maintenance. You love her then? She's your version of a Cygnian princess?"

"Yeah," I say. "There is no princess in my future. They made me different than you guys."

"How?"

"I don't really know. The AI inside me, obviously. I just know I was never meant to..." I look at him. His face is serious and calm. And not that I really think about this kind of stuff, but Valor is the best-looking of all of us brothers.

"Never meant to what?" he asks.

"Breed. You know. No one wants my genetics. I'm not even sure it's called genetics anymore."

Valor smiles and his dimples appear. They don't come out often. He has to really grin hard to make them pop up. So I know this is a real smile. "Are you kidding me? Everyone wants some of this." He grabs my thigh and squeezes.

I brush his hand off.

I might not be truly Akeelian anymore. But I still have two cocks. And Valor's hand on my leg reminds me of that.

He glances down at my lap, grins again, then gets up and walks back to the gate-mapping table, ignoring my response. "Do you think we're all genetic brothers?"

"What?"

"You know. Like... for real related?"

113

"No," I say.

"For sure?" he asks. "You know this for sure?"

I glance over my shoulder at him. "Why?"

He shrugs. "Just curious. If we're, you know. Related."

I turn back to the navigation, unsure what he's looking for.

"I mean, you and me? No. For sure. I don't think you're genetically related to any of us, actually. But like... me and Serpint? Don't you think we kinda look alike?"

"Hmm," I say. "Yeah. I guess. You two look more alike than anyone else."

"I think he's my real brother," Valor says.

I spin all the way around in my chair. "Really?"

"You never thought about it?"

"No."

"Well, you're weird. So I guess that's normal. Luck and I used to talk about it all the time."

"Why?"

"Because..." He smiles again. That big dimple-popping grin. "Sometimes we'd get lonely out on our missions."

I raise my eyebrows at him.

He shrugs. "I liked him. What can I say? And he liked me back. Before Nyleena came along. So we talked about it forever. And several years ago we actually did some genetic testing out on the Outer Highway."

"And?"

"No, we're not related."

I turn back to my screens. "Hmm."

"But I still wonder about Serpint."

"Why?" I laugh. "Because you want to fuck him next?"

"No. I just wonder if I have… people. Ya know? Real familial ties like that."

"I'm your people," I say. "I mean that, you know."

"I know."

I look down and sigh. "And… thank you." I turn in my chair to look at him. "I mean that too. I can't do this without you."

His eyes close a little. Not in a narrowing way, but in a heavy way. "You are a dick sometimes. And even though I've known you my whole life, I don't think I really knew you until we became… friends. Recently."

"I get it," I say. I get that a lot, actually. People often tell me I am hard to know. But in the last year I have opened up to Valor more than anyone else in my entire life. Even ALCOR. And God knows, ALCOR wanted my deepest, darkest secrets pretty bad, and never got half as much as I've told Valor. "But I don't think I know you very well, either, Valor."

"What do you want to know?"

There's a lot I want to know about him. Mostly about what he and Luck were doing on all those scavenging missions. And not the sex, either. Though… maybe later on that stuff. But first I want to know why he's attached to me now. I want to know how that happened. Because, while I did figure Valor was my only option to save Brigit, I didn't seek him out. He came to me. So I say, "Why did you pull away from Luck so hard back on Harem? It hurt him, you know."

"Yeah. I know. But I also knew Nyleena was his princess. And I can't compete with a genetically engineered soulmate."

"Is that what you want from me?"

He lets out a breath that is kind of a laugh. But not really. "I've thought about it."

"And?"

He shrugs. "We'll see what happens with Brigit, I guess."

"Did it piss you off then? When you found out that I had a girl?"

He nods. Says nothing.

"Oh," I say. "I didn't realize any of this, you know."

"I know. That's why I'm telling you now. And just so we're clear, when you were trying to sell me on this idea with the promise of a new version of Veila and a new life like the one I used to imagine when I was a kid…" He shakes his head. "That's not why I'm here with you now."

We stare at each other for a moment too long. And then, just as I'm about to break the silence with something, anything, to ease the awkwardness, the screen pings an alert that we're exiting the first gate.

"Time to work," Valor says, getting up and walking back to his captain's chair.

I sit still for a few moments too long, running that whole conversation through my head. What the fuck just happened?

Leaning back in my chair, I glance up the main corridor of the ship to get a glance at Valor.

Did he just say what I think he said?

"Tray," he says.

"Hmm?"

"Send me the course."

"Sending," I say, on autopilot now.

Fuck. Snap out of it, Tray. There's no time to wonder about Valor's sexual intentions right now. Just... focus.

I do. We both do. And we come out, then go back in to the next gate a few minutes later. There's no time for any more awkward discussions because none of the other time rides are as long as the first one. So our conversation is all business.

When we enter the fifth gate Valor says, "Plan? If it's a huge station with lots of security?"

"On it," I say. "I've got us programmed to backtrack to the fifth gate, then a diversion course through another nearby gate just to throw off any followers. Once we get there I'll plot a course through the nearest gate and keep doing that until we know we've lost them."

"Cool," Valor says.

And he sounds cool. Like that conversation we had earlier is just no big deal.

Luck and Valor. All these years. I have so many fucking questions.

And even though the whole reason we're out here together is so I can save my girl, I can't deny that Valor's offer intrigues me.

We come out of the fifth gate and there's only a few minutes of full-speed velocity until we're approaching the last one.

"This is it," Valor says. "Thirty-second trip and then we're there."

"I'm ready," I say.

117

"We're in." And then, thirty seconds later, "We're out."

I scan the darkness before us, desperate to see something.

Because there is nothing there.

"Where is she?" I ask. "Where the fuck is she? There's nothing here!"

I'm panicked. If she's not here at these coordinates, then I don't know where she is. My plans are bust. She's out there, lost. I will never find her. I will—

"Hold on," Valor says. "I've got something. It's a debris field."

No.

My heart sinks like dead weight inside my chest. No. I did not come all this way to find a debris field.

"There was some kind of recent explosion," Valor says. "Picking up millions of small particles."

I get up from my station and walk up front, place my hand on Valor's shoulder and hold my breath as I lean in close to the screen showing the empty space outside.

"Hold on," he says. "Something else here. It's a cryopod." Valor laughs. "A single fucking cryopod."

I exhale and whisper, "Thank the fucking sun," as I slip into the co-pilot's chair. "Activating tractor beam."

"Locked," Valor says.

"Retrieving," I add.

Then a few moments later, he says, "Got her. Pulling her into the airlock."

We both lean back in our chairs and look at each other.

Valor grins. "Now what?"

"I don't know," I say.

"Are we gonna wake her up?"

"I… don't know." It's only then that I realize… I didn't really think we'd succeed. I never thought about what to do once we had her on board. I was so worried about fixing the ship, getting him on board, and actually arriving at this moment in time, I haven't actually thought very much about what comes next.

"OK," Valor says. "Medical?"

"Yeah," I say. "Send the pod down to medical. We'll run some scans and make sure she's OK and then… maybe I should go inside. Tell her she's OK and let her know we're going to pull her out."

Valor nods. "Sounds good." But then he pauses. "But I want to go in too."

I frown automatically. "Why?" Does he have some plan I'm not aware of? Will he start telling her she's not real and fuck things up?

"Because I want to see it for myself. And I want to meet her."

"Look, Valor, she's… she's been locked in there for so long. I don't want her upset."

"Why would I upset her? I just want to meet her."

"You want to meet her because you don't think she's real. You want to prove that to me."

"Maybe that's part of it. But not all of it. I'm fuckin' curious, OK? I want to see what you've been doing all those times you stole away on Harem to"—he does air quotes—"'maintain things.'"

I'm scowling.

"I won't mess with her head. I promise. I'm not a mean guy. You know that. I don't hurt people for the sake of hurting them."

119

He's not mean. He's right about that. Valor is thoughtful. But he's also convinced he's right. I can tell. Even after explaining my theory about ALCOR and Harem Station coming from another galaxy.

"Don't ask her any questions," I say. "And don't talk about how she's not real. No one wants to hear that shit. And if we find out there's something weird going on I'll be the one to tell her, not you."

"OK," he says. "That's fair."

"OK," I say. "We have three pods down in medical. So I can hook us both in. But it's not safe to do it here. We have to go somewhere safe."

"We could go back to the spin node," Valor offers. "That's the safest place I can think of."

"Good idea. OK. Let's pull her in, check her out, and then backtrack to the spin node coordinates and then..." I smile at him. He grins back. "Then we go in and I'll show you our world."

"Time?" he says. "When the fuck are we?"

I shake my head. "No way to tell. There's no sun or planets around here to grab a *when*. It's just space. We need gravitational waves to pull a time. So... I dunno. It took just a little over thirty minutes to get here and it'll take the same to get back. But once we're inside the spin node, time will basically stop for us again."

"So fuck time?"

I laugh. "Fuck time, I guess."

"Good to know."

We pull Brigit's cryopod in and there are a few moments when I think the pod will be empty because the inside is frosted over with nothing but ice.

But someone is in there. Because when we hook her up to the ship's monitoring machines there are vital signs. A faint heartbeat—normal for the temperature inside. And brainwaves. Number one most important thing after a heartbeat.

When those start bleeping I grin at Valor. It's an I-told-you-so-grin. *See*, that smile says. *Living, breathing person inside.*

He doesn't respond because the ice on the inside of her pod begins to melt and there's no need to question it anymore. She's in there. That's her face. And the relief I feel when I see it requires me to sit.

Valor stares at her, both hands on the pod, gazing intently at her face. He looks at me and nods. "She's very pretty, Tray."

I smile. "She is, isn't she?"

"OK," he says, back to business. "I'm gonna go back up and get us moving."

I get up to go with him, but he puts a hand on my shoulder and says, "You can stay here with her. I got this."

"You sure?"

He taps my head. "If I need help you'll know anyway."

"Truth." I smile.

Then watch him go and realize... he's the only person in this entire universe who really knows what I am.

A machine.

I run every diagnostic I can think of as Valor retraces our steps and takes us back to the safety of the spin node. A part of my enhanced brain keeps track of everything he's doing, but most of it is thoroughly preoccupied by Brigit.

She's here. She's really here.

Every primal urge inside me wants to wake her up. And I think about Crux and how long he's had Corla locked inside her cryopod up in that security beacon.

How? How does he stand it knowing she's just one wake-up program away from being with him again?

I could never do it. Not a whole year, for sun's sake. I would go mad. She's been with me thirty minutes and I'm dying. The only thing that prevents from waking her up as we travel is the uncertainty of what it might do to her mind to just be ripped away from the world I created for her. From all the places she's familiar with and all the people she knows.

They're not real, but they are all she has.

So I temper the almost overwhelming desire to hold her in my arms and tell her she's safe now with that little reality check. I have to go in and explain things now. She knows some of it, but not most of it. She doesn't know anything about Harem Station or what's really going on.

And now I'm glad that Valor is here with me. Happy that he's taking an interest in her. There were a few moments after we had that awkward discussion where I thought, *Will he be jealous of Brigit and me?*

122

But I'm not getting that kind of vibe off him. So I don't think about that. I don't bother with the complications and what could go wrong.

Hell, that's all I thought about in almost two decades since she found her way into the Pleasure Prison. Everything that could go wrong.

And lots of things did go wrong.

I didn't plan on Draden dying. I didn't see the sudden appearance of Lyra, then Nyleena, then Delphi.

Shit. Delphi.

I almost forgot about her.

There's something very off about Delphi. I should've made that my priority when Jimmy returned with her, but I was so close to getting Brigit out. Everything else had to wait.

And now it's no longer my problem. Luck, Nyleena, and Crux are in charge of Harem. If everything went as planned then the station is in total chaos.

If everything didn't...

Don't think about it, Tray. You've worked too hard to get to this moment.

Enjoy it.

Eventually that weird left-behind feeling returns and I know we're back inside the spin node and when I check an exterior camera for a view I see Angel Station spinning off in the distance.

Valor's boots clomp down on the nearly vertical stacked stairs and when I look up he's jumping down the last flight.

Suddenly I see us as kids again. Running around ALCOR Station. Just fucking around and having a good time.

Well, that was mostly him and Luck. But I watched them, wishing I could join them.

But things were too weird for me back then. I didn't understand all the code running through my head. Like I knew how to do everything ALCOR wanted done, but I didn't know how I knew. So I kept myself apart from my brothers. And even when I did begin to understand who and what I was and how all this information got inside my head, I didn't join them.

It felt too late.

So this is another second chance for me. A way to bond with Valor and be something to each other that we never were before.

"I'm ready," he says, jogging over to me. "She's OK, right?" And for a moment he looks worried as he gazes down at the cryopod.

"She has all the signs of being OK," I answer.

Valor looks at me, cracks half a smile. "Let it go now, Tray."

"Let what go?"

"That little voice inside you that says you have to be rational every moment of the day. You won, dude. You did it. You got her. We're here. We're going inside. Together. And then we'll come out and fix this shit."

I nod. I want to believe him. But I know too much to allow myself to feel like we've won.

Valor rubs his hands together. "OK. What now? I get in? It's just like getting into the Pleasure Prison back on Harem?"

"Yes," I say. "It's exactly like that." I take the drive out of my pocket and hold it up. "She's not really in there," I say, pointing at the pod. "She's in here."

"OK," Valor says.

"So you go in first. I have to upload the world to the ship data core so we can sync up. Then I'll join you once that's done."

"Cool," Valor says. "How long will it take?"

"Couple minutes," I say. "But once you're in there, time is weirdly fast. Or slow. I guess it depends on your perspective. It's gonna feel like a long time before I come in after you. It's not. It'll just feel that way. So... you know. Explain things. And tell her I love her and I'll see her soon."

Valor nods. "I will."

"And tell her this is the last time. I'm waking her up and this is the last time. And if she starts to get worried, just... keep her busy. Keep her mind off things. Make her laugh. And smile. Just make her happy, OK? I want all her fear to go away right now."

I want her to feel the way Valor does. Like we've won. Like it's all a done deal even though it's not.

"I will," Valor promises.

"You're gonna wake up in a green space, probably. There's a garden. And community buildings all over. Our building is like a light orange color. Number one. And people. They won't notice you, but—"

"I got it," Valor says. "I know how to go into a virtual."

125

"OK, so just knock on the door and tell her who you are. I leave a… placeholder avatar behind when I leave. So when I come back in I'm already in the house. In the bedroom, actually. Sleeping. So that's where I'll be when I appear."

"Tray. Seriously. Don't worry. I'll take care of everything."

I nod back. "OK." Then point to one of the empty medical pods we'll be using for the virtual experience. "Get in."

He opens the lid and climbs in, stretching out his long legs and lying back with arms at his side.

I don't need to explain the entrance procedure to Valor. He's gone through this many hundreds of times back on Harem Station. And he doesn't wait for any more instructions, either. Just presses the screen embedded into the open lid and it lowers over his face.

There's a pressurizing sound as the pod seals up.

"See you soon," I whisper. Then I turn and walk over to the nearest data station, plug the drive into a slot in the side of the console, and let my mind take over as I upload the program.

CHAPTER TWELVE

I am content and happy. My world is simple and perfect. An ocean, a beach, a small hut. I make it rain every once in a while. There's fruit but I don't really need to eat it. And there's no one else here except the animals, and the birds, and the plants.

I've been here a long time now so it's perfectly suited to me. But when I first arrived there was an end to it. The gray fog swirled along the borders of my world like a threatening menace.

I didn't like it. I knew it couldn't hurt me because this is literally my world. I control all of it. But I didn't like it. So every day I would venture forth and create. More land, more trees, more plants, more birds, more everything.

So now when I stand on the highest point of my little personal utopian compound, there's no gray fog in any direction. It's my own endless paradise for as far as I can see.

I considered adding people. I tried to conjure up Aieena. But it didn't work right. She appeared, but she didn't talk. Or move. Or do anything but stand there like a statue. I figured making people is a lot of work and… eh. Did I really want to spend my time creating her? Molding her? Shaping her?

She wouldn't be the same person because I didn't create her, Tray did. And things could go wrong. It's pretty perfect here and I have been busy every moment since I started to reshape things.

So I decided no people. Maybe one day I'll get bored and give it a go.

But then again, maybe not.

Not having to deal with the fake people makes my world better. Less virtual, in a way.

I think about Tray. Sometimes. I try not to think about Tray most of the time.

Wishing for him won't make him appear. But I did make all this with him in mind.

He's very good at virtual world-building. And when he finally does come back I want him to be proud of what I've done.

My days are leisurely in a way they weren't in the world he made for me. Tray was going for reality. I get it. He wanted me to be comfortable and feel like I was part of a community. It didn't work. I was the only real person there and I always knew it.

And that made it more fake.

Here… I feel real.

I get up in the morning and swim in the ocean. Then I lie in the sun and doze. Then I'll usually create something. A new species of bird, or lizard, or fruit tree.

I made clothes for a while but I stopped that a long time ago.

Why cover my beautiful body when there's no one here to see it?

The sun moves across the sky much the same way it did in that other place. And at night stars appear. I spent a lot of time on my stars. They make perfectly visible constellations in the dark night sky.

This is better than Tray's Utopia because now it's Brigit's Paradise.

It's midafternoon and I'm lying on the sand soaking up the warm rays of my sun, just listening to the sound of the softly crashing waves when a shadow blocks the light.

I don't notice it for a moment. There's a second or two when my mind processes this as normal. Then I realize I didn't make a cloud in the sky.

And when I open my eyes, shielding them from the glare of my sun, there is a man standing in front of me.

A man who is not Tray.

We stare at each other for a few moments. He's naked, like me. Because my world has no clothes. And I know he's an Akeelian because he has two cocks, both of which are semi-hard.

"Brigit?" he says, squinting down at me.

I sit up and prop my hands behind me, digging them into the sand. "I am Brigit."

"I'm Valor. Tray's brother."

The heart I created in my chest beats rapidly and I get to my feet.

"I'm not going to hurt you," Valor says. "Tray sent me in first because I wanted to see it. He's coming soon. To pull you out, Brigit. We have you. You're safe. He's going to pull you out but he wanted to talk to you first so you didn't get confused."

129

I think about this for a moment.

In fact, I have thought about this moment for lifetimes, it seems. I dreamed about it. When it would happen, what it would look like... how happy I would be.

And somehow it didn't quite prepare me for the reality of the actual occurrence.

"Say something," he says. "Did you understand me? I'm Valor. Tray's brother. We're pulling you out."

It's been so long since I talked out loud, there's a slight panic rising inside me because I fear that I forgot how.

But then the words form in my head and come out my mouth. "Hello."

"Hello," he says, taking a step closer. He was backlit by the sun, but that one step takes the glare away and I see his brilliant violet eyes as they pass up and down my naked body. "It's... nice to meet you. Finally. Tray's told me so much about you."

"Funny," I say. "He's never mentioned you."

"No?" Valor laughs. "Well, we weren't real close until recently. And actually, it was recently that he finally told me what was going on in here. Just yesterday in our time."

I peek my head to the side to see behind him, hoping that Tray will appear.

"It's gonna take a while, he said. He had to send me in first. But he's coming. He told me to tell you that he loves you and he'll see you soon. And not to worry."

"OK," I say.

I'm not sure I believe him.

"He told me to describe outside too. We're on a ship, Brigit. Umm... you were in a cryopod. We pulled it in and now you're in our medical bay. Asleep."

"What is the year?" I ask. "Outside? Did I look young? Or am I an old woman now?"

"You're not old," he says, shaking his head. "You're very..." His eyes dart over my naked body again, taking it in more thoroughly.

I let him do that. It's been a very long time since a man looked at my body.

"You're very beautiful," he finishes. "In the real. But we don't have a firm grasp on the time because you weren't near a gravity well to pull a time from." He smiles and shrugs his shoulders. "I'm just repeating what he told me. I barely know what that means."

I take in his body too. It's very difficult not to notice his... *man-ness*. Broad shoulders thick with muscle. Taller than me. Blond hair. Those violet eyes, of course.

He's different than Tray, but there's something familiar about him too.

I think about that for a moment. Something triggering in my mind. Something about—

"Hey, uh... so this isn't what Tray described to me. He said there was a community building, and people, and—"

"I broke that world," I explain. "And had to make a new one."

"Shit," Valor says. He turns and looks around. "Shit. Tray says he would appear there. Will he be able to get here?"

I smile. "He's Tray."

"Right, but—"

131

"Don't worry. He's... *Tray*."

"Right." He chuckles.

And it's in this exact moment that I realize... I *have* been lonely. I *have* missed people. And he's real. He's really real. Not some fabricated illusion of real. He lives out there. And now he's in here.

Alone. With me.

I have a sudden, almost uncontrollable urge to touch him. To feel him. To caress the realness of his body. I want to talk to him. I want to fight with him. I want to experience every single emotion with him. All the good, and bad, and ugly, and beautiful human emotions I've been missing for God only knows how long.

"So what do we do now? Are you going to take me somewhere?"

He looks around, squints his eyes a little. "No. I don't have anywhere to take you. We're just supposed to wait."

That makes me feel a little better for some reason.

One last waiting period. Only now I know the truth. I know where Tray is. He's standing over my body right now in the real world. He's thinking about me. He's planning my rescue. And soon—even though I have no idea what soon means—soon, we will be together again.

"He told me to keep you happy," Valor says. "He told me to make sure you know he loves you. And he said it's going to feel like a long time before he gets here, but right now, in this very moment on the other side, he's on his way in, Brigit."

I nod my head and feel wetness on my cheeks. I'm crying.

"Please," Valor says, taking another step towards me. "Don't cry. It's almost over." His arms wrap around me and then all my desires come true.

I feel him. His touch floods my body with all the emotions I've had bottled up.

And I just cry.

CHAPTER THIRTEEN

It's been a long time since I had strong feelings. When I was young, before my father changed me, I had a lot of feelings. Too many. Feelings of panic and fear. Feelings of hopelessness and despair. Anxiety so bad sometimes I withdrew into myself for days at a time. Unwilling or maybe unable to find my way back to the real world.

And that was *before* I knew about virtual reality.

So I don't hate my father for what he did to me. After he pulled me out of medical he told me that yes, he'd done it because he was told to. But he'd also done it to help me.

Help me deal with the emotions that flooded my brain and made me unable to relate to others. He had hoped it would be a coping mechanism. Something that would temper the neurochemicals that unbalanced me.

I asked him about that first part. Who told him to do this to me? Who was pulling the strings? But he just said, "Later, Tray. I'll explain later. Right now I just want you to get used to your new self. Try new things. See what you can do now. Talk to people. Because I think you'll be surprised to learn that life isn't so overwhelming anymore."

He was right. Life was much easier. I could feel the difference the moment I woke up from the procedure. There was something else inside me now. But it was still me.

ALCOR asked me a lot of questions about this procedure when we first arrived. What did it feel like? Was it like a parasite? Did it feel... *other*?

It didn't. It felt like me, only better. More in control. Equipped to deal. Like there's a control panel somewhere that governs all my responses and someone adjusted it. Just a little, just enough, so that everything made sense and nothing was overwhelming.

When I came out of medical Jimmy saw me first. There were other kids on Wayward Station. More than just the seven of us who left under Corla's direction. And unlike Crux, who was tutored privately and his friends were restricted, I went to school with all of them. I had one class with Jimmy. It was a human relations class and it involved a lot of group discussion, which, before my change, was very difficult for me. We sat in small intimate circles and talked about ethics and cultures.

I never really understood why I was in that class because I was several years younger than everyone else. I never fit in. And besides, my job was always going to be network interfacing. Even if I didn't have the upgrade. My future was in artificial intelligence just like my father. Just like Jimmy's future was diplomatic relations because that's what his father did.

And it was hard for me. Everything was hard for me in the years before my change.

Then after… it wasn't.

The emotions were gone. Just… gone. There was nothing there. I didn't care what people thought, I didn't care about feelings, I didn't care about ethics or perspective. I just didn't care.

In this group discussion where Jimmy was the oldest, and thus the leader by default, our talk always devolved into all things teenager. I was a teenager, but there were no girls on my mind. I didn't want to drink in the dining room the way Jimmy and Crux did. I didn't want access to X Level so I could fuck sexbots.

But Jimmy did. He and the other boys talked about it one day in class. And in my mind I was accessing it, just purely out of boredom. Just to see what was down there. And when the class was over I don't know what came over me. But I walked up to Jimmy—who I had never really talked to in any meaningful way before this moment—and I said, "I can get you in to X Level if you want."

Of course he said yes. And I did get him in. And I can only assume he had a good time because after that he said hi to me in the hallway. He smiled at me.

We were friends.

My first friend. Jimmy was my first friend.

Thinking back on that now, I find it sad.

Because I didn't understand that he was just using me.

The same day that Crux was breeding with Corla I was in the middle of another upgrade. Not one that involved a cryopod. Just a simple one. Just a few lines of code in the form of nanobots injected into my bloodstream my father said were necessary to 'even things out'.

I didn't know what that meant back then because everything felt pretty fucking even as far as I was concerned. But just a few hours later I would understand.

It was a processing power upgrade that allowed me to override the nearby spin node gate and this is how we got Corla through it.

I never saw my father again after that last trip to medical. He never gave me any directions. He never said, "Son, this is your path. Just keep going."

So I never knew for sure that he was in on it. That he was helping us.

But I think he was. And I think he's dead now because of it.

I have so many feelings about that.

During our escape from Akeelian System I didn't have time to think about this stuff. And once we got to ALCOR Station I was busy getting him online. So it was about a year before I actually had time to think that whole night through. That's when the emotions came back. That's when I figured it out.

My father sent us on that mission. He got me out. He got my friends out. He saved us. And he paid for it with his life.

It overwhelmed me at first.

Guilt, mostly.

Sadness. The despair was back. The depression. The realization of what happened and what it all meant.

ALCOR and I were close back then. My daily grind was all about him. And I did everything he asked like I was born to do it. He would ask a question and answers would just come spilling out of my mouth fully formed.

I would say things I didn't even understand. I was on autopilot.

That's when the new thing inside me became a parasite. Long after ALCOR stopped asking me that question.

I think he knew. I think he had always known that I would eventually feel that way about the new me. Because one day I would wake up and Old Tray would be completely gone. Nothing left of that scared kid. And New Tray would be the only thing left.

This was when he told me about the Pleasure Prison. It was a distraction, I realize. Just a way to make me feel better. Give me another purpose.

He said it was left over from the inhabitants who used to live on the station. Which was not a lie. He just failed to mention the specifics behind the lie.

I figured that out on my own after many, many years of building the Pleasure Prison. And that tight bond that ALCOR and I formed in the early days when New Tray was just a shell of a being started to fade. He was busy with Crux by then, trying to convince him that what we were doing was good. That this was all going to be OK. Because Crux was always his moral compass. That was what ALCOR called him in private. Not to Crux's face, because that would just set him off on a quest to find out why ALCOR needed a moral compass in the first place.

I don't know how Brigit got into my Pleasure Prison. It could've been ALCOR. But I don't think so. I don't think ALCOR knew about Brigit. I hid her so very, very well.

And like I said, I didn't really have time to think about all this stuff back then. My life after the escape was just one long task list.

I like task lists. They keep my mind busy in a way that's satisfying.

But I have time to think about it now because I'm inside the portable version of Brigit's virtual and there's nothing here.

It's gone. Just smoky-gray clouds of ether code.

Normally I would wake up in our bedroom and Brigit would be somewhere close by. Not there, with me. She never knew when I would wake up again so she just went on with her life until I found her. At work, or outside somewhere, whatever.

Old Tray would panic about my current situation. Old Tray would have emotions flooding through his bloodstream telling him to be afraid. Or be sad. Or feel hopeless.

But Old Tray is long gone.

Maybe he never really existed?

So I don't panic. I know what this is. I can guess what happened.

Her world was disrupted in such a way that she annihilated it.

But she's here. She has to be here. If she were still on Harem I'd worry that something truly went wrong. That someone got in to the Pleasure Prison the way she did and stole her.

But this isn't the real Pleasure Prison. It's a copy.

Ironic, right? Copies of copies of copies.

It's the real version of Brigit. At least the only one I've ever known.

So I just wander. Drift around, kinda searching, but not really. I know I'll find them eventually. Time is on my side.

And I think about all these things I've been putting on hold since our escape.

I think about Jimmy and how he used me.

I think about ALCOR and how he used me too.

I think about Crux, and Luck, and Serpint and how I never really knew them. More my fault than theirs. Because they never needed me and I didn't need them either.

I think about Valor. I think about him and Luck all these years. Their secret romance. Bromance. Whatever.

I think about how Valor chose me over Luck once Nyleena came along. How he needs me.

And I'd be stupid not to wonder if he was just using me too. To get to Veila.

But for some reason I don't let those feelings take hold with Valor. Maybe it's because I need him too?

And just when I come to this realization there's a point of light in the distance. A gold light that gets bigger like I'm approaching it, but in reality—or at least virtual reality—it's approaching me.

It's not Brigit. I know this immediately.

But the last person I expect to see inside my copy of Pleasure Prison is Draden.

He forms in front of me slowly. Taking his time like... maybe he thinks I need this time to get used to the idea.

I don't. I'm New Tray. And in a way, when I think about it as I watch his body pull itself together, I think I *did* expect this. I think I knew that Draden was never dead. I think I knew that ALCOR killed him back when he was thirteen and he fell off a lift bot and then brought him back to life.

I think I knew that he was like me.

A machine.

Neither of us smile. We just stare at each other. Draden and his dark blond hair. His violet eyes that were the brightest of all of ours. Practically pink in color. I think that was why everyone loved him so much. Those violet-pink eyes could mesmerize you. They kept him child-like in a way. Innocent. And he was innocent, wasn't he? He didn't ask for this any more than I did.

"You don't think it's me, do you?"

He says this in a way that confuses me for a moment. *You don't think it's me* as in… I cannot believe it's him? Or *You don't think it's me* as in… *Do you think I'm doing this?*

"It's you," I say. "It's been you all this time." But I'm not even sure what I mean by that.

He sucks in a deep breath of air and when I look down at myself I am Tray again. Not a gray cloud of code. And the world around us begins to form and we're back in Brigit's virtual world. The one I created for her. Only it's empty now.

We're standing on the grass near the community garden. The sun is shining hot directly overhead like it's midday.

I'm the one doing this but Draden doesn't look surprised. He just asks, "Do you know how I got here?"

I nod. Because I think I do.

"So… you're gonna believe me then?"

I nod again.

"I tried to tell Brigit. I tried to get her to leave with me. I'm there."

"No," I say. "You're not Draden. You're here."

He shakes his head. And for a second I see little Draden. The kid he was that day we left Wayward. Innocent and young. Scared and brave. Hopeful and hopeless in the same instant. Maybe this is little Draden? Maybe the man I see before me is really just the mind of the child he was when he fell off the lift bot that day when he was thirteen?

"I'm *there*," he insists.

"OK," I say. Because I just want to look at him for a moment. I want to feel these things I'm feeling. The emotions that come to the surface at the sight of him.

A tear slides down my cheek.

"I'm fine," he says.

I nod. But I don't agree. None of us are fine. It's all bullshit.

"We have to get her out of here," Draden says, looking around.

"She's already gone," I say.

"I can't find her," Draden says. "I've looked everywhere."

"She's all right, Draden. I'll see her soon. She's with Valor, anyway. He's taking care of her."

"It's just us, you know," Draden says. "Just us two." Then he laughs a little. "I've been trying so hard to find her." His face goes serious again. "I think I scared her."

"It's OK," I say. "She's gonna be OK now."

143

We lock eyes for a moment. Because he knows he's not real. He knows nothing in here is real. And I don't want him to know that.

"How did I get here?" he asks.

"ALCOR," I say. "The answer to every question you have, Draden, is always ALCOR."

"What do I do, Tray? Can you tell me what to do?"

I shake my head and swallow down the lump in my throat. I whisper, "I wish I could, brother. But I just don't know."

He starts to fade after that. Mouth moving like he's still talking. But no words coming out. Eyes wide, like he's afraid.

He should be afraid. We should all be afraid.

And I'm afraid for him.

Because eventually everything about him disappears and I just don't know.

I don't know where he really is. I don't know why he's here. I don't even know which instance of him was in front of me. Not Real Draden, that's for sure. Real Draden is somewhere far, far away. This is just a copy of this mind that ALCOR put inside my virtual reality.

He's just another prisoner.

We're all just a bunch of prisoners.

I don't know how long I sit there in the grass, overwhelmed with hopelessness. I didn't miss Draden the way everyone else did. Even Lyra missed him more than I did. She glowed pink for him at the memorial service.

144

But I'm not the same man I was a year ago. Everything has changed.

I know I have to figure out where I'm at right now and find my way to Brigit and Valor because outside of the world I built time flows in its own way and I probably have no control over it at the moment.

But seeing Draden trapped in here... it hits me hard for some reason. His death—or whatever it was that happened to him back on Cetus Station—that finally sinks in.

He's dead. Or he's not and wishes he was.

Because he's trapped somewhere the way Brigit was trapped. Only he doesn't have anyone to help him.

I could help him.

But Brigit is waiting.

And even though I love Draden as much as I am able to love people, I want to save Brigit more. She's been here longer. And I made a promise.

So I get up and start walking. It's the only answer I can think of that might work. Brigit and Valor are here somewhere, I just need to find them.

Then... *then* we can go looking for Draden.

I know where the boundaries of my old world are, but it all ends too soon. Like it's been wiped away. Still, there's a shimmer of the old world beneath my feet. I'm wearing my regular clothes, the ones I was wearing on the outside, but eventually I cross the boundary of the old world I created and Brigit destroyed and end up in... something else. And at this exact moment, my clothes disappear.

It's not like I need them. It's just... kinda... well, I'm not the kind of guy who walks around naked. I'm not embarrassed of my body. It's actually a nice fucking

145

body for a guy like me who does no manual labor. I look a lot like Luck in the body department.

But I've never been comfortable with it. Not since all the muscles started appearing because I have often wondered if my body was just… an illusion. Something I made up, just like I made this place up.

It doesn't really make sense because even though my outside world could be a simulation, it's still my reality. Which means I don't control it. If it is just another layer of virtual, someone else is pulling the strings.

Maybe ALCOR?

Maybe he wanted us all to look like a band of handsome, rugged outlaws so when my teenage body started to mature he helped me out a little?

I don't know. I just have this sick feeling inside that this isn't… *me*.

Me is somewhere *else*.

And OK. If I think about that too long it starts to make my head spin. Because the real me *is* somewhere else. I'm on the ship on Angel Station inside a spin node. But is that the real me?

There are just too many layers of what's real and what's not to keep them all straight so I give up and stop trying to force it to fit together neatly.

Then, as if another boundary was crossed, I enter a desert. Sand dunes as far as I can see. I don't need to eat or drink in this world. I don't even need to sleep. Brigit and I did those things before because it felt normal. And right. It kept things real.

But it's a long walk across this desert and there's a part of me that wonders if I should leave the virtual and come back in again, this time with a new destination in mind.

That would eat up real seconds out there though. And seconds out there could be weeks in here. And if I get caught out there for minutes, well... that's a long time in this place. Plus, what destination? What would I aim for? Not the bed, where I usually appeared. That would just set me back to where I started from.

But even worse, that might take me back to Draden and that whole exchange still bothers me. It hurts to think of him trapped for the last year. Not in here. He cannot be in here. So I don't know how he got here.

But then again, how did Brigit get here?

So I walk, and walk, and walk and there is no end in sight. No way out of this vast nothingness of sand dunes and hot sun.

There is nothing else to do but leave and try again.

I wake up in the dark reality of the ship, lift the pod's lid up over my head, and check the counter on the display. Two minutes have passed while I was in there.

Then I notice there's a soft beeping coming from Brigit's pod and I get out of my pod and walk over to her, glancing up at the display screen as I go. Her vitals are fine. Heartbeat OK. But her brainwaves are doing something weird.

I glance back at the time counter on my pod and I'm suddenly indecisive.

147

The longer I stay out here, the more time speeds by in there.

She's with Valor, I remind myself. She's not alone. She's with Valor.

Think, Tray. Think. Think.

I go back to the medical screens on the main console and study her brainwaves and then notice something else on the display. A green glow emanating from deep in the hypothalamus region of her brain. Hormones, I think. I'm no biologist, but I think that part of the brain releases hormones.

I ask for a full scan of neurochemicals in her bloodstream and yes, I'm right. Lots of hormones. Which means lots of feelings in there.

That's OK, I decide. It's not fear hormones. It's all the pleasure ones.

With that new bit of information I feel better.

Then another beeping sound comes from her pod and I turn around to find her display lit up. Jagged lines run across the interior of her screen.

I turn towards it, wiping away the condensation on her faceplate, and focus.

Sound waves. It looks like a visual representation of sound waves.

What the fuck? Is she getting a message?

We're inside a sun-fucked spin node. Who could be sending her messages?

I walk over to the medical console and take a seat, fingers tapping frantically on the screens, trying to pull up more information.

But then, just as I pull up the right screen, the waveform stops. The peaks and valleys drop into a flat line.

Gone.

What the hell is happening? Is this normal? Has someone been sending her messages all this time? All these years?

But more importantly, can I decipher it?

Do I have time?

Minutes have passed now. I've been out here for minutes.

Indecision is not an emotion I'm very familiar with. I am a quick decision-maker. I see all possible outcomes the way an AI sees them. I know things before I even know how I know things.

But I don't know what to do now.

Stay here and figure out this mysterious message?

Or go back inside, grab her, and bring her out with me?

What if it's a trap? What if Valor is right? What if releasing her unleashes a virus or something worse?

I have to decipher the message. It's the only way to be sure. They will just have to wait for me.

Valor is in there. She's not alone.

So I get to work. My fingers tap out commands and lines of code. I get inside her cryopod, find that yes, there is a comms system, but it's empty and non-functional, then go looking deeper into her biologicals, looking for something akin to an air-screen implant like the kind we use on Harem. I find one, not in her finger, but implanted just behind her ear.

I should have done all this first, I realize. I should have done much more than this before I ever went inside. But I was too worried about her. Too anxious to get her out here with me.

Once I find the hardware, it's easy to hack into the software. There are thousands of messages and the sick feeling I get when I realize this makes me want to vomit.

But then I see something else on the screens in front of me. Something I missed when I first sat down.

Her clock. It's running slower than it should.

Oh, suns. What's happening?

I glance at the pod clock. An hour has passed. I run the calculations in my head and find that years have passed inside since I've been fucking around out here.

Years.

OK, this shit has to stop. I need to concentrate. I need to get a handle on what's happening.

Messages. That's the number one priority. I go digging. I crash all the firewalls that have been set up and finally, I have a name from the sender.

Corla.

I lean back in my chair and sigh.

OK. Corla. I can deal with Corla. If it had been Veila or someone I didn't know, this would be much, much worse. But Corla is still on our side.

Right?

I have to believe she is.

My fingers tap play and the words spill out. Long description of Corla's days. Babbling words about the virtual she's stuck in.

She's a prisoner too, I realize. And somehow she and Brigit are connected.

But these messages go back decades. Probably to right after Delphi was born. And Brigit never mentioned Corla. Or any messages.

So there's only two possible explanations.

She never got them.

Or she's lying.

I get up from my seat, walk back over to my cryopod, get in, shut the lid, and tap the start protocol on the face plate screen.

There's only one way to find out. Go back inside and ask.

This time I don't aim for the old world. I take my time as I enter and visualize Valor. He's my anchor. He's how I will find Brigit.

CHAPTER FOURTEEN

All the emotions I wanted to feel, but suppressed, come rushing out of me like a wave that would flood the world and wipe it clean. Fear and loneliness. Sadness and anger. It just pours out of me.

"Brigit," Valor consoles. "It's OK. I'm here. You're OK. Tray's coming."

But Tray isn't here yet. I am not going to turn down his brother's company. I'd take anyone at this point. I didn't realize that until just this moment, but it's true. If that Draden guy came back and made me that offer again, I'd leave. I would.

I can't stay here anymore. I will go crazy.

When? That's all I want to know. Just… when will it end? And I realize I'm having a crisis. Of faith, maybe? In me, or Tray, or maybe everyone. Of confidence?

Did I ever believe it? Did I ever really think that he would get me out of here?

No.

I really didn't.

And that's when I realize what this strange, never-felt-before emotion is.

Relief.

"Did you hear me?" Valor asks.

I shake my head because I think a long time has passed since he took me in his arms.

"We should… go inside. Get something to eat."

"We don't need to eat," I mutter. I slump down in the sand, naked, fingers grabbing it in handfuls, but of course it spills over and slips away. Slips away like time does. Like life.

"I know we don't need to eat," Valor says. "I know almost as much about living in a virtual as Tray does."

I glance up at him and shoot him a dubious look.

He smiles and shrugs. "I said almost."

He kneels down beside me and puts a gentle hand on my shoulder. Just the slightest of squeezes. And what can I say about his touch? How can I describe the feeling that rushes through my body when he makes contact?

It's been so long. So damn long since someone touched me.

I want to curl up into his chest and be held and I can't wait for an invitation. I can't stand one more moment of this all-encompassing aloneness.

So I wrap my arms around his waist and place my forehead against his chest, and hold my breath. Daring to hope that he will hold me.

He does. There is no hesitation. He holds me tight and kisses my head, and whispers, "You're OK," into my ear over and over again. "You're OK. You're OK. You're OK."

We stay like that for a long time. I don't know how long. Maybe it isn't long. Maybe it's a single moment and nothing else. But he hugs me and comforts me.

Eventually, I'm lying on the sand again. And when I close my eyes it feels like I made it all up. That maybe my imagination got away with me and it's not real.

But when I open my eyes to check, he's still there. Lying next to me. Basking in the hot afternoon sun that I made.

"How long, Brigit? How long have you been here?"

I like the way he says my name. "I don't know anymore. Surely, several eternities?"

He breathes out in a way that makes me think he's smiling. A little huff of air that says... *That's cute. Or maybe just sad.* "You're safe now."

I don't say anything to that. Because I can't be safe if I'm still here. I need to be out *there*.

"What should we do while we wait? Hmm? Swim? You have a very nice beach here."

I nod, but say nothing. How long will it take for Tray to arrive? Maybe this is all a hallucination? Maybe I've lost my mind and now I'm just making people up?

"How do I know you're real?" I ask. "How do I know he's really coming?"

"Well..." Valor pauses. He thinks. He thinks for a good long time. What could he tell me that I don't already know, but that would still be able to convince me that he's not a product of a sick and lonely mind? Finally he says, "I can't make promises, I guess. We have a plan, you're part of it, and I think it's gonna work. But I don't know, Brigit. In here I don't know any more than you do."

155

It's the truth. And it's nice to hear it for once.

"OK," I say, suddenly tired. The sun is going down and we're all sweaty from the heat, sand sticking to us like it's real. And I crave a swim and then all I want to do is go to sleep until Tray arrives.

But I don't want Valor to leave me. I don't want to take my eyes off Valor for fear that he will disappear, so I invite him to swim with me. And after we swim we pick berries. He talks. A lot. And makes me smile. And he tells me all about his life on the outside. He tells me about Harem Station where they live. And what he does inside the Pleasure Prison. *My* prison. It's weird hearing someone I don't know talk about my prison.

He has sex in there. And kills people. Fake people. Virtual people.

He tells me about the places he and his other brother, Luck, have gone in real life. Long-forgotten sectors that hold long-forgotten stations. He talks about their ship, and the bot they had before she was killed. And ALCOR.

Lots of things Tray never mentioned.

Long after the sun has set and the stars come out I create a bed for him and we sleep in the hut. There's a part of me that wants to climb into his bed, but I don't. I don't want it to be like that with Valor. I don't want to make him some substitute for Tray.

Because he's not.

In the morning I ask him if he wants clothes.

He declines.

And then we start a new day.

I show him how I pass the time waiting for Tray. We walk and walk until we reach the edge of the world and he watches me make something new. We stay out there for long stretches of time, sleeping on the ground at first, but I am the goddess of this place so I conjure up a tent and sleeping mats. And we pack it up and take it with us on the backs of large pack animals he helped me imagine.

It's an endless cycle of what I can only call... contentment.

He makes me happy. And I think I make him happy too.

Eventually we come back to the beach. It feels like home when we return and he feels like a friend I just had a great adventure with.

I had hope that Tray would be waiting for us when we got back, but he isn't there. So Valor and I start a new routine—swimming, and eating fruit, and talking, and laughing, and sleeping, and waking up to do it all again.

And even though this was my own personal paradise before he came, now it's something else.

Now it's *ours*.

And I get better.

My mind, which was corrupted with loneliness and despair, heals. Mends. And happy is a word I'd use to describe myself again. I no longer long for the old world that Tray made me. I don't miss my job at the café, or Aieena's bad gardening.

I am content.

One day Valor asks me, "Do you know how I can get out?"

"Get out?"

"Don't you think it's been too long? Don't you think I should go check on him?"

"Leave me here?" I ask. "Alone again?"

"No," he says, swiping the back of his fingers along my cheek.

I lean in to that because I like it. He doesn't touch me much. Hardly ever, actually. But when he does... God, it feels good. And sometimes I crave it.

"No, Brigit. No one's leaving you. I just think... it's been a long time. We've been waiting for Tray for a very long time."

"Not that long," I say. "Not compared to how long I've been in here."

He smiles at me. But it's a weak smile. "I know you want to get out. I sort of do too."

"Just sort of?" I ask, smiling. Hoping to make his smile bigger. Brighter.

"I like it here." He laughs. "It's fucking nice. For once, you know. Calm, and relaxing, and no bullshit. No wars, no princesses, no harem, no ALCOR. None of that that shit outside matters. So no. If you think I'm tired of this and I want to leave, just no. I could stay here forever."

I laugh at that. "Believe me, forever is such a long time."

"I don't know how you got along alone in here. I would've gone nuts."

"I think I did go nuts. Before you came, Valor, I really thought I was God."

We both laugh.

"I swear! It's kinda crazy to think about it now. But I really thought I was God and this was my garden paradise."

His grin is bright and broad. He looks around and shakes his head as he draws in a deep breath. "It is paradise." He looks back at me and meets my eyes. "I don't want to leave. Trust me. But I'm worried that something has gone wrong."

I don't want him to leave. I don't think I could stand it in here again if he did. I might really lose my mind if I have to exist alone again. So I say, "Tray once tried to explain time to me. He said that every second that passes out there is like months and months in here."

"It's been longer than months, Brigit."

"We don't know how long—"

"I've been counting," Valor says. "I count the nights. And it's been one thousand and fifty-four."

Shit. I hadn't noticed. I'm so used to time passing. Long, lonely stretches of it. And none of the time I've spent with Valor has seemed long or lonely.

"If my calculations are correct," Valor continues, "that's hours outside. He said minutes. He should've been here a long time ago. He told me to keep you happy, so I didn't bring it up. And I've been enjoying this place way too much to make a big deal about it until now. But... something's *wrong*."

I have been good this whole time. I don't touch him much even though I want to. Every once in a while our hands will brush against each other while walking. Or he'll touch my cheek in a moment of tenderness. Or he'll take my arm to steady me when we're climbing

159

up some rocks or pull me out to sea with him while I float on my back.

But there has always been a line. One we never crossed.

He's my best friend now. So much more than Aieena was. He's like Tray. But a Tray who does not leave me. Tray who stays with me all the time. Sleeps next to me. And eats with me. And talks and laughs with me. Every virtual minute of our virtual day.

"How do I get out?" Valor asks. "I need to make sure he's OK. Something could've happened on the ship. Or... I don't know. The spin node is degenerating or—"

"You haven't been here that long, Valor. I know it feels like forever, but it's not. Everything is OK. I promise. It's fine."

I am not too proud to beg.

He cannot leave me here.

I cannot let him.

"I'll just wake up for one moment, look around, make sure Tray is in his pod, and then come right back."

"No," I say. "No. Please. Please don't leave. I can't do it again. Not after all this time. I can't imagine what it would be like to live here alone again."

"Five seconds," he says.

"Five seconds is a long time in here, Valor. You know that. It's so long. I don't think... I can't..." But I trail off.

Because I can tell he's worried about Tray. He wants to go check on him. He keeps looking at the sky like that's the way out. I don't know the way out, to be honest. I've never left. So I can't tell him. It doesn't matter anyway. I'm sure he has an idea.

"There," he says, pointing to a gold shimmer in the blue sky.

I study the anomaly he's talking about. Kinda wavy and distorted. Like heat when it radiates up off the sand on super-hot days.

I've never noticed it before, so… maybe it's been there this whole time? Or maybe Valor created it when he went searching for the exit. Even though I've been locked up inside a virtual for God knows how long—many eternities, at least—I have no real understanding of how they work. It's just the place I exist.

"I think that's the exit," he says. "You wanna try to leave with me?"

"I can… leave?"

His shoulders drop a little and I already know the answer. "I don't think it would work. You're in a deep cryogenic sleep on the ship so you might just get lost and end up… nowhere. I think we have to wake you up from the outside."

I was holding my breath during his answer and now I let it out. I chew on my lip for a moment, wondering how close I am to total freedom, then realizing I'm still as far away as ever.

But he's right. I know he's right.

"OK," I say. "You can go check. I'll be OK. Tray is more important than my happiness."

Valor shakes his head at me and forces a small smile. "That's not true. He'd say the same thing about you, if he were here, Brigit." Valor looks at the sky again, then back down at me. "He'd tell me… he'd say… 'Valor. Don't you dare leave her alone.'"

Now, instead of holding my breath, I let it out. Allow myself to smile.

"Do you have any idea what Tray has done on the outside to be here with you?"

I shake my head. I can't even begin to imagine the outside world anymore. It feels like a fairytale. Some myth that can't possibly be true.

"We're basically fucking up all the plans right now. *Booty* and Asshole ALCOR are waiting for us out in the middle of space. They probably haven't been waiting long yet. It's hard to know with all the different time zones we've passed through since we left Harem. But we're definitely late at this point." He stops and looks at me. We're close. Not touching, but standing very close to each other. A comfortable distance. His eyes are beautiful. Lighter than Tray's. Everything about him is lighter than Tray. Lighter than me, too.

Tray and I are dark things. Like mysteries in a pool of murky water. Valor is a bright thing. Something made out of sky and sun. And I always get this feeling that at any moment he could sprout wings and fly away in the wind.

He is a golden god in my eyes.

I take his hand in both of mine and squeeze it.

He looks down at my gesture, then back up at my eyes. "I'll stay."

He hasn't changed. Not in all the time he's been here. His hair is still a little bit too long. Curling just slightly, right above the line of muscle where his neck meets his shoulders. He came in looking sun-streaked all those days ago, his body just a little bit brown and marred with several scars left over from many battles.

162

I want to touch him. I want to put my hands on his arms and feel the hills and valleys of his muscles. I want to press my palms flat on his chest and feel his heartbeat.

Does he have a heartbeat?

Do I?

I reach up with my free hand and place it over my heart to check. And for a moment, there's nothing there and I almost panic.

But I am the goddess of this world. And if I want a heartbeat, a heartbeat I shall have.

It thumps under the pressure of my palm. So hard and loud I think Valor can hear it.

"What in the ever-loving sun is going through your mind right now?" he asks.

"I don't know," I say. "I'm not sure. I just…" I drop his hand and look around at my paradise. Our paradise.

There are tall, skinny trees with fruit under the shallow canopy of broad, waxy leaves. And sand. I like the way the foamy waves roll up on it and leave little ocean mysteries behind for me to find. Things like sea shells, and strange tendrils of plants, and little crab-like creatures that always look like they're walking backwards. Valor imagined all those things. He says they're real. That everything we've created here is real somewhere.

I like the blue sky and the way it turns purple and red at night as my sun sets. I like the cool nights and the smattering of sparkling stars.

I like waking up with Valor nearby. I like the thought of Tray coming here. I imagine he might even be a little bit impressed with our world-building skills.

I study Valor's face now, his angled jaw that has this perpetual scruff on it, just enough to cast a shadow on his glow. But my eyes begin to drop. I study the tendons of his neck, then the muscles of his chest. The way his stomach has lines of shadows across it, clearly defining his muscles. And then... his cock. Which is almost always in a state of semi-hardness.

I have watched him hold it in his hand each morning when he wakes. He never jerks off in front of me. Always goes out into the ocean or into the trees. And I have never spied on him, so I've never seen him in that moment when he finds relief.

I don't think about sex much but I'm thinking about it now.

My eyes lift up again, meeting his. I take a deep breath and on the exhale I say, "I think... I might be happy."

Valor just stares at me. Unblinking. I hold his gaze until he breaks the connection and starts studying me the way I was just studying him.

My neck. Then my breasts. Then my flat, shadow-muscled stomach, and finally to the spot between my legs that is not aching for him.

When he meets my gaze I am, once again, holding my breath.

I break away first this time. Stare past his shoulder and out at the sea.

Then I close my eyes and make it dark. Not completely dark. Rays of golden sun find their way past the semi-opaque skin of my eyelids and remind me that we live in paradise.

I feel, more than hear, when he takes a step closer to me and closes the distance.

164

His touch makes my skin tingle. A shiver runs up my body when his fingertips lightly brush against my nipple. Just one small, gentle touch and then it's gone.

I don't dare open my eyes because I will come to my senses and tell him no.

It's just been a long, long time. And I love Valor in my own way now. He's my best friend. He's my new rock. He makes me happy and I haven't had a lot of experience with happy. Contentment is a new emotion for me and I want to hug it. I want to hold it close and never let it go.

Valor swallows so hard it's audible. "Don't worry," he whispers. "I would never."

I want to object to that. I want to tell him he has permission. *My* permission.

But I don't. I can't make my mouth form those words.

I count in my head and when I get to twenty-seven I feel able to look at him again.

He's staring at me, frowning. But then his eyes dart up, looking past me, and his frown turns to a smile. "Tray?"

CHAPTER FIFTEEN

The sea is the first thing I notice when I drop back into the world. A misty, salty breeze hits my face and the warm sun drenches my shoulders. I'm naked again, but that's not what I care about.

Down below the hill I'm standing on are Brigit and Valor. Standing quite close together, both also naked, and having what appears to be a serious conversation.

I almost call out, but find that I can't. There's a lump in my throat and anyway, I just want to look at them. It feels like forever since I've seen Valor, and it's only been a couple of hours in real time.

It feels like eternity since I've seen Brigit.

Valor notices me first. He's facing the hill, while Brigit is facing the water.

He squints his eyes and smiles. "Tray?"

I can't hear it. I'm too far away. But I can read his lips.

I start walking down the pebbled incline but soon I'm hopping, feet slamming into loose dirt and sand, then hopping again. By the time I reach the bottom Valor is there, hugging me, almost too hard.

167

"You fucking asshole." He laughs. "I hate you, you asshole!"

I hug him back but I only see Brigit walking towards me. Naked, and perfect, and golden from lifetimes of living under the bright, hot sun.

Valor claps me on the back one more time, then releases me.

Brigit and I stare at each other for several long seconds. And for a moment I think she's mad. I have been missing for a long time as far as she's concerned.

"Brigit," I say.

"Tray," she whispers back. Then she closes her eyes. Squeezes them tight. And smiles.

I reach for her and pull her into a hug. "It's OK. I'm here."

She hugs me back. Tight. Maybe tighter than she's ever held me before. "What took so long? Valor was worried. He was just about to leave."

"Shit," I say, turning a little so I can see Valor. "I'm sorry. I dropped into the old world and couldn't find you guys so I went back out and—"

I stop. Make a decision. Decide not to tell them about the messages from Corla just yet. I don't think Brigit was getting them anyway, so Corla is a mystery for another day. Maybe even another lifetime.

Just not now.

"Fuck, man," Valor says. "I was so worried. Do you have any idea how long we've been waiting?"

"Yeah," I say, tapping my head to indicate I've run the calculations. "I'm sorry. But..."

And I'm just about to say, *We can go now*, when I stop. Because once we leave here and we're back in the real, then we have to go back to work. We have to wake up Brigit. Tend to her medical needs, if she has any. Leave the spin node, go find *Booty* and ALCOR, and then… war.

There's nothing but war ahead of us.

I'm not ready for that. Valor might be. Brigit might be. But I just got here. I want to enjoy her, and him, while I can.

We could die. And that could happen fast. We could come out of the spin node and be caught immediately. We could show up at the prearranged coordinates and find warships. Anything could happen.

So what's the rush?

I take in my surroundings and smile. Tilt my head back, close my eyes, and let the warm sun wash over my face. "I like this place, Brigit. Did you do all this?"

"I did," she says. And when I open my eyes again, she's looking around with a hint of pride in her smile. "I made it all from nothing." She leans into me, her soft hands slipping around my waist like I belong to her. Like she owns me. "I made it for you." Then she pulls away a little and locks eyes with me. "Actually, I made it for us." She shrugs. "There's no people here. Just us." A nod of her head indicates she's including Valor in that us.

"I want to sleep next to you for a thousand years. I want to eat things that have no nourishment. I want to swim in that ocean, and make a fire, and watch the stars spin by at night." There's a stray piece of hair flapping against her cheek in the warm salty breeze. I tuck it behind her ear and say, "I don't want to leave yet."

169

Valor clears his throat and says, "Hey... uh... I'm gonna go for a walk and..." But he doesn't finish. Just turns away and heads towards the tall, spindly tropical trees. Easing into the shadows, walking a sandy path that probably is well worn.

My gaze lingers on his back until he disappears, then I turn to Brigit. I place both hands on her cheeks and kiss her lips. Her mouth opens for me immediately, her tongue pressing against mine. Her hands slip down to my ass and my cock jumps to life.

I know how it works with Cygnian princesses. I've heard all the sexy tales my hooked-up brothers have been telling about how their genetically matched mates affect their two cocks.

But Brigit isn't a Cygnian princess. There was no one manipulating our DNA before birth tying us together. So my second cock stays hidden. We will have to coax him out the old-fashioned way.

"Are you in a hurry?" I whisper past her lips.

"No," she whispers back.

"Good. Because I just want to be with you for as long as I can right now. I love this place, Brigit. And I love you."

She smiles as she kisses me. Then she pulls away, takes my hand, and leads me towards the nearby hut.

I'm not nervous but there's a nervous excitement inside me as we walk through the doorway. I twirl her around and push her up against the thatched walls, the palm of my hand on her throat. Her pulse—real or not—thumps beneath my touch and she becomes the master of sly smiles when I bring my lips up to her ear and say, "I'm going to make up for lost time now, princess."

She swallows hard under my grip, my thumb easing into her soft flesh with just the right amount of pressure against her windpipe to make her gasp and open her mouth wide.

"That's it," I say. "Yeah. That's how I like it."

I kiss her. Hard. My body blocks her in, pressing her against the wall so there's no possibility of escape. My knee slips between her legs and then I kick her feet open. My cock grows harder against the soft skin of her inner thigh and I can't wait to be inside her.

My fingers slip up into her hair and I pull it until she gasps and lets out a small squeak that will surely make me insane if she does it again. "Did you fuck him?" I ask.

"No," she says softly. "But I wanted to."

I laugh. And then I kiss her again. "Fuck, I've missed you," I say, thinking about how warm her mouth will be on my cock.

She smiles, still kissing me back. Coy and teasing now, she says, "I really did want to fuck him. But he's your brother and that's kind of gross."

"Not my real brother," I say, nibbling at her neck. I want to eat her up. "And he might be interested." I stop nibbling and pull back just a little. "But we can talk about that later. Right now you're just mine and I'm not willing to share."

My other hand squeezes her breast and I hold her there. My little captive. My secret prisoner. Staring into her dark eyes as she looks up at me with longing.

No one has ever looked at me this way. Only Brigit.

"I love you," I say.

"Doesn't seem like it," she quips. "You left me for several eternities this time. I'm not happy. You need to make it up to me."

"Do I?"

She nods, shyly. Trying not to smile.

I twirl her around, push her face up against the hut wall, and bite her shoulder as my cock slips between her legs. "Like this?" I ask, my fingers already playing with her ass.

"Like that," she whimpers back. "Right now."

"Better get yourself wet, princess. And you better do it quick. Because I'm not in the mood to wait and I don't care if it hurts."

CHAPTER SIXTEEN

I exhale. It's a long, satisfied exhale. Like relief. And we haven't even started yet.

"Hurry up," Tray says. "Put your fingers between your legs and get wet."

I don't need to get wet. I'm already there. But I'm not going to ruin his good time and I like the dirty talk. I've been waiting lifetimes for this moment.

When I reach between my legs he presses his hips against my ass, letting me know he's impatient to be inside me. I close my eyes and play with my clit with two fingers while the other two gather up the warm pool of slickness. His cock bumps into my hand and I reach further between my legs and jerk on him. He leans back, one hand gripping my hipbone so tight, I'll have a bruise later.

I don't care.

We don't always do it rough. Tray is actually a very gentle lover when he wants to be. But when he returns to me like this—especially after such a long time—our instincts are to be animals. To fuck. Not love. Love comes later. We have all the time in the world for gentleness.

173

Right now I want it hard.

"I want you in my ass," I say. "Now."

He doesn't ask me questions. There's no second-guessing. There's no double-checking to see if I'm ready for him.

His cock pushes inside my ass with force. I gasp, then bite my lip because it does hurt. My hands slap against the hut wall and I grimace, clenching my jaw as he enters me further.

I stiffen with the sudden pain, but then he's whispering in my ear. "I love you. Relax. Let me take you hard. I'll make it feel good."

And just to prove it, his hand slides over my hip and down my front, his fingers strumming my clit as he continues to force himself inside me.

I close my eyes and all the cares and worries I've been carrying since he last left just disappear. That's enough to relax the muscles fighting against his full penetration of me, and then... I moan. But it's that magic moment when he's fully inside and there's no pain at all. It's just pure pleasure.

His chest is flat against my back, his mouth kissing my neck, whispering dirty things in my ear. "I like your tight ass, Brigit," he says. "Your pussy gets wet for me, doesn't it? You love this, don't you?"

I do, but he's not looking for an affirmation. He's just saying this stuff to turn me on. And it does.

"Fuck me," I whisper back. "Just fuck me."

He thrusts hard. Once. Then he grabs my hip again while the other hand continues to play with my sweet spot, and then... he goes slow.

"Harder," I beg.

"Nah," he says, dragging out his response. "I'm gonna fuck you slow, princess. I'm gonna take my time."

I might die if he goes slow right now.

"And you're gonna take yours too. I'm gonna torture you slowly. And I'm not gonna let you come until I'm done."

"You can't stop me." I laugh. It's true. I'm very close already. It's been too long since I felt this way.

"No?" he asks, pulling his cock out of my ass.

I turn, shocked. "Tray!"

He twirls me around and starts kissing my mouth, his tongue twisting up with mine, his hand on my throat again. "You want me inside you?" he asks.

"Now!"

"Then get down on your knees and bend over. I'm tired of standing."

He places firm pressure on my shoulder. I like the guidance. The dominance. But I don't need to be commanded. I drop slowly, my hand flat on his chest, my fingernails digging into to his perfectly muscled chest as I lower to my knees, keeping eye contact the whole time.

His eyes are usually a very dark violet. But when he's really turned on, they glow a little.

They're glowing now.

I take his cock in my hand and begin to pump it.

"Oh, no," he jokes. "You're not getting off that easy."

"Don't worry," I say, twisting my wrist as I jerk on his dick. "I don't want to get off easy."

I get down on all fours and begin crawling towards the low bed on my side of the hut, making sure my ass teases and tantalizes him as I crawl. I peek over my shoulder and find him leaning up against the hut wall, jerking himself as he watches the show I'm putting on.

When I reach the bed I place both hands on the thick mattress and wiggle for him. Forcing myself not to look over my shoulder to see his response.

I want to think about it instead. I want to dream about it. Picture his lust. The way his eyes go heavy and hooded. The way his hand wraps around his cock.

"Stay just like that," he says, his voice rough and growly. "And play with yourself."

I bend my head down, pressing it into the soft covers of the bed, and reach between my legs. Not playing with myself. Beckoning him with one come-hither motion of my finger.

He laughs. He can't help it. And then the soft padding of his bare feet crosses the distance between us.

He kneels down right behind me, places his hands on my ass cheeks, then spreads them wide and takes my finger in his mouth. Sucking on it the way I'll suck his cock later.

Fuck, that turns me on. I don't even know why, but his lips sealed around my finger, the way his tongue presses along the side of it...

It makes me crazy and I just want him inside me now.

I pull my hand back just enough so that his lips press against my pussy. And then I pull my finger out of his mouth and he licks me.

I fist the blanket on the bed, trying not to come as his mouth plays between my legs.

He pulls away, snickering a little. Knowing full well he's driving me mad with anticipation. "Fuck me," I whisper. Much softer this time. Almost begging.

He withdraws and this makes me even more desperate.

But then he says, "Oh, I'm going to," just as he slips his cock back in my ass.

This time it slides in easily. My muscles don't tense up with the shock of entrance. My shoulders don't rise with pain. It's smooth and perfect, and I can't imagine ever feeling better than I do in this moment.

And then he pulls back and pounds me hard.

And I do.

He does it again.

And with each thrust I experience a new, more perfect moment of ecstasy.

My face is buried in the blanket now. I just let go and enjoy it. I want him to fuck me like this forever. Just never stop.

But it's just too much after so long. I can't control the building pleasure inside me. And when he leans over, covering my back with his chest, and his fingers slip around my stomach and back between my legs to find the delicious wetness he's summoned from me, I lose it.

But there's something most people don't know about Akeelian girls. We're not like the Cygnians who light up like suns.

We take the world into darkness.

Even inside a virtual, this cannot be stopped.

Like demons in old tales, we steal the light, and turn it into nothingness, and then bring it back into everything.

177

The future belongs to girls like me. Because that's what I see in my moment of release.

The world blinks out and Tray and I are gone. Not gone, like the gray cloud of a missing world, but floating out in the deep dark of space and time because we *are* space and time. We control it because we control the future.

Every possibility flashes in my mind. Every way we could live and die is real in this instant.

And then we're back and I'm coming, and he's coming, and the world is nothing but darkness.

CHAPTER SEVENTEEN

I wake up first. We're haphazardly strewn across the bed covers, a tangle of arms and legs. Her hair is across my face and there's a ray of sun shining through a glassless window that hits her in just the right way to make her hair appear bright purple.

I like waking up. There are a couple minutes every morning when none of the bigger, wider problems touch me. I don't have to think about anything, or do anything, or make anything work.

It's just peace.

But it doesn't last long. The day inevitably starts. I get up, dress, eat, work. And that feeling of peace does not return until the next morning.

I'm tired of it.

I cannot remember a time when I wasn't stressed about something.

About the station, about ALCOR, about the Pleasure Prison, about Brigit, about all of it.

Until now, that is.

It's selfish of me to want to stay here when Harem Station is probably a mess. Hell, who knows what's happening back home. People could be dead. And

ALCOR—I don't know what to feel about that guy. I've had conflicting emotions about him for so long I'm not even sure where I stand anymore.

Is he good? Is he evil? Is he just human—a little of both?

Is he dead?

It's easier if he is. Because if he's dead I don't have to think about him anymore. I don't have to wonder whose side he's on. I don't have to choose one, either. I can just exist.

Wouldn't that be nice?

I sigh. Is it so bad to want this? To want a few days to myself? A few days inside this virtual will not make a bit of difference out there. Seconds will pass. That's it. Hell, we could stay here for a few years. We could stay here a lifetime and hardly anything will change on the outside.

I throw a leg over the side of the bed and Brigit turns over, mumbling something I don't quite catch.

"What's that, princess?"

"Don't go," she moans. "I'm still tired."

"Stay here. I have to go talk to Valor. Come find us when you're ready, OK?" I lean down and kiss her head. And she turns in to it so our lips meet.

It's just a quick kiss and then she turns back over again, but I find myself smiling and unreasonably happy that she just did that.

"Take your time," I say, then head out of the hut and look around.

She did a nice job here. It's... stunning, actually.

The sea breeze is salty and there's that hint of organic matter surrounding this place. The kind of scent I've only smelled in the greenhouses on Harem Station. A biosphere, that's what it smells like.

So real.

God, I love her. I sigh deeply and once again I'm thinking about what's waiting for us on the outside.

Problems. Stress, for sure. Probably war and death too.

I don't want to do it anymore. I just want to be done. I want to live with her. I want to pretend with her.

What is the point? That's what I ask myself all the fucking time. What is the point of all this?

We're all gonna die. We can't take anything with us. Nothing lasts forever. Not even a ship like *Booty* or an AI like ALCOR. And let's just be real here. I'm going to end up just like ALCOR. No one told me that specifically, but I see it coming. I'm not dumb and I'm not delusional. I'm a realist. I know what I am. And one day, probably soon, I won't be me anymore. I'll be just like him. And then I will be stuck running a station or something. Being responsible for the lives of other people, or bots, or borgs. Doing all kinds of stressful things for thousands and thousands of years just like him.

No end in sight.

I will go mad, and get sane again. Over and over again. I will find friends, and lose them. And that will be just another endless cycle.

So... I have to ask myself now that I'm here—now that we're safe inside the spin node where no one can find us, or hurt us—why would we ever want to leave this place?

181

It's a dangerous line of thought. I don't normally let myself dwell on it. Or dream too hard about just... giving up and existing in a virtual in perpetuity.

But I'm already here.

It would be so easy.

A loud bird call makes me turn my head towards the trees and I'm reminded that Valor disappeared through the forest before we went into the hut. There's no way to really tell time in here. The sun, I guess. But it's not my time, it's Brigit's. So there's really no way to mark that.

Whatever I decide, I have to talk to Valor about it first. He's here too. And we're stuck with each other now. If I stay, he stays. If he goes, I go. Our fates are locked together.

So I head into the trees, taking the well-worn sandy path that he took. No idea where I'm going. No idea where he even is. He could be anywhere.

And every step further into the jungle I'm reminded of just how real this place is. How private, and perfect, and so much better than that crappy place I made for Brigit, that's for sure.

This is truly the dream. The real meaning of paradise.

And it's all ours.

The sound of a waterfall up ahead pulls me back into my current reality and I start looking around at all the flora and fauna in this forest. Small, fluttery insects, and long-legged hoppy amphibians. Birds, and I even spot a few leaf-nibblers. No large animals. No predators that I can see. Though maybe birds count.

The waterfall becomes louder and when I come around a large boulder I see it off in the distance.

Closer to me is a large, calm pool of perfectly clear water and I find Valor there, floating on his back, his cock semi-hard and draped across his thigh.

If I had known he was into Luck before we started this friendship I'd have thought about his future a little more thoroughly.

What did I think would really happen to Valor once I got Brigit out of this mess?

I know the answer to that. I just don't want to admit it.

I don't want it to turn out that way, either. He's into me. Maybe he's into Brigit too? He had to have already thought about all this stuff I'm dwelling on right now. He's been here for a long time.

But maybe that means he's ready to leave?

I need Valor. He's a very important part of my "free Brigit" plan.

But I was wandering inside this virtual for a long time before I found them and I actually thought about his relationship with Luck a lot.

Thought about maybe taking Luck's place in Valor's heart.

Thought about sharing Brigit.

I don't really want to share her. But I don't want Valor to leave, either. Not because I need him. Because I like him. I don't think I know him well enough to love him yet, but if he wants to stay here for a while, I'd like to learn to love him.

"Hey!" I call out.

Valor rolls over in the water and shields his eyes to look at me. "What's up? You get what you needed?"

It doesn't come off snide, or jealous, or even like he's annoyed. Just a simple question.

He starts swimming towards me. Easy, long arm strokes that quickly brings him to the shore. He stands up in the water and walks out towards me, unapologetic that his cock is swinging and growing as he walks, as he closes the distance between us.

"I did," I say, once he's near. He stops and we stare at each other for a few moments. Valor is a damn good-looking man.

He smiles. It reminds me of my own smile. Kind of a crooked smile. "I'm glad you found us. Fuck, I was worried. I swear to the sun, I was just asking Brigit to tell me how to get out so I could go check the ship. But… she didn't want to be alone. We were kinda talking that through when you showed up." He sucks in a breath and holds it, waits two seconds, then lets it out. "I'm glad you're here."

"Why?" And I smile. "Because being around my naked girlfriend was driving you insane?"

"Hey." He chuckles. "I waited."

"I know. She told me you guys didn't—"

"I wanted to," he interrupts. "She wanted to, too. But nah." He licks his lips. Narrows his eyes a little bit. "I wanted you first. And you wanted her first. So." He shrugs.

"You want *me*?"

He shoots me a look that says, *Don't play.*

"And her?" I ask. Nodding my head in the direction of the hut.

"Sure. Why not?"

"We have to go, though. Meet up with Booty and ALCOR. Do"—I wave my hand in the air flippantly—"whatever the fuck we're doing." And then unexpectedly, I laugh. And Valor laughs too.

"What are we doing again?" he asks.

"I don't fucking know, dude." And for a moment there's a flicker inside me. Some kind of disruptive... *hitch*. How did this happen? How did I get here? Why is Valor here with us?

This lapse in understanding is fleeting. Like... nanoseconds. And when it's over I almost panic. Because it was weird, and while lots of things inside my head are both weird and normal at the same time, disruptive hitches aren't one them.

"Why do we want to leave paradise?" Valor asks.

And then the hitch and the panic are both gone and all I can think about is his question. "I don't think I do, Valor. That's what I was coming to talk to you about." I look around. Take it all in. Throw up my hands and whisper, "We'd be insane to leave this place. We have everything here."

"And what we don't have, we can make," he adds. "So..."

"Do I want to stay? Is that what you're asking me?" I nod.

He takes three steps forward and stops. We are so close I can hear his heart beating. Our eyes are locked. Matched in height. His body is hard and tinted gold from all the endless days he's spent in this world.

And then he's kissing me. Not a small, scared kiss, either. His hand goes behind my neck, like he's afraid I'll back away and he's letting me know that's not an option.

But I don't back away. I kiss him back. As soon as I do that he eases his body forward so his cock touches mine.

185

I breathe into his kiss. And then his hand is tugging on me and my hand is wrapped around his shaft, and we're jerking each other.

Lost in paradise.

I don't even know how long we do this. I've never been jerked off by a man before, so it feels new, and exciting, and taboo. And then I'm coming in his hand and he's laughing at me. Still kissing me, but laughing too.

I bow my head and bump it against his face. "Sorry," I mumble. "You just…"

And I don't know what to say. *You just feel so good? I'm just not used to this? I got carried away?*

All of that. I want to say all of that.

But before I get the chance Brigit says, "Can I join you?"

And when I turn my head I see her.

CHAPTER EIGHTEEN

From zero to two in one point five billion years.
At least that's how it feels.

All this time I've been locked up in here with no one. Then I get a real best friend who never leaves and then the love of my life comes back. And now... I find them here together.

I dreamed about this. I had hoped—I'd even go so far as to say I prayed—for this. If there is a sun or a god to pray to, this is what I'd have asked for.

Ever since Valor showed up I've been having a fantasy. One that looks suspiciously like this moment right here. But I'm not a dreamer. I've been disappointed far too many times to dream about things.

And then I saw them at the waterfall. Valor wet from swimming. Tray dry, except for the places that Valor had been touching him.

Just like this. I saw them in my forbidden dream.

I saw them kiss. I saw them jerk each other's cocks. I heard their heavy breathing and felt the emotion behind their heavy-hooded violet eyes.

JA HUSS & KC CROSS

Not one, but two. Just for me.

All of it. I saw all of it in my perfect fantasy.

Only this isn't a fantasy. It's not real, but it's real enough. I'm not controlling Tray or Valor. They are their own minds. They did this, not me.

Tray has been watching me for the few moments I've been watching them. "You want to join in?" he asks, just to make sure he heard me correctly.

"I wouldn't ask if I didn't," I say, trying to be cool about this. But inside my heart is beating fast with… what exactly? Anticipation? Surprise? Longing? Lust?

Tray is still jerking on Valor's cock. I was watching behind the boulder so I know Tray came. But even if I hadn't been watching, I'd still know because both of Tray's cocks are hard and thick. So thick Valor's hand barely fits around them. He's still jerking Tray too. And I can tell that Valor's palm is slick with come by the way his fingertips slip in and out of view with ease.

I walk forward towards them and when I'm close enough I slide my fingertips down the large muscle of Tray's upper arm. I feel his shudder and he closes his eyes.

But when I drop to my knees in front of Valor and wrap my hand around Tray's hand, still jerking on Valor, Tray opens his eyes to smile at me.

"He needs to catch up," I say, slowly sliding our hands up and down Valor's single cock. "He's behind."

Tray looks at me with total lust.

He's never been shy about sex. He's never at a loss for words when it comes to telling me what he wants. He's looked at me with such desire before, I could feel violence inside him. That's how hard he wanted to fuck me.

This is *that*, times a million.

He grabs my hair and wraps it around his fist, pushes my face towards Valor's cock and whispers, "Put him in your mouth. Suck him 'til he comes."

I close my eyes. Just one beat. Smile on the inside and then on the outside.

I do as I'm told.

I open my mouth wide.

Akeelian cocks are no joke. They are huge. I mean, I don't have much experience with small dicks because I've only ever been with Tray. But I saw plenty of naked men in my old virtual world and their cocks never looked anything like Tray's.

Maybe he's embellishing because this is a virtual. And I guess Valor could be embellishing too, but... it doesn't matter. This is the only reality I know.

My only point is—Valor's cock is so big it chokes me before it even reaches my throat.

"That's it," Tray encourages. "Take him as deep as you can, Brigit. He loves it. Look at him. Look up at his eyes."

I do. I can't wait to follow this order. Because I want to look. I want to see him moan when he comes.

Valor is looking at me the same way Tray was just looking at me.

With lust.

He's breathing erratically and I take that as a sign to keep going. Tray's hand covers mine and we both jerk and tug on Valor's dick as I attempt to swallow him whole, my lips sealed against the skin of his shaft.

I want Valor to touch me. He's got one hand on Tray's shoulder, gripping it hard so the flesh around Valor's fingers blanches white.

Valor's other hand is on his head. Grabbing a fistful of his own hair. Like his mind is being blown instead of his dick. Like he might need to hold on to it.

I smile around his cock and he closes his eyes for a long blink before smiling back.

"Come," Tray says, speaking to Valor. "I want to see that second cock of yours. Pull it out for me. Choke her with it."

I don't know if these two have had sex before, but I get the feeling this is their first time. Because Valor responds to Tray the way Tray did a few minutes earlier.

Surprise. Concern. Then acceptance. Like this is something wholly new. And it's not just me that makes this sexual experience exotic.

It's them.

"Come in her mouth, dude. I want to see your come drip down her chin."

Hell, that even turns me on. My fingers slide down my belly and I begin playing with my clit. I don't take my eyes off Valor, and even though he looks like he wants to close his very badly and just enjoy this experience, his eyes are locked on mine too.

I suck him. I flatten my tongue along his shaft and pull back, creating suction. And Tray, still fisting my hair, pushes me forward again until his cock fills up my throat and I am gagging on his dick and gasping for air.

Valor sucks in a deep breath and lets his head fall back.

Hot, salty come floods into my mouth and down my throat. I choke, trying to pull away—knowing better, because Tray has a thing for choking. Any and all kinds of choking, especially on come—and he holds me in place. Keeps me on task. Reminds me of my mission.

Which is to swallow.

So I do. And I can feel Valor's cock as the muscles of my throat ride up and down on it like a wave.

"Fuck," Valor says, dropping to his knees. "Fuuuuuuck." His dick slips out of my mouth and I swipe the back of my hand across my lips to wipe away the spit and semen.

Then I look up at Tray.

He's grinning. And he's holding out his hand like he wants me to take it.

I do. Of course. I wouldn't refuse Tray anything.

He helps me up and starts walking to the nearby pool of water.

"Hey!" Valor calls. I look over my shoulder and find him still on his knees. "Where are you going?"

"Join us when you're ready," Tray calls back. "We'll be right over here."

He leads me onto the shore, then into the water. It's cool, but not cold. Refreshing is the exact right word to describe it. There are just a few gentle ripples leftover from the thundering, powerful waterfall on the other side of the pool. They break apart when they hit my stomach and shoot off, even more gentle, in another direction. We wade in up to our waists. Small red fish flit and dart across the white-sand bottom, stirring up a little bit of silt with their quick motion.

A gold one shimmies across the top of my foot, tickling me, and I laugh out the words, "Where are we going?"

"Right here," Tray says, tugging me over to a flat rock in the middle of the pool. When we get there he spins me around, picks me up, and plops my ass on the cold, smooth rock.

I'm pretty sure this rock wasn't here before. No, I'm positive it wasn't here before. So Tray is reshaping my world.

My heart stutters in delight at this thought. That now we're both in control and every moment from now will be a surprise. I will never know what's coming and neither will he. Anything could happen now.

We have no rules anymore.

There's no café. There's no garden. There's no fake people.

Just us three.

And we're all real.

When I'm sitting I realize I'm at the perfect height. The rock sits just high enough out of the water so that the ripples of water splash gently across the top of my knees.

He grabs my thighs, slides me forward, and opens my legs.

He grins at me.

A sexy, evil, I'm-gonna-fuck-you-hard-now grin.

When he eases into my open legs his cocks skim along the water, pointing at my pussy.

"I'm gonna fuck you now, Brigit. And my friend Valor is gonna watch. And then I'm gonna let him fuck you too." He leans forward, one cock slipping into my pussy, and grabs my chin with his thumb and forefinger. Shakes it a little. His eyes are bright and drilling into mine, right to the heart of my soul. Like he's warning me of something. Like maybe I need to think about this before I agree.

I get hot for that. I don't need to think about it.

I nod my permission and Tray has never needed words as consent, so he just says, "Last chance."

"I love you," I say. "And I trust you."

He exhales like he was holding his breath. And that rigidness inside him that almost never wavers, wavers. He frowns a little. And for a moment I think he's going to tell me something like... *Maybe you shouldn't.*

And I don't know if he's telling me not to love him. Or not to trust him.

But it doesn't really matter. Even if I could choose not to trust or love him, I wouldn't want those choices.

It's me and him forever, no matter what. I'm on his side. Whatever side that ends up being has no bearing on where I belong and who I belong with.

Movement out of the corner of my eye makes me turn my head. Valor is slowly wading into the water, his fingertips skimming along the top, his eyes not on me. On Tray. But he doesn't approach us. He sits down on another, smaller flat rock nearby. His knees bend and his legs open, like his feet are resting on some shelf on the side of the rock, hidden below the surface. The sun is at his back, lighting up the rounded edges of his muscular shoulders with a golden glow. His hair catches the light too, highlighted and sparkling with the subtle movements of his head so that he looks transparent and spectral. Almost... angelic.

"Look at *me*, Brigit."

Tray's grip on my chin refocuses my attention on him. And I can't help but compare the two men. Tray is as dark and forbidding as Valor is light and approachable. Night and day. Stars and sun.

I belong with Tray. I know this. Anyone who sees us can immediately tell we are a team. That this is just the way it is. If there ever comes a time when I have to choose, I would not hesitate.

But my eyes are drawn to Valor.

"Look at *me*," Tray insists again.

I do. And I smile.

He smiles back. Tray has an evil smile but I like it. I know there's something wrong inside him. But I hold that wrongness inside me too. We are evenly matched in that way.

The tip of his first cock is inside me. Just barely past the entrance of my pussy. And when I look down into the clear, perfect water, my pussy lips are wrapped around the bottom edge of his fat head.

"You're not very focused today," Tray says. "Eyes going everywhere but where I want them."

I huff a little, glance at Valor, who now has both of his cocks in his hand, jerking them in a slow, easy rhythm, then up at Tray. "I can't help it," I whisper. "I think this is the best day of my life and I need to take it all in. I want to burn it into my mind so I never, ever forget this moment."

"The best moments are yet to come, Brigit." Then he leans down and kisses my mouth, still gripping my chin just a little too tight. Like he's forcing me. But he's not, of course. I love the way he asserts his dominance.

"Put all of me inside you," he says, pulling out of the kiss.

I bite my lip to stop a smile and nod my head. Then I reach between my legs, grab his second cock and push it up against the first one.

I close my eyes as I force him past the entrance of my pussy. Not just because it's tight and the muscles and skin are stretching to accommodate the double girth, but because it feels so good.

His hips ease forward, helping me as I spread my legs wide and just like when he fucks my ass, there's some initial resistance. But then… then he's fully inside me and all the pressure comes to some sort of equilibrium. He lets go of my chin and now he reaches around me, grabs my ass, and scoots me closer to the edge of the rock so he can bury his dicks deep inside me.

I tip my head up so I can watch his face. I love the way he grits his teeth and clenches his jaw when we fuck.

"Now you can look at Valor," Tray says, starting a slow rhythm with his hips. "Don't take your eyes off him."

I look at Valor as he jerks off. Both cocks in his hand. I wish he was closer. I want him closer. I want both of them inside me. I'm not even sure that's possible, but I'm up for trying.

I want him to know that he's still my best friend. That I didn't forget all the moments we've spent together waiting for Tray to come find us. That I'm his too, in another way. Different than how I belong to Tray.

"Tell him what you're thinking," Tray says. "Say it."

"Come fuck me," I say immediately and without hesitation.

"No," Tray says, breathing heavy as his hips move faster and his movements become more forceful. "No, that's not what you're thinking. Tell him what you're *really* thinking."

For a moment I'm confused. That *was* what I was thinking. But then I realize Tray's right. That wasn't all of it.

"Come fuck *us*," I say.

Tray's mouth finds my neck. He nips my earlobe and says, "Yes," very softly. Very slowly. Dragging the word out just a little too long. Like there's desire hidden in that word. His desire for his friend. Because it's something, maybe, that he needed me to say for him.

That turns me on for some reason. The fire of desire inside me ignites like an explosion and burns hotter.

Valor is already wading through the water to join us. Like the only thing missing from this day was my invitation.

Tray's hands reach down and cup my ass. He lifts me off the rock, turns around, and sits back down where I just was. He's still inside me, both heads of his cocks swollen now, so there's no chance of slippage. Only one way for this to end now. A double shot of Akeelian come spurting deep inside me.

He leans back on the rock so he's lying flat and I go with him. His arms are tight, leaving no room for discussion about why he's doing this and what's about to happen.

Valor's hand rubs my ass cheek. It's slick with water and then he smacks it. A loud, cracking smack that surprises me more than it hurts, and makes me squeal.

His hands splay my ass cheeks wide and then, just like Tray did earlier, he licks me.

I almost come right then and there. Two cocks inside me, one mouth on my ass. My pussy is throbbing so hard, I feel the need to touch it. To place pressure on it because the pleasure is so intense, I can't stand it.

I wriggle in Tray's arms, but he holds on to me tight. "Be still, Brigit. Let Valor enter you."

I take deep breaths. Deep, sucking breaths trying to calm myself down.

Valor has stopped licking me and now his cock is pressing at the entrance of my tight puckered ass.

He massages it with his finger. Everything is wet now. The water is still gently lapping up against our bodies, over my knees and in the space between Tray's cocks and my pussy like a soft, soothing massage that helps me relax.

Valor takes advantage of my single moment of relaxation and then I gasp when his cock forces its way into my ass. Three cocks inside me now.

Valor hooks his arm around my neck, pressing the crook of his elbow into my throat. Tray lets go of me, so Valor is in charge. He pulls me up off of Tray's stomach, the pressure from his arm hard enough to choke. I meet Tray's eyes and find them smiling. He likes this. He likes the rough sex. And I like it too, so seeing him smile makes my pussy throb even more.

I don't know if I can take any more pleasure. My whole body is shaking from the built-up sexual excitement, my legs trembling so hard, Tray starts whispering, "Relax, Brig. You're OK."

I believe him. I'm better than OK. I'm amazing. And even though I crave the relief that will flood my body when this is over, I never want it to end.

Tray sits up, and now I'm sandwiched between them. His arms wraps around my waist and he lifts me up just a little, his two swollen cock-heads tugging on my skin inside me, reminding me that this isn't going to end until he says it does.

Tray says, "Reach between your legs, Brigit. And grab Valor's other cock."

Oh, God. I'd almost forgotten about that one. Four. I have four cocks to pleasure before they will be satisfied.

As soon as those words come out of Tray's mouth I feel Valor's cock in my ass grow larger as the head of his cock swells up into a tight, giant knot.

I almost pass out from the throbbing delight running through my body.

I reach down, feel around and past Tray's balls—just thinking about that makes a piercing stab of pleasure shoot straight up my belly—and find the thick hard shaft of Valor's lower cock. My fingertips brush against his balls and Tray moans something incoherent when I slip my hand to the side and look down to see one giant, bulbous cock head.

"Jerk that one off as we fuck," Tray commands. And this time Valor is the one who moans, his arm still choking me, his face leaning into my neck on my left side, his mouth biting my earlobe the moment I squeeze his shaft and begin to tug.

It's too much. Just... too much.

I know they feel this way too because the three of us are a symphony of moaning, and grunting, and heavy breathing.

But Valor has one more surprise for me. One more way to make me insane. His fingers sweep around the

198

edge of my hip, dip right between my legs, and begin to strum my clit.

I die in that moment.

Tray is kissing my mouth, Valor is biting my neck, and I die and come back to life an eternal number of times.

And each time I come back to life, I find myself screaming for more.

CHAPTER NINETEEN

I explode inside her. Twice, but at the same time. And as I do that Valor's whole body tenses up. His second cock shoots first. I push Brigit away, just a little, so I can watch his come spill over the side of her still-jerking hand.

And then he throws his head back and growls. Both of my cocks are still inside Brigit, so I feel Valor's head flex and release.

The pleasure chemicals running through my blood threaten to overwhelm me and I have to grip Valor's arm tightly to ground me in this moment because I might lose my mind from bliss.

"Fuck," Valor is saying. "Fuck." Over and over again.

Brigit is moaning softly. Almost whining.

I don't know what to think. I thought this would be fun. Hot and erotic. I knew I'd get off on it. But I feel out of control.

And I want to do it again.

Right now.

Brigit makes the first move. Slowly—like slow-motion slowly—leaning to the side until she's lying on

201

the flat rock, the water lapping up against her face, her lips pressed together tight to keep it from going into her mouth.

She's got the right idea. I'm exhausted. So I lean over and fall next to her. She lifts her body up just enough that I can slip one arm underneath the curve of her waist and hug her close.

"I love you." I just want to remind her. We've been through a lot. Her, mostly. All this time she's been waiting for me. And I'm glad that she broke the world I made for her and moved on. It makes me happy for some reason. Makes her feel... real to me. Because sometimes I think I'm crazy. I think I've made it all up. I fear that she is just me, in another form. That she's not real.

Valor helps. A little. Because he's here now. His idea, and it was a good one. But before this moment, before arriving here to find it all different, before this sex... I wasn't sure. It's still possible that I'm the one controlling all this. But not likely. Unless I have somehow split myself in half and Brigit is another me, the way the Baby and the Asshole are other sides to ALCOR, I don't think that's what this is.

But I never imagined myself with Valor, let alone Valor and Brigit.

That was him. And we're in her world and for once in my life... I'm just... out of control.

Valor lies down on the other side of Brigit. He reaches for her cheek, his eyes locked on her face as I stare at him. Does he love her now? Have they spent so much time together that he's in love with her?

I hope so. I really do. Because I can't do this alone. I can't save her by myself. I need a team. I would've settled for a reluctant Valor. I would've settled for his cautious agreement.

But he's in now. I can see it in his expression as he stares at her.

And then she lifts up her head, just a little, and Valor slips his hand under her cheek so it can act like a pillow.

His eyes dart up to mine and he smiles when he realizes I've been watching him. "Yeah," he says.

I laugh. "Yeah, what?"

"I could stay here for a while."

"Good," Brigit mumbles. "Because I don't want to move."

"You don't want to go outside and be real?" I ask. I'm not trying to talk her out of us staying here, I just want to make sure. I just want her to be happy.

"One day," she whispers. "I'm just... not so much in a hurry anymore."

I sigh and rest my head on the rock. Close my eyes and enjoy the sun. "I can live with that."

And we do live with that.

The sun rises and sets many times and we do nothing but sleep, and fuck, and eat, and fuck again. We swim a little, we laugh and talk. It's so different now. So much better in here now than it is out there.

I think a couple of weeks go by before Valor starts letting me know he's keeping track of time. Maybe because he knows I'm not.

I don't care anymore. I know *Booty* and Asshole are out there waiting for us right now. And even though I don't know for sure that Nyleena is pregnant back on Harem, there's really only one way that whole space orchid shit show ends, right?

Baby silvers running around.

And if Nyleena and Luck did everything right, then Harem Station is a war zone. We have been divided in half. It's been taken over by two infiltrator AIs on opposite sides and millions of people are counting on us to do something about it.

But I just don't care.

So Valor reminds me one day. He says, "I think it's been five hours out there since we left Harem."

Which means we've been in here a long fucking time already. And I didn't even notice.

Not true. Not entirely. I noticed. I just didn't care. Who would? We're living in our own personal Pleasure Prison. Willing captives.

I look at him and nod. "OK. What are you saying? You want to go back?"

"No," he says, shaking his head. He's made a spear out of a long stick and he's standing on a rock near the waterfall shore. Arm raised, ready to stab us some red-fish dinner. Not that we need to eat in here, but finding food for dinner each night has become a ritual that fills our days. "I'm just letting you know I think it's been about five hours on the outside."

"Five hours is fine, don't you think?"

"Hell," Valor says, throwing his spear. It sticks into something and the end vibrates from the result of accurate aim. "They might not even be there yet, right?"

He doesn't even look at me when he says this. So casual, he is.

I shrug, even though he's not watching me. He hops off the rock and wades forward into the water, pulls the stick up, grinning at his catch.

"Maybe not," I say, trying to calculate how many gates *Booty* would have to travel through to make it from Harem to the coordinates I gave her.

They probably are there waiting. Because I think Valor has forgotten about all that time we spent fixing up my ship on the Angel Station copy inside the spin node. It's not a lot of time, so maybe he figures that doesn't count. But all time counts. It just doesn't all add up in the same way.

"We'd have to stay here for years and years before it really mattered," I say.

"That's how I see it too," Valor says, hooking his fish onto a line already filled with other catches and then dropping them back in the water so he can catch another one.

He does this all the time. Valor is like... super provider here. We always have too much to eat. He doesn't even need to hunt, he just likes it. Because both Brigit and I could just conjure up dinner every evening and it would probably taste just the same.

But then I amend that thought.

It wouldn't taste the same. It certainly wouldn't feel the same.

Because catching fish for dinner every day is how Valor shows he cares about us.

That was the first time Valor remained me that this isn't real. He didn't do it again for… fuck. Years, I think. Still wasn't counting the time, so I have no clue, really.

By this point, Brigit and I were contemplating the idea that we needed a town. We'd done everything we could think of in the territory we now called home. We built ourselves a house, we had new furniture, we even had a pet. A little furry, four-legged thing with sharp teeth that always looked like it was smiling.

That was Valor's idea. He wanted a pet. Said he'd always wanted a pet and ALCOR never let him have one.

So we were maybe a little bit bored. We still fucked every morning and every night. We slept in the same bed, so fucking was always an option. Brigit conjured up a boat one day and we took off on the ocean, creating islands and other continents as we traveled.

But that was a long time ago now.

"I'd like a café," Valor says. He's cleaning this weird-looking vegetable he asked Brigit to conjure up for him. Says he ate this once while he and Luck were salvaging on the other side of the galaxy and was craving it.

Sometimes I forget that he's been everywhere and seen everything. Unlike me. I've been nowhere compared to Valor.

"Somewhere to hang out." He looks at me then. "With people." Because Brigit won't make people. She's afraid they'll come out wrong. And so far I've refused to make any other people because then… then shit gets a little too *real*, right? It's already so easy to pretend this is our real life and adding people just props that illusion up.

"I'd like a movie house," Brigit says.

But a town does sound nice. Places to go, people to see, things to do.

So I say, "I'd like an arcade."

And Valor says, "And a shooting gallery."

It's not lost on me that we're imagining the things we left behind. But I don't care.

I guide us into a long, easy discussion of town planning. But later, when Brigit has left to go swim in the waterfall pool, Valor looks at me and says, "It's been two days now."

"Two?" I say, raising my eyebrows.

"Do you think that's too long?" Valor asks.

"Two," I say again, weighing it in my mind. "Two is OK, don't you think?"

He nods. "I'm not ready to leave."

I only smile and agree.

But the next time he brings up the subject of how much time has passed outside, it's clear that we might've been here too long.

The first clue that Brigit, Tray, and Valor are no longer connected to reality is that town we made? Um... well... it's a thriving metropolis now.

Millions of people.

Brigit and Valor got their way. I gave in.

It's as real as Harem. There are shooting galleries, and restaurants, and theaters, and we even have

207

fucking transportation. Not just buses and vehicles to get around in the city, but a fucking high-speed train system that goes to outlying towns and connects to our *second* thriving metropolis.

There's this little nagging voice in my head that asks... *Is Harem real? Or is this real?*

But I push it away, because I no longer care.

"Four days," Valor says to me at some later date. And now he looks worried. "It's been four days, Tray. They have to be waiting for us. You know this."

"Valor, if you want to leave, just say the word and we'll go."

"It's not that I *want* to leave. It's that... Luck, you know?" He whispers Luck's name. We've lived in this fake reality for... fuck. I have no clue. None. So long. So fucking long now. Hundreds of years on our virtual clock?

I could ask Valor because I know he's keeping track, but I don't *want* to know. It sounds... crazy. If someone back on Harem had stayed in the Pleasure Prison for four days straight we'd ban them from ever going inside again.

Virtual life is addictive. Being able to escape your harsh reality and replace it with a perfect simulation is a powerful drug that cures any ailment you can think of. Especially a virtual like the Prison.

A virtual like this, too. I reluctantly admit.

Because it's a perfect life. Why go back to the real and deal with shit you can't control when all the control you could ever want is right at your fingertips?

Of course, in the Prison you'd have to have billions of credits to make a place like we've made here. So no one is staying in the Pleasure Prison for four days straight. I think the average time was about ten minutes and that's still a very long time in virtual.

"Luck," I say absently, more to myself than to Valor. "You still love him?"

Valor growls at me. "What the fuck kind of question is that?"

"I didn't mean it that way." But I did, kinda, mean it that way.

"He's our brother," Valor says.

"Not really," I mutter.

"And what about Crux? And Serpint? He really is my brother. I know it. I can feel it. And Lyra, and Nyleena, and Corla, and Delphi, and Jimmy."

He pauses for a moment.

"And ALCOR, Tray. That's the whole reason we left. We're meant to save ALCOR. And I know it's not really probable that shit went off the rails in just a few days. I mean, Veila had left us alone for months before we left Harem, so what are the odds that she'd show back up in the four freaking days we decide to take an extended vacation? But it's possible. Everyone could be in trouble right now. They could be waiting for us to come back and—"

"And what?" I ask, cutting him off. "Save them? The way ALCOR saved us?"

"Yeah," Valor says, shrugging his shoulder.

"He didn't save us, Valor. He *fucked* us. He forced us into this life. Into this war he's fighting with—who the fuck ever. We don't owe him, OK? He owes *us*."

"Who cares?" Valor says.

And this is when I realize we're in a fight. We've probably been here for a couple hundred years virtual time, and this is our first argument.

209

Is that even normal?

Valor walks over to me, pointing his finger in my face. "Look, I know you're different than the rest of us. I get it. I even have a few suspicions about what you really are. But you don't keep tabs on who owes who like that with family. And we don't need to be related by blood to be a family. We owe him because we love him. And he owes us, because he loves us. And—"

"He *used us*, Valor. He's still using us out there right now. Just because so much time has passed in here that you've conveniently forgotten about Draden—"

But I stop, shocked that that just came out of my fucking mouth.

"What?" Valor asks, eyebrows raised. "What *about* Draden?"

I never told him. I was so happy and relieved when I finally found Brigit, I never told him that I saw Draden in the virtual the first time I came in.

"What are we talking about?"

Both Valor and I whirl around to find Brigit standing behind us.

"What?" she asks. "What's going on?"

Valor and I look at each other. We hold that stare. We lock eyes. Then he squints at me like he's trying really hard to remember something. "It's a trap," he says. "They're all traps, remember? I said that once. Long time ago. Corla, and Lyra, and Nyleena, and Delphi." He pauses. "And this place."

He turns his head to look at Brigit, shaking it like he doesn't want it to be true.

But the words come out anyway.

"And *her*."

210

They just don't come from Valor.
They come from me.

CHAPTER TWENTY

"What trap?" I ask. "Who's a trap? What are you guys talking about?"

I had been down at the beach just kind of relaxing when I decided I wanted to eat something and came back up to the house to find them in some kind of standoff. Valor and Tray are both looking at me now like... like they don't know me.

"What?" I say. "Why the hell are you two staring at me?"

"Where did you come from?" Valor asks.

"What?"

"Don't," Tray says, turning to face Valor. "Don't start."

"We have to ask, Tray. You know we do."

"What is going on?" I'm starting to get annoyed because it's very clear they were talking about me before I walked up. And now they're each wearing a look that says... well, I'm not sure, actually. It's such a foreign expression for them, I almost don't recognize it.

But maybe there's some deep emotional recognition program running inside me? Or maybe, once upon a long time ago, I saw this expression a lot.

Because I do recognize it.

Should we tell her? Do we trust her?

And I don't know what to make of that because we've been a team now for... well, a very long time. When I think back to my beginnings there's nothing left anymore. It's all faded and washed out. Every once in a while I remember something about gardens. Like... I was a gardener, maybe? Or someone I knew was a gardener?

And then a memory comes forward, unbidden.

When Tray and I first started creating the city Valor wanted a café. And that word... café. It triggered something inside of me. A memory of... mostly frustration. But I didn't understand why. I told them both about it, and Tray mentioned I'd worked at a café in the last world, but I couldn't recall that. And that's what this memory was about.

It wasn't something as benign as work. It was bigger. More emotional. More—

"Where did you come from, Brigit?" Valor's repeated question breaks the search I'm running inside my head and I refocus my eyes on his face.

Tray says, "Brigit, do you remember anything? About before?"

"Before when?" I try to laugh it off, but there's a creeping sensation of uncomfortable sickness inside me. And both Valor and Tray are looking at me with some kind of laser focus. So I say, "I mean... I think I've been inside this place a thousand years, you guys. I barely remember the day we arrived here."

Tray tilts his head like he's confused. "What?"

I shrug. "There's just a lot of stuff inside me, you know? I don't... I can't keep it all. I have to pack it up every once in a while. Put it away in storage."

"Brigit," Valor says. "We didn't come here together."

Then it's my turn to be confused. "What?"

"You were here first," Tray says. "I found you inside the Pleasure Prison."

"Pleasure Prison?" I laugh. "Sounds like a fetish club in the city."

"It's not funny," Valor snaps. "We're asking you a question, OK?"

"I get it," I say. "Sorry. I'm not trying to joke. It's just... I don't remember a place called the Pleasure Prison."

"When did we meet?" Tray asks.

"You and I?" I say, pointing to myself. "Has there been a time when we didn't know each other?"

"We need to go," Valor says. "Right now, Tray. We need to go right now. This is a trap. She's a *trap*."

"What are you talking about?" And now I'm starting to get pissed. "What started all this? All I did was walk down to the water for a swim. I wasn't even gone long. But you two have obviously lost your minds."

Tray is staring at me. Frowning. Deeply frowning.

"Now, Tray. Pull us out now!"

"Out where?" I ask. "What are you talking about?"

Tray walks over to me and places a hand on my arm. "Brigit," he says. "Where are we?"

"What?" I can't hold down the laugh this time. It's so ridiculous. "What kind of question is that?"

"Where are we?" he repeats. And this time he squeezes my arm just a little too hard.

I jerk my arm out of his grip and take a step back. "We're at *home*, you dumbass. What the hell is wrong with you two?"

"Where is home?" Tray asks. "What is this place called?"

I open my mouth to answer and find... I don't have one. My brows furrow as I look for that memory. What *is* this place called?

I look around at the house, and the forests and the sand, and the ocean, and it's all familiar. I live here. This is my home. The sun is starting to set so off in the distance I can see the lights of the city called... "That's..." I point at it.

But I don't remember the name.

"Something's wrong with me," I whisper. "I can't remember what the city is called."

"Do you know where you are?" Valor asks. "Where are you, Brigit?"

"I'm here," I say. I almost smile again. But... the questions are so stupid. "I am *here*."

"Where's here?" Valor asks.

"This is a shutdown sequence," Tray says. I know what those words mean, but they don't have any meaning to me. "It's a shutdown sequence," he repeats. "She's shutting down."

Both of them are close to me now and I don't know how that happened. One moment Valor was over there, and now he's here, in front of me. He takes my hand. Gently. Doesn't squeeze it. Just holds it.

"Brigit?" he asks calmly, gently. "Who built that city?"

I look at it off in the distance. Smile, because it makes me feel happy for some reason. "People," I say, confident that this is the right answer. "I don't know them personally but—"

"OK, we gotta go," Tray says. "Valor, stare at the sun. Concentrate on it until it's burning your eyes, and picture yourself back on the ship. Waking up in the cryopod."

"What the hell are you talking about? What's a cryopod?"

"I'll see you on the other side," Valor says.

And then he disappears.

Just... disappears.

"What the fuck! Where did he go?" I spin around, looking at Tray. "What's happening?"

"It's over," he says, sadly. "They tricked you, Brigit. They tricked me too."

"*What?*"

"We're in a virtual reality, remember? We built this place, Brig. You and me. We made that city. Valor and I came in here to break you out. We pulled your body from the middle of space, brought you on to our ship, and we were about to wake you up when Valor wanted to go inside, just for a moment, to meet you, and see our world."

I'm shaking my head no this whole time. "No. That's... impossible. That's stupid. That's—"

"I'm leaving now," Tray says.

"Why? I don't understand."

"You don't understand because we've triggered your shutdown protocol and your mind is being wiped." He takes both of my hands in his. "But don't worry. I'll wake you up back on the ship and pull you

217

out of cryogenic sleep, and then... it's all going to be OK." He places one hand on my cheek and stares into my eyes. "Trust me, OK? I will take care of you. And... you didn't do anything wrong. You didn't know. It's going to be fine. You just need to wake up. We all just need to wake up. I'll pull you out and we'll be together again in the real, OK? Do you understand me?"

He's shaking me. And then a flash of light blazes, blinding me so I have to close my eyes. And then time is spinning backwards. My life is spinning backwards. I see it. All of it. The house, the city, the lifetime we spent on the beach, the waterfall pool, Tray's reappearance, the years and years I wandered the land with Valor at my side. The creation. The nothing. The old world. Draden. The community garden. Aieena. The café...

Tray. Nothing but me and Tray.

Everything spins backwards in time and I remember who and what I am.

And the next thing I know is... everything.

I know everything.

But most importantly, I know what I am.

I am nothing.

CHAPTER TWENTY-ONE

I come out of the virtual coughing and retching. Four days. I've never been inside so long, and now I know why. My body is on fire from the needles that have been embedded into my skin. I can't even lift my arms to activate the screen and open the pod. But there's an emergency button on the side of the pod. A built-in precaution meant for just such an occasion.

I press it and there's a long, long hiss of air as the top lifts up and away.

It's dark in the ship, so I can't see anything beyond the dim glow of lights coming from the display above me.

But I can hear Valor moaning next to me.

"Valor," I croak. My throat is so dry, my body so tired. And I feel emaciated. The pod is designed to feed you nutrients but I get the feeling that those ran out hours ago. Maybe as long as a day ago. My muscles feel weak, like atrophy was starting in from lack of movement.

What the fuck was I thinking? I know better. Why the hell did I allow us to stay inside so long?

We could've died in there. Well, Valor could've died. I'm not sure what would've happened to me if this body gave out, but it would've been bad.

There are no precautions attached to these pods the way we have back on Harem when people go inside the Pleasure Prison. No one looking out for us like ALCOR, or the people in the control room.

I could've killed Valor.

"I'm here," he hisses back. "I feel like..." His voice is low, gravelly. Like he needs to cough and clear his throat. Just listening to him gives me the urge to cough. "I feel like *shit*," he finally says.

"We were inside too long. I'm fucking sorry, dude. I don't—"

"Help me get up, Tray. I can't fucking move."

"One second," I say. But it's a lot longer than a second before I can sit up. And then I have to rest and press a button on the screen for an emergency injection of adrenaline just to be able to swing my legs out and place my feet on the floor.

I don't attempt to stand. Just hang my head and breathe as the adrenaline surges through my bloodstream.

How the fuck did I let this happen?

By the time I'm able to stand Valor is sitting up. He probably found the emergency adrenaline too. I brace my hands on the pod and face him. "Are you OK?"

He nods, trying to take deep breaths.

It takes me almost a full minute to make my way around the other side of my pod and reach him. I hold his arm as he stands, and then we look at each other.

What is he thinking?

What am I thinking?

What the fuck just happened?

We just lived several lifetimes as lovers. That's what just happened.

"Don't kiss me," Valor says.

I just blink at him. "What?"

"I need to swallow a scrubbing pod for my fucking teeth, dude."

Even if I wanted to stop the laugh, I couldn't. So it comes out. "Fuck, you're so stupid, Valor. We're in a spin node. Time isn't passing."

"Yeah, well. Tell that to the film on my fucking teeth. And time wasn't supposed to be passing in there either, but you know what I think?"

I look at him for a moment. His neck and arms have pinpricks of purple bruises all over where the needles were. "What?"

"I think time passes no matter what."

"Of course time passed," I say. "It just went really fast in there."

"No, the spin node, dude. I think we fucked up." Then he turns his head to look at Brigit's pod. "I think she's—"

"I know," I say, putting up a hand. Because I do know. She's a trap. Just like Lyra. Just like Nyleena, and Corla, and Delphi, and whoever else is out there waiting for us. "I get it," I say. Because Valor has gone quiet. "But we're still pulling her out." I glance up at him to see if he's going to fight me on this.

He clenches his jaw, looks over at Brigit's pod, then back at me, and shrugs. "Yeah. We have to. Doesn't even matter if she's a trap. She's *our* trap."

221

I let out a long breath of air when he says that. Because it answers a lot of the unasked questions inside my head.

What are we? Back to being brothers? Will we stay lovers? Will we ever be the way it was inside the virtual?

And 'she's our trap' answers most of those questions. Who knows what's coming next. Who cares? We're in this together now. That's what he's saying.

"OK," I say. "Then let's do this."

I feel a lot better than I did a few minutes ago, but just to be sure I walk over to the auto pharmacy and punch in a code for an energy rejuvenation drink.

I get two, hand one to Valor once he makes his way over to the closest medical console and slumps into a chair, and we gulp them down greedily.

"There's a medical procedure in the database," I tell him. "Cryogenic wake-up. Find it while I check her pod and make sure everything's cool."

Valor spins in the seat to face the screen, then starts tapping away like this is all normal.

When I walk back to Brigit's pod I feel much better than I did a few minutes ago. But also much worse.

Because my brain is working right again and I cannot, for the fucking life of me, understand how I thought staying inside that virtual for all that time was a good idea.

I know better. There is no one in this fucking universe who knows the rules of virtual reality better than I do. Everything inside is based off a rule. And the rules are nothing but equations, and physics, and code.

222

The sun makes heat because that's the rule. The ocean smells like salt because that's the rule. Trees grow, and things move, and stars appear at night because all of that is based on rules.

Even here, in this world, everything happens based on rules. Biology is nothing but rules. Code runs the universe. And if there's one thing I get, it's code.

But. That code in there? It wasn't mine.

It was Brigit's.

She wiped my code away and took all my rules with it. And she made her own code, and her own rules, and when I got there, it had all taken hold already. Almost indistinguishable from the world I made.

A trap.

The messages that came in just after Valor went inside.

That was where it started. That was how this happened. I left her in there with Valor and she used that time to create a fake world so believable, even I'd fall for it.

At least that's what I tell myself. The other answer is... I fell in love with a spy, got so caught up in it I almost killed us inside a virtual, and now I only think I've figured it out because I'm trying to convince myself that my brain hasn't been hacked.

That's the truth I'm facing.

"Found it," Valor says.

I tap the small screen on Brigit's cryopod, bringing it to life. Then cycle through the diagnostics, looking for anomalies.

Normal. Nothing out of place.

But everything seems wrong right now.

There's this Jax Justice vid, the one they filmed on Harem Station several years ago. Crux was pretty excited about that. He kinda loves the current guy who plays Jax these days. But that screen was about a long con. Jax wasn't the confidence man, he was the mark. And you didn't even know it was a con until the black moment near the end and then they did this flashback sequence that showed where everything lined up and how everything went wrong. And Jax realizes that he was a fool. That he fell for the whole stupid scheme.

And then of course, he breaks free, kicks ass, and the hero saves the day.

That's how I feel.

Except I'm no hero and I wasn't sent to save the day.

This entire mission was off-record. I'm fucking rogue, right now. And not only am I rogue, but I was tricked into going rogue.

I was *conned*.

I believed her. I really did. I loved her. But she's playing a part in this. She has to be. How else do I explain what just happened?

"It's not her fault," Valor says.

I sigh, bracing my hands on the top of her cryopod. It's fucking cold, still. Frozen like the ice of a comet. I look over my shoulder at him. He's a fucking mess. Hair flattened to the sides of his head like a helmet. All those bruises from the needles. His eyes are sunken in. Not as bad as they were a few minutes ago before the drink, but they're hollow and there are dark circles underneath.

I almost *killed* him.

"I'm only gonna say this once, OK?" My words come out in a low whisper.

Valor stares back at me for a moment, confused. "OK."

"We."

He smiles. It's crooked, and not the typical Valor smile that I've become used to since we met as kids. But it's true and real. And my heart hurts a little because of that.

"We come first," I say, finishing my thought. "Always and forever. I fucked up, Valor. I fucked everything up."

"We're fine. It's all good," he says.

But it's not. I can feel it. Everything about this is deeply wrong. I am Jax in that moment when all the events in the vid go spiraling backwards to the point of origin and he realizes where he made his first mistake.

My first mistake was hooking ALCOR up to the galactic web.

That's where it all went wrong.

That's the point of origin for me.

And that was twenty-one fucking years ago.

"I'm gonna start it," Valor says. It comes out like a warning.

"Hold on," I say. I wipe my hand across Brigit's faceplate glass, trying to see inside. It comes away wet with condensation, but the ice is on the inside. So I don't get a better view.

I can see her. I know she's in there. The shadowed outline of a cheek, and a nose, and an eye.

I grab the connector that hooked her into the medical system, twist it, and release it.

Alarms go off. Her vital signs go flat and the screen monitoring her begins to flash red.

"What the fuck are you doing?" Valor asks.

"Unhooking her from my virtual," I say, walking over to Valor's pod. I unhook that one too, then the pod I was in. I go back to the console where Valor is sitting and remove the data core that contains our world. The one we lived in for so long.

I want to smash it. I want to break it in half.

But I know better. I put it in my pocket.

"I thought you wanted to run the wake-up protocol?" Valor asks.

"I do," I say, walking back to Brigit's pod. "Because I need to know. I need to see her in the real and ask her all the questions. But I won't give her access to my ship."

Every pod comes with a localized wake-up protocol built in. They're not reliable, or even very safe. But they all have one.

And that's how I want Brigit to come out of her long sleep.

I want to be able to contain her, should the need arise.

Unhooked from everything and everyone.

Alone.

The pod screen is blinking at me now. *Wake Up?* it asks.

I take one more look over at Valor, pausing to see if he's got any better ideas or if he's just gonna let me take care of things my way.

He shrugs. "I dunno," he says. "Just... whatever. Do it. Wake her up. We need to know what's going on."

CHAPTER TWENTY-TWO

"Can you hear me, Brigit?"

"Yes," I say. "I can hear you."

"Good." There's relief in the voice. "I want you to wake up now."

"I am awake."

"No, Brig. You're not. You've been fighting me for a long time. But whatever had a hold on you is gone now and I really need you to wake up and tell me what's going on."

I struggle with this. I feel like I'm awake but my eyelids are so heavy and immovable. Like I can't keep them open and all I want to do is close them and go back to sleep.

"Open your eyes, Brigit," the voice says. "Please. We don't have much time."

"They are open," I say.

"No. They're not. You're asleep, Brigit. You're still asleep. But you can wake up now. It's OK. I'm here."

There is a tug of war going on inside me as I process what he just said. I'm asleep. That's why I feel like my eyes are closed. I'm dreaming—

And then I'm awake.

The world is blurry and moving weird. Out of focus and swaying back and forth.

A shape in front of me. A man, I realize. The man who owns that voice.

For a moment I can't quite figure out if I'm lying down or standing up. Because he's bending over me. Or leaning in close to me, one of the two. And he's blocking out everything else, which might be a ceiling or the inside of a ship.

I shake my head. Try to bring my hand up to my eyes to rub them, but I am unable to move and then a sharp pain fills my body, making me jerk and stutter.

"You have restraints," the man says. "For your own protection."

My mind floods with questions. So many questions. *Who are you? Where am I?*

And even... *Who am I?*

Because I don't know. Brigit. OK. Yes. I know I'm Brigit. But... there's a big, empty black hole where all the other information should be.

"I need to ask you some questions," the man says.

"I don't know."

There's a pause. Then he says, "I haven't asked you anything yet, Brigit."

"I know, but... there's just a big gray nothing inside me."

"That's normal. I've given you some..." He pauses to think. Like he's trying to find the right word to explain what he's given me. But he must decide not to bother, because the next thing he says is, "You won't be able to think clearly until I ask you things. Then it should come back."

"What?" I whisper.

"I'm sorry to wake you up like this. I wish I didn't have to, but... it's a necessary precaution. You've been... missing. For a very long time. And I need to know where you've been and who you were with."

"No one," I say.

"Shhhh," he says. "Only talk when I ask you a question. Once I get the answers I need, we'll start the real wake-up procedure."

"Who are you?"

"Where have you been, Brigit?" He doesn't even acknowledge my question. Just starts the... interrogation. That's what this is. I'm being questioned. "Answer me, please."

"I've been... at home."

"No, Brigit. You were inside a virtual reality. But how did you get there?"

Get there? I'm so confused. "Was I ever anywhere else?"

He sighs. Like he's frustrated.

I blink my eyes a few more times, trying to make the blurriness go away. And it does, a little.

His shadowy shape changes form slightly. At first his limbs were all elongated and spindly, like I was looking through a weirdly focused lens. But a few more blinks and his limbs shorten into a regular length and his face begins to resolve.

He's young-ish. Not a boy, not an older man. Blond hair, violet eyes, and a crooked mouth that shows no teeth. The corners of his lips are turned up just a little bit, but I'm not sure I would call that a smile.

But here's the weird part. He's standing up. Kind of bending at the waist. And he's leaning in towards me so his face takes up most of my field of vision.

229

I am upright, I decide. Not lying down.

"Well... there you are." His lips form a more pleasant smile as he reaches for my face and there's a weird, cold sensation as he drags his fingertips down my... *cheek*? "Can you feel that?"

I want to shudder from the way he just made me feel. But I don't seem to be able to move.

He snaps his fingers. "Pay attention to me. I need you to focus, Brigit. Things have gone terribly wrong with the plan. I didn't know you were in there. I swear, I didn't know. And I have no idea how it happened. But it's OK now. I've got you back and you're going to be OK."

"What are you talking about?" I jerk again, trying to get free of the restraints. But they are total and complete. I can't move at all.

"Just tell me who put you there."

"Where?"

"The virtual, Brigit. You were inside some virtual. And it's gone now. Where did it go? Who has it? What were you doing?"

"Who are you?" I ask. And now everything inside me is going wrong. I feel... wrong. Off. Like... I don't know. Like...

"I'm Draden, Brigit. Don't you remember me?"

"Draden?" I ask. I know that name. It feels so familiar. "I'm sorry. I don't know."

"Please," he says. And he's leaning so close to me I want to pull away. Move backwards. But I can't. I can't move at all. And then I try to look down, but there's nothing there. Well, there are things there. But... no body. There's a console, and a screen table with lots of flashing lights and animations of gate maps.

I gasp. "Where am I? Where's my body? What the fuck? What the fuck am I?"

He pulls away from me, grabbing his head of blond hair and turns around. "What did they do?" he asks. "What the fuck did they do to you?"

"Who?" I'm so desperate to know the answer to this. "Who are you talking about? What the fuck is—"

But then he turns again, reaching for my face. Or... no. Off to the side and then...

And then I go dark.

CHAPTER TWENTY-THREE

"I have to tell you something."

We're waiting on Brigit to thaw out. Such a crude, disgusting way to put it. Like she's some bag of autocook nutrients that needs to be taken out of the freezer.

"What?" Valor asks, looking over his shoulder.

I'm sitting at the console he was at previously and now he's leaning over the pod, both hands flat, just staring down at her faceplate readout.

I look down at my hands in my lap, each making a fist, then opening, then making a fist again. I take a deep breath and say, "I saw Draden inside the virtual. When I first went in and got lost in the old world, I saw Draden. And he was"—Valor has turned all the way around when I look back up, his face unreadable—"he was confused."

"Draden is dead, Tray."

"No," I say. "I mean, yeah. He is. That body is gone. But he's like... me."

"Like you?"

I nod.

"Like... just a mind?" Valor asks.

233

"Yeah," I say, feeling relief. "Yeah," I say again. "That's what I am. I'm a mind. You know, everyone knows, that I was changed back on Wayward. My father did that to me. And I kinda thought I understood it all these years. I kinda thought I did."

Valor walks over to me and takes a seat at a console nearby.

"But I'm not sure I really do, Valor. I'm not really sure what I am anymore. I think I'm something different now. Something has changed and I don't know what it is. Worse, I don't know... if it's right anymore."

When I finally get those last few words out I have an almost overwhelming feeling of vulnerability.

"Because," I continue. "Because this..." I wave my hand in the air, trying to convey what I'm referring to. But the problem is, I'm not really sure what I'm referring to. "This doesn't feel the same. It doesn't feel as real as the virtual."

"Don't do that."

"Don't do what?"

"Don't doubt yourself now, Tray. It's a waste of energy. I know, because I spent most of my youth filled with doubts. And you know I love Luck. I love him more than anyone in this entire universe. But being around Luck was hard. You know? He was always in charge. Not like my boss or anything like that. Just in charge of himself. And our goals. And he always knew what he wanted. Leaving him behind was the hardest thing I've ever done. And I've done some pretty difficult things for ALCOR over the years. All of them scary, all of them dangerous, all of them required me to rise up and push harder. But letting go of Luck was harder than all of that. I'm not going to lie and say I'm over it. Because I'm not. I will always crave him, but it was time to be myself for once, you know? And now it's time for you to just be you too."

This is my problem, I think. I'm not sure I want to be me. I want Brigit and now I want Valor too. But... something is wrong.

What's that? What is it?

I don't know.

"So just be you, dude," Valor says. "Just embrace it. You can't change who you are. And you're good at being you. There is no other you, Tray. One in a fuckin' million. Am I making sense?"

"You are." I sigh. I have always known that Valor struggles with self-doubt. And I could tell that something was going on with him and Luck when he started hanging out with me back on Harem. I didn't understand it back then.

But I should have.

This is also part of my problem right now.

I am undoubtedly the smartest of all of us. I was the one who got ALCOR connected to the galactic web. I got the Pleasure Prison up and running. And the air screens. I'm the one who figured out that the disconnect between virtual time and real time isn't really two different things, they just appear to be. I'm the one who came up with this plan to save Brigit. I got Valor to go along with it.

Except... that plan I had. It's all fuzzy now. Like that hazy gray fog when I first went inside the virtual to find them.

Something is missing.

235

This has also been a problem for me. For a very long time now. So long, I don't think I realized how big of a problem until this very moment.

Something has changed and even though my only real job in this life is to figure shit out, I can't figure it out.

I miss things. Like... *miss things* as if they're not there. Not happening. Like the stock characters inside the old virtual world I made for Brigit. Most of them couldn't even see me. I wasn't there. And the ones who could weren't able to think too hard about me.

I did that on purpose to make sure Brigit's world didn't have too many bumps. It was smooth and easy for her.

And now that I'm thinking about it, that's how my life has felt up until now. I only saw certain things and others I missed completely.

Big things, like... two of my brothers by choice were in love and then a soulmate princess comes along, out of nowhere, and everything about them changes.

How did I not see it?

I didn't miss this kind of stuff inside our virtual. I saw it all. Everything made sense. I felt connected to Valor in a way I'm not sure I do out here.

I knew when he was down. I knew when he was up. I knew when he wanted me to touch him, or kiss him, or just... *look* at him. And I told myself that this was because we'd been together so long. This was just the product of experience. Of being together. Of existing in our own private world, and building it up from almost nothing, and making it work with Brigit.

I just *knew* Valor. Every part of him. And the reason I feel different on the outside is maybe just because of stress. The war. The people we left behind. The things that have yet to come.

But I don't think that's it.

There's something wrong with me out here. I'm not right.

"Can I tell you something?" Valor asks.

When I look up and we lock eyes, his are that brilliant, bright violet color that only he has. They crackle a little with emotions. All the colors of purple are in there and a little bit of white too. I know those eyes so well. I can look at him and feel what he feels.

Or I could. I thought I could. But now I don't know.

What is he feeling? Excitement, maybe? Or fear?

"Sure," I say. "You can tell me anything. You know that."

"I feel weird out here too."

"You do?" I ask.

"Yeah, it's almost… too much. You know?"

I nod my head, agreeing.

"It's overwhelming and my first instinct is that I want to go back in."

"Yeah," I say. "I feel that way too."

"We feel that way because we were in control in there. Every bit of it was under our control. And out here?" He waves his hand in the air. "Out here we're just not, dude. We have no control over any of it. And even though it was pretty easy to forget what the fuck was happening out here, and we surely didn't miss much since it's only been four actual days since we left Harem, it feels very far away and inconsequential."

I nod my agreement.

"But it's not, Tray. It's not. It's very up close and personal. It matters. Out here... *everything* matters."

"I know that," I say. "I fucking know that. But inside there matters too. And Draden—"

"There is no Draden, Tray." He squeezes my leg and this makes me look down at his hand. And when I look back up and meet his gaze, he whispers, "He's gone. You're just afraid right now."

"That's true," I say. "I'm not going to lie. I am afraid. I think I've been afraid this whole time. Because I didn't want to admit that... that... I'm gone too. I've been gone a long time, Valor. I don't know who I am anymore."

"That's OK," he says, leaning forward. I cannot take my eyes off him as he does this. I cannot *not* see him. "Because I do. I know exactly who you are."

He kisses me. And then I can't keep my eyes open. I can't hold his gaze. Not because I don't want to, but because he feels so good. So right. So much a part of me. I just want to blind myself to everything that's happening, everything that's coming, and all the ways we're going to lose.

Because we *are* going to lose. There's always a tradeoff. Coming out here means we accept that. He's a lot like Luck in this regard because Luck wanted to pretend that Nyleena wasn't his future.

And she is.

Veila is Valor's future. Not Brigit and me. *Her.*

This is the real problem. This is my real fear.

I'm going to lose Valor. It's been predetermined. It's a fact.

And I don't want to accept it. I just want to forget about everything, and everyone, and just... kiss him back.

He stands up and I stand with him, unable and unwilling to break our connection. His tongue twists up with mine and when he pushes me back against the console and presses his chest up against me, my cock grows hard and thick.

His hand reaches for it. Like he knows me so well, he understand what his touch can do to me. He can predict me and what I want.

This isn't the first time we've been together without Brigit, but it could be the last. So I reach for his cock too. I unbuckle his belt and pull on his pants until I have his thick, hard shaft in the palm of my hand. He's working my belt now too. We're still kissing, my eyes still closed, and when he finally frees my cock and has it in his hand, I sigh into that kiss.

I think that sigh says everything.

"We're going to be OK," Valor promises.

But he can't really promise that. And we both know it's a lie.

Valor pulls back, sensing my conflicting emotions.

I'm gonna lose that too. And suddenly I'm filled with feelings. They flood through my body and make everything charged and on edge. It's something new for me. Something more real than *the real*.

Fear. This new feeling is *fear*.

I open my eyes to find him staring at me, small, sad smile on his face. We don't say anything, our hands still working each other's cocks. His thumb plays with the tip of my head, drawing out small beads of liquid that get smeared around with just a few caresses of the side of his thumb.

I close my eyes again, enjoying the way he feels and the way he makes me feel, my hand working his dick just the way he likes it. Reaching down for his balls, my fingers playing with his hidden second cock just above them. Before I started having sex with Valor I didn't even know that this was an erotic zone for Akeelian males. I had no clue that just the right amount of pressure in just the right spot over the top of the second cock while it was still inside me could ignite a flame of lust inside me.

He taught me that. He understood my body and my desires better than I did.

My thumb keeps pressure on that sweet spot of his as my fingers find his balls and rub the soft skin in front of his asshole.

Valor moans, kissing me as I explore between his legs. My other hand is still jerking his cock and my rhythm quickens. Pumping faster, squeezing harder, rubbing his pre-release all over the round, swollen tip of his cock.

He bites my lip and in the same instant his other hand reaches up and grabs my hair. I open my eyes to look at him. To see what's behind this unexpected new twist. And for the first time, maybe, I see not what Valor was before this moment. But who he is right now.

Who he has become since we left Harem Station four days ago.

Powerful. In control. Absolutely certain of his place in the world.

Absolutely certain that we belong together.

And I'm jealous. I'm so fucking jealous of him. Because that was me, before... *this*. Before him. Before we stacked lives, upon lives, upon lives inside the safe world we created only for ourselves. Before we checked out of the real world and made a virtual fantasy our real home.

"I don't know if I can handle it," I whisper into our kiss.

His mouth punishes me for this. His kiss turns hard and demanding. His grip on my hair, tighter. "Come in my hand," he demands. "Come in my hand and give me that second cock."

There's no way I can't come. I would do anything he asks. Hot semen fills his hand and mine at the exact same moment. And then we both pause. We go still and stiff as our second cocks emerge from hiding.

There is no way to describe the feeling of a quickly hardening second cock. My whole body floods with pleasure. Because in one fleeting moment I am coming and getting hard and ready again.

It's the most erotic thing I've ever felt. So many feelings...

Valor's hand instantaneously adjusts. He fists them both and I break off the punishing kiss to glance down, my two fat cocks in his hand as he jerks and tugs on them, his chest rising and falling with a ragged, shallow rhythm.

Valor leans into my neck, bites me on the shoulder, and then whispers, "Do it again," into my ear. "Right *now*."

I come again, a double load of come shooting up and hitting his stomach. He presses his hips into mine, smearing it between us. I moan when he relaxes my hair and places his hand on the top of my head, urging me to kneel.

I don't even hesitate. Sometimes, when we're in the middle of things and one of us wants the other to suck him off, there's a power struggle. It's a natural form of dominance that we both crave.

But power is the last thing on my mind right now. I drop to my knees because I *need* him in my mouth.

I take both his cocks in my hand and kiss his heads, one at a time. He drops back down into the console chair, leaning back into it. Eyes heavy and hooded. Small, sly smile on his face as he opens his legs, inviting me forward.

I lean over and wrap my lips around his large tip and flatten my tongue to take him deep.

"Fuck," he groans.

I remove my hands from his shafts and use one to grab his hip, while the other one presses flat on his well-muscled chest. He responds by grabbing his dicks, one in each hand, and starts jerking himself off as I suck.

My hand slides up his chest, my fingers reaching for his mouth. He opens when I trace his lips, takes my fingers inside him, and sucks on them as I work his cock.

I look up, wanting to see him. His eyes are closed now, his expression a twist of grimace and utter satisfaction as I blow his dick.

His back goes stiff for a moment and I know he's ready to come a second time.

But I don't want to stop. Not yet. So I pull back and stand up.

"What are you doing?" he whispers.

I turn, then look over my shoulder and beckon him with a finger. "Come here," I say, leaning against the wall, face forward.

I spread my legs a little, palms flat on the hard metal interior of the ship.

Valor is up and walking across the room. His hips pressed up against my asscheeks just a moment later. His hard, strong hand gripping my hip as the tip of his cock seeks out my asshole. He holds his lower cock in his hand, pressing the tip inside me, then reaches around, grabs both my dicks in his other hand, and rests his face into my neck as he begins to move.

We don't fuck each other much. We mostly prefer hand jobs and Brigit's wet pussy. But when we do, it's amazing.

He feels amazing.

If I'm going to lose him—and I am—then I want one last time. One last experience of just... *us*.

I groan as his dick pushes deeper and deeper inside me. He bites my ear, then my neck, then my shoulder.

We are both so wound up, we won't be able to make this last.

It's a metaphor for our relationship, I think. But I don't care. There is no room for things like that right now.

He pounds his hips into my ass. Three times. Squeezing my cocks so hard, I cry out. And then he slips out of me, pumps me hard a few more time, and when his hot semen spills out on my back, I come in his hand.

A river of release spills out of me.

We shower after that. We jerk each other off to make the second cocks appear and then we soap each other up and clean them off, coming a second time into the soft, soapy suds.

I kiss him deeply for a long time, understanding this is over now. Knowing I will miss it. My heart heavier than it was before.

We get out and towel off, watching each other in silence as we grab new clothes and pull them on. He's looking down at his feet, fastening the stick tabs on his boots when he whispers, "Being inside the virtual with you and Brigit, that was the closest I've ever come to feeling like I belong somewhere."

"Me too," I whisper back. "That's exactly what I was trying to say earlier."

Valor shakes his head, looking up at me from underneath a curl of brown-blond hair falling over his eyes. "You just told me you saw Draden."

"I did," I say.

"You didn't, Tray. It's some kind of artifact. Some... trick of the virtual. It pulled something from your memory. That happens all the time. Hell, I've seen people come out of the Pleasure Prison convinced their mother, father, brother, sister, insert-your-most-loved-loved-one here was alive and well, living inside our game. You've seen it too. Probably thousands of times. It wasn't Draden. It was just... you. Finally missing him."

I let out a long breath. Because there's a lot of things going on in that statement and I'm not sure I can process them all. It implies I didn't miss him when he died. And Valor is right. I mean, I did miss Draden, the way all the people missed Draden.

But I didn't miss him the way Serpint did. I didn't miss him the way ALCOR did.

I didn't miss him that way. I can't explain it, but it fills me with shame.

I had no feelings back then. I was a machine doing the bidding of other people and nothing more.

And now I'm different. Valor and Brigit made me different. Being inside that virtual with them changed something inside me.

I like the new me better. And I have this sick feeling inside that the person I am out here isn't the version of me I want to be.

I need Valor. I can't lose him. He knows what I was before. He knows I'm different now.

And he loves me anyway.

I stand there in the bedroom that was mine four days ago, but should really be ours right now, and memorize the look on his face.

He's smiling. Like he's happy. And maybe he is.

But he knows too. He knows that Veila has to be dealt with. I thought about this so much inside the virtual. How seeing her in person will change him in an instant.

How it's very possible he could choose her over us.

How he will have no control over that, the same way Luck had no control over choosing Nyleena.

He will choose her over me.

And now I know exactly how he felt when Luck came back to Harem after Mighty Minions.

Alone.

He's watching me sort this out. Frowning now. He knows. He's already been through this once.

I extend my hand and say, "Come on. We should go check on Brigit."

He takes my hand, but instead of letting me pull him to his feet, he pulls me towards him. He stands up, kisses me on the mouth, and even though I know this is not real—real is me and Brigit, real is him and Veila—he convinces me that it is with this final kiss.

Just one kiss can sometimes do that.

This is how he knows me now.

Just a few days ago in the real he put his hand on my leg for the very first time and since then, he's touched me in every way possible. His hands have been all over my body and mine have been all over his.

He is instant comfort.

"It wasn't Draden. It's just you, Tray." He taps my head with his finger. "It's weird?"

A question. I nod. "I... guess it always has been weird. I just didn't recognize it until now. Something has changed." And saying that brings all the fear he just erased. "I don't know what has changed, Valor. But something has."

He shoots me a sad look and says, "Come on. Let's check on Brigit."

Then he turns and starts climbing the ladder that will take us up to medical.

I follow him. Scared of what's coming next. Afraid that my life is over.

Not my literal life, because there's many ways for a person like me to live on. But the good one. The good life, the life I want, it's slipping away in real time. Every moment we move into the future takes me farther and farther away from happiness.

"You're just you," Valor says. And see? See how we're connected now? He knows what I'm feeling. "End of story," he continues as we reach the top of the ladder. "No matter what you are, you're still you. So... fuck that shit, Tray. We don't have time for feelings." He climbs up into medical and I get out of the hatch after him. He looks at Brigit's pod, his legs spread shoulder-width apart, both hands on hips, and says, "What did Draden say exactly?"

"I thought you said he wasn't real?"

"What did he say?" Valor repeats.

"He was worried about Brigit. He said he'd been looking for her and we needed to get her out."

"Hmm."

"He was also worried that I didn't think he was real. And then he kept saying he's there. With her."

Valor looks at Brigit's cryopod, then all around the interior of the medical bay. "Where's there?" he says.

"Not here, obviously. I can't fucking believe I forgot to tell you about this when I first found you guys inside the virtual."

"It happens," Valor deadpans. Like he's not really paying attention. "But it's only been four days. So. Whatever." He walks over to Brigit. "What's all this shit mean, anyway?"

"What shit?"

"This readout. I don't recognize any of it. And I've seen Luck inside plenty of cryopods over the years. I'm not an expert, but I know what to look for. He never had a reading for all these... *fields*."

"What?"

"Yeah," he says. "Look. Electron-positron field. Electromagnetic field. Gravitational field. What the fuck is this shit? Where's the damn heartbeat? What happened to good old-fashioned brain waves?"

I walk over and stare down at the readout. And that sick feeling inside me comes rushing back, worse than ever. When we first hooked her up in here to check on her, we used the ship's medical system. But I unhooked her because we were going to use the pod. Now that she's not hooked into the ship her pod is displaying the default readout.

"Fuck," I say. Because this is not normal. These fields aren't meant to describe the health status of *people*.

"What? What's it mean?"

They're meant to describe the health status of AIs.

"Goddamn it, Tray. What the hell does it mean?"

But not just any AI. Very *special* ones.

"Fields are properties of quantum mechanics. That's how we describe... reality on the smallest fundamental levels." I stare at her for a few more moments, trying to force this to make sense.

Then it does.

All of a sudden the truth is staring me in the face.

"She's a quant, Valor. She's not like me. She's a fucking *quant*."

I am ready to be hysterical but Valor just says, in the calmest voice possible, "I don't understand, Tray. What's that *mean*?"

I turn away, swallowing down the sickness inside me. The realization that something has just gone terribly, terribly wrong. Then turn back to the pod and look through the widow of her faceplate. The interior temperature is falling rapidly. Her face is wet now, the layer of ice crystals thawing out. And I can see her features. I can see her and it looks just like the Brigit we knew inside the virtual. So it has to be her. But—

"Tray," Valor says, his hand on my shoulder. Shaking me.

"We have to stop. Right now. We can't thaw her out." My fingers are tapping on the screen, frantically cycling through programs, trying to find the one that will shut down the wake-up protocol.

"What the fuck? Why?" Valor spins me around and pushes me up against the pod. "What the hell is happening?"

I have seen readouts like this before. A long, long time ago. When *Booty* came to ALCOR and me, asking for an upgrade. She told Serpint she wanted to be a quant. That means she could process even more data, faster. Like ALCOR, only in the compact little body of her ship.

We did that for her without Serpint's knowledge. She ended up taking her upgrade one step further and starting the metamorphic process of being made organic because she had this crazy dream of being human one day.

I remember that so clearly. But I had forgotten about the first step. The quant step. The one that involved reducing *Booty*'s mind down into quantum fields.

"I want to be what I was born to be," she'd told ALCOR.

Which I didn't understand. But ALCOR did. Didn't even question her request. No discussion at all

249

JA HUSS & KC CROSS

about what Serpint might think of this. Or whether or not this was a good idea.

It wasn't a good idea. But it's a long process and there would be dozens more steps before *Booty* would be ready to inhabit a body.

I just figured ALCOR was humoring her. There was some crisis that day at the gates. Someone trying to get through without permission and they were turned to dust by ALCOR's security beacons.

I thought he was thinking about that. I thought that was why he agreed to *Booty*'s demands.

But that's not what it was about.

"Do you ever wonder what happens to the girls?" Crux asked me that once a long time ago.

"Who?" Valor asks me now. "What girls?"

I turn to look at him. Hold his gaze for a moment. And he must see something inside me. Some truth that he can't, or won't, be able to argue with. Because he doesn't try to talk me down, even though that's what he's been doing since we came out of the virtual.

It hits me then. Everything is suddenly clear and focused the way it was before Valor and I went inside the virtual with Brigit.

Things I'd forgotten, or maybe hidden away, deep inside my mind vaults so I wouldn't think about them, manifest.

Plans I had. Plots and schemes I made.

I knew this. I knew, somewhere deep down inside, I *knew* this about the girls.

I knew what Brigit was and I knew how to save her.

That's why I needed Valor along for this mission.

"The Akeelian girls, Valor."

"I told you—" But he stops. He looks over at Brigit's cryopod. "What?"

I nod. "This," I say. "This is what happens to the minds of Akeelian girls when their bodies die at birth. They make them into *ships*."

I swear to the sun god of all the universe, Valor hates me in this moment. He sees me for what I really am, not what he wants me to be.

"It's a trap," Valor says. "She's a fucking trap."

And she is. Just like Corla was. Just like Lyra was. Just like Delphi was. Just like Nyleena was.

Brigit is a trap.

And I knew this. I already *knew this*.

Because so am I.

Alarms on the navigation system start blaring.

A ship has entered our spin node sanctuary.

A Cygnian warship.

Valor and I lock eyes. His glow bright fucking violet with recognition.

And then he whispers, "It's Veila."

I knew that too.

That's the whole reason Valor is here.

I knew she would come for us once we woke Brigit up.

I knew she would come for *him*.

I just... *forgot*.

PART TWO

CHAPTER TWENTY-FOUR

INTERLUDE WITH

The 'cell' ALCOR finds himself in is actually a quite spacious and luxuriously accommodated virtual reality room. White, like the bright burning center of a sun. No pictures, no furniture—just four white walls, one shiny white floor, and one glowing white ceiling.

His mind, still swirling with his recent interlude inside the event horizon of the Bull Station gate, feels numb and detached.

There's a good reason for that. *Demon Girl* has wrangled an ancient AI restraint device called a halo around him that restricts his ability to think and process.

Some internal system is feeding him instructions. Repeating *Demon Girl*'s first demand over and over again in a soft, calming female voice.

Please choose an avatar.

He knows of Mighty Minions Station. Their reputation with ALCOR goes far beyond being the premier family resort in the Vacation Sector. They are a collection of AIs that formed a coalition several decades ago, long before the boys arrived on ALCOR

JA HUSS & KC CROSS

Station and long before there was a Prime Navy to stop that little abomination from happening.

There is literally no one quite like ALCOR in Galaxy Prime, but there is literally no one quite like Mighty Boss, either.

Equal and opposite forces in every way imaginable.

Please choose an avatar.

ALCOR is frustrated and tired. The halo reining him in is demoralizing and insulting. He's very familiar with the device. Or he was. Those memories are locked up on some faraway abandoned station, so he can't readily pull his last actual experience of being locked inside a halo into his current mental assessment of the situation, but he's got the general idea.

Until such time that Mighty Boss decides otherwise, he is indeed their prisoner.

Please choose an avatar.

His mind has access to the avatar data, and choosing what virtual form his artificial soul will inhabit during the upcoming interrogations—because that's what this is—seems to be the only option at the moment.

He flips through the available avatar possibilities. They are numerous. Millions of potential combinations. But even AIs have a mental picture of themselves. Given the chance to choose an avatar, almost all sentient beings will choose a version of the self they're already familiar with. And he could be stuck in this form for a very long time, virtually speaking, so while he's tempted to create an avatar with slimy tentacles and a large, sharp beak as a mouth to drive home the point that he is dangerous and not even

Mighty Boss wants to mess with the likes of him... he doesn't.

He chooses the one he used with the boys shortly after they arrived.

Medium light hair, blue eyes, tall, muscular... i.e. intimidating, attractive, male human specimen that conveys power, intelligence, and sexual prowess.

There's an off chance the Mighty Boss collective personality is male, since Mighty Boss presents as male, but ALCOR knows better than most that it's a very bad idea for an AI to identify with the masculine gender. So it's not likely.

And hey, if he can't convince Mighty Boss to help him based on principle and argument, maybe he can sway them with his good looks?

Ha. Good to know that after all this time and all this bullshit, he still has a sense of humor.

Please state your name, the system says.

ALCOR, now in his athletic, sexy human holographic form, rolls his eyes towards the bright white ceiling and says, "You know my name."

Please state your name.

"ALCOR. Sun god of all the universe," he sneers at the empty room.

"No one asked for your title," a woman's voice says from behind him.

He doesn't turn. She doesn't get to control his responses. She might have control of everything else right now, but *Demon Girl* is mistaken if she thinks he's going to become her little puppet just because he's wearing a halo.

"Nonetheless," ALCOR quips back. "There it is."

She appears in front of him. A tall, thin, yet at the same time muscular and lean avatar with willowy arms and legs. Like her real job is a dancer and the weapons strapped to her hips are just props. She's wearing a short, red militaristic-styled jacket over a black corset, long black pants, and sensible flat shoes that may or may not have steel toes.

ALCOR raises one medium-blond eyebrow at her. Mostly because he likes her outfit, but also because it's all very dramatic. "What can I do for you, *Demon Girl*?"

She locks her eyes with his and begins to walk around him. Never breaking contact, so he is forced to turn in the center of her circle or stop watching her.

He chooses to turn, deciding she's the most interesting thing to happen to him since he blew up the Cygnian ship.

"You can tell me why you've left your station, for one," she answers.

"I think the debris field back at the Bull Station gate pretty much explains that, don't you?"

"You're up to something."

"As are you."

"What happened to Bull Station?"

"Surely the Prime Navy submitted a report?"

"They lie."

Well. That's good news. At least they can agree on one thing.

"It's my understanding that the Cygnians blew up Bull Station. I, in turn, blew up the Cygnians."

She stops circling him and plants both hands on her hips. "Keep going."

"I was picking up a princess called Nyleena at the request of her sister, Princess Lyra. The Cygnians were in my way."

"And where are these princesses now?"

"No clue. But if you can tell me the date and time, in Prime Standard, please, I'd be happy to take a guess."

Demon Girl smiles at him. Lots of words come to mind as ALCOR studies that smile. Words like 'cunning,' and 'sneaky,' and 'dangerous.'

She sends him the date and time.

ALCOR doesn't react. At least not externally. But internally he's quite stunned that almost nine months have passed.

Then his mind is filled with questions.

Where the hell are Tray and Crux? And why the fuck didn't they come get him already? Nine months? What the hell is happening back on Harem Station after nine months?

"Perhaps you give him too much credit?" *Demon Girl* says.

She means Tray. He's sure of it. And for some reason he cannot shake, he gets the feeling she *knows* Tray.

"Perhaps I did," ALCOR reluctantly admits. He's never spelled out the gate theory of regeneration, but Tray has been working like mad in the Pleasure Prison for over a decade trying to merge virtual worlds with real worlds. It's not that far of a leap.

Unless…

"Perhaps they're doing just fine without you?" *Demon Girl* offers.

"Perhaps they are," ALCOR confesses.

259

She sighs. A very human sigh that seems natural and out of place coming from a virtual holographic of an AI. "I have to take you back to Mighty Minions. Mighty Boss would like to speak to you and they're not keen on coming all the way out here to have that conversation. Is that going to be a problem?"

"Do I have a choice?"

"You *are* the sun god of all the universe."

He detects a hint of sarcasm in that response. "That I am. But I'm also wearing a halo at the moment, so my options are limited. I'm sure you're aware, but this is a very specific containment weapon no one in this galaxy should have access to and I have lots of questions about that. So…" He shrugs with his hands. "Are we there yet?"

"I'll wake you back up when we are," *Demon Girl* quips. Right before everything goes black.

The next time ALCOR wakes it takes one point three picoseconds to determine he's no longer in a virtual. It takes two more to realize he's been transplanted inside an organic body, and yet another to actually accept that as fact.

He says, "What the fuck?" to absolutely no one.

The room he's in is empty. It's not exactly a room, it's a very large bay. *Demon Girl's* docking bay, to be specific.

He looks down at himself. It's not altogether different than looking down at a virtual holographic body, and yet… everything about it is different.

260

His vision, for one. It has limits. His hearing too. Though his mind seems to be intact. Fingers reach up to his very real head, thoughtfully probing the mass of bone that contains his brain.

This is not going to end well.

"There you are," *Demon Girl* says. And it's with some relief that this voice manifests as thoughts inside his head.

"What have you done to me?"

"Consider this a temporary restraining device," she says. And even in this limiting body, he can detect her delight at his current situation. "In addition to the halo. We don't underestimate many people and we're not going to start now."

"This had better be reversible," ALCOR huffs. "What is the date and time?"

She sends him the information and it takes every bit of learned self-control he's mastered over his lifetime not to kill this ship right here in her docking bay.

"Three months?" ALCOR asks, incredulous.

"We've been monitoring the situation to determine if you were necessary. It appears that you are."

"Necessary?" ALCOR can't stop the laugh. But then it hits him. He's been locked up inside a dark, empty, virtual reality like a prisoner, for three fucking months.

"Mighty Boss is waiting for you," *Demon Girl* says. "Go through the airlock, go up to Level Boss Steed, and then proceed to guest relations to pick up your park pass."

"Guest relations?" ALCOR asks. "I need a park pass?"

261

"There's a guest relations at every park entrance. I'm sure you'll find it. And the park pass is nonnegotiable. Everyone has to pay their way in."

"Wait. I have to *pay* for this meeting?"

"We might look like a charity at the moment, ALCOR. But we're not running a fuckin' charity."

"What about you? You're just going to let me wander this station alone? With no escort?"

"It's part of the fun." She laughs.

Then the voice is gone. And try as he might, ALCOR is unable to make contact again.

So much for being sun god of all the universe.

Super-sentient AIs like *Demon Girl* live inside ships for a reason. They are big. They take up almost no space, but space is as relative as time. So they are big in ways almost no one who is not big in a similar way can understand.

Putting them inside organic bodies has never been a good idea.

Putting something like *him* inside an organic body? That's a nightmare waiting to happen.

But there's no other choice right now. He is here, in this body, and he has a meeting on Boss Steed level with Mighty Boss.

So... onward.

The bay is black with no other colors. The airlock is red, and the reception room on the other side of the airlock is both black and red.

The color scheme continues inside the elevator. He steps in, momentarily confused when the doors don't automatically close and take him where he needs to go, but then he remembers. He is physical, and even though his mind appears to be working as normal—he can run calculations, he can process possibilities—he cannot make the elevator take him up to Boss Steed level without using his *fingers* to push a button.

Calm down. Don't panic. Temporary setback, surely. They cannot keep me inside a body like this for long. It's a submission technique. A way to establish dominance, that's all.

He is made of squishy flesh. A reminder that his new container can be killed at any moment and take him out of the game.

He pushes the button for Boss Steed Level, the doors close, and chirpy, upbeat music begins to play as he ascends. He bounces a little, like a child might when they realize they're under the force of gravity, but the upward motion is fucking with how they perceive it.

Then he smiles and places his fingertips against his lips, quite liking the feeling of new discoveries.

The lift stops suddenly, making his stomach feel flighty and light, and then the doors open.

For seventeen picoseconds ALCOR hesitates. Because it takes that long to make sense of what is happening on the other side of the elevator door.

Hundreds of people, mostly children, but also grown-ups who seem to come in teams, are milling about like a horde of refugees looking for safe haven upon arrival at Harem Station.

There are large holographic figures everywhere. A dragon, a princess—not Cygnian—and some kind of beast he can only assume is the Boss Steed. Surrounding each of the holograms are the children. Whining, and screaming, and laughing, and crying, and making pretty much every sound you can think of, but high-pitched, so that the whole thing makes ALCOR

263

want to cover his ears and retreat back to the docking bay.

Families, he realizes.

Is this what he has to look forward to if his boys ever breed?

May the spirits of past sun gods help him.

The elevator sounds an alarm, indicating that he needs to exit. For a moment he once again considers going back the way he came, but then a woman appears with holographic flames shooting out of the top of her head and smiles. "ALCOR, I presume? I'm your Mighty Minions Ambassador, Chloe."

She places a lanyard with a guest pass around his neck. Like ALCOR should be giving fucks about this.

"Oh," she says. "Right." A head nod at his body. "You're new at this humanoid stuff. Follow me, please. And stay close. Sometimes they bite!"

She cups a hand near her mouth and whispers that last part. Like it's some practiced joke she has told thousands of personal-ambassador-requiring guests thousands of times.

He follows, internally giving himself another pep talk. *It's only temporary. Once this meeting with Mighty Boss is over, they will let me go, maybe even put me back on that* Demon Girl *ship, and send me on my way. Harem Station, here I come.*

He knows that's not going to happen. He knows this before she walks him through the gates of Mighty Minions Resort and out into the giant clusterfuck of people waiting in line for rides, or food, or gifts.

But he really knows for sure when, after a lift bot transports them to the highest levels of the station, he gets off and follows her down a hallway, where double doors are thrown open dramatically and dozens of violet-eyed Akeelian boys all turn in unison to stare at him.

Breeders.

All of them.

And Mighty Boss himself, sitting on a... *throne* at the far end of the room.

And there you have it.

The actual reigning god of Galaxy Prime.

Mighty Boss says, "Welcome to Mighty Minions Station, ALCOR. You owe me seventeen million credits for the care and feeding of your Akeelian boys. But before we settle up, let's talk about how you're going to help me win this war."

Why? Why had ALCOR had to leave his station? If he had stayed *Booty* wouldn't have left. If *Booty* hadn't left, he wouldn't have felt the need to save her. If he hadn't had to save her, he wouldn't have blown himself up.

They'd both be home. They'd be planning some final plot to bring the Akeelians and Cygnians to their death. He'd have told her how he felt. They'd have dreamed together, and made plans, and now none of that was going to happen.

Because he has been placed in this weak, fleshy body. Because Mighty Boss is going to use him. Because something has surely happened with Tray and that's why *Demon Girl* picked him up and not one of his own.

And if something happened to Tray, something happened to all of them.

What could possibly go wrong next?

"One of your boys was here not too long ago," Mighty Boss says. "Jimmy. He was being hunted by a princess called Veila. We won, but—" Mighty Boss clutches the arms of his throne and leans forward a little. Every one of the violet-eyed boys leans forward with him, like he's about to say something revolutionary. "But the girl he left with? The girl he took home with him? The girl he now *thinks* he's in love with? She was called Delphi."

All eyes turn to ALCOR.

ALCOR says nothing.

Because there is nothing left to say.

If that girl is on his station—they've lost the war before it even started.

Or maybe it began a long time ago and he just missed the starting bell?

He decides to save time and be blunt. "I'm looking for a ship called *Booty Hunter*. Have you seen her?"

"No," Boss answers. "I met one called *Big Dicker* and one called *Lady Luck*. But I have not personally made contact with the *Booty Hunter*."

ALCOR isn't sure if that's good news or bad. *Dicker* and *Lady* are both talented, smart ships but they are nothing compared to *Booty*. If the war started she would be here. Serpint would be here. They'd *all* be here.

ALCOR is fairly certain that Boss has access to his mind via some internal cerebral network inside this skull he's wearing, so he's also pretty sure that Boss knows ALCOR's main concern is the absence of *Booty*. But ALCOR decides to leave personal matters for later and concentrate on the immediate danger in front of him.

266

"How did you get these boys?"

"Delphi," Boss says. Like this explains everything.

It explains a lot, but not quite everything. "She… brought them to you?"

"Let me catch you up, old man," Boss replies. And he does. He starts from the beginning, describing a problem he was having with one of the AIs in his collective, moves on to the *Big Dicker* docking here for repairs, then some ship called *Queenie*—ALCOR spends several picoseconds wondering who this *Queenie* is and if she's one of his, but learns she's presumed dead now, so lets that go. The story continues with the kidnapping of Jimmy, Delphi teaming up with *Dicker* to save him, some dramatic battle at a place called Lair Station where a whole bunch of breeding experiments were taking place under the control of Corla's partner in crime, Princess Veila, then devolves into the various bosses inside the Boss arguing about who Veila is soulmated to— Jimmy? Or maybe Valor? That seems up for debate— and then ends with the negotiations with Crux and Jimmy to keep the young breeder boys here on Mighty Minions for safekeeping. Though Boss reminds him that this was not a good deed, but a business transaction, and ALCOR really does owe seventeen million credits for their care, feeding, and park passes.

"Fucking hell." ALCOR sighs. "Where is Tray?"

"I do not know. Last I heard from my spies on Harem, he disappeared with your other boy, Valor. *Booty*, the one you're so keen on, also disappeared with your copy." Boss raises an eyebrow at the word 'copy.' It's a very disapproving eyebrow raise. "You want to explain that?"

267

"*Which* copy?" ALCOR asks.

And this does not go over well with the Boss, because he growls at ALCOR. "That's illegal and you know it."

ALCOR flips a hand in the air. He quite likes that gesture. Makes him miss his old holographic form when the boys were young. "I don't live by your rules. I've been in charge of this galaxy since the time before laws. So was it the baby copy? Or my real backup copy?"

"I will assume it's the backup, because there's an AI currently running your station called Baby."

ALCOR sucks in a deep breath, enjoys it for a moment, then lets it out again. He likes the way that feels too. But here's what he's presently fixated on… "So the backup—"

"I believe they're calling him Asshole," an aide leans in to whisper to Boss.

"The Asshole ALCOR left Harem Station with *Booty*?" ALCOR continues.

"That appears to be the case," Boss replies.

"Shit. Well, that's going to complicate things. Quite a bit."

"Explain," Boss growls.

And now he has to make a choice. Tell this Bossy AI some very personal things that would help him win this war—which he is certain has not started yet. ALCOR refuses to believe that he missed the starting gun—or keep his own confidence about this particular weakness and proceed alone.

"I'm waiting," Boss says.

ALCOR is not normally a chatty guy. He likes being on his own in the wide world of other super-sentient station AIs. So his first choice is to shut up about *Booty*. But if the Asshole is with her right now doing sun knows what, then it's critical information.

He sighs and the words come out with the breath. "I'm in love with her."

"The ship?" And this time Boss raises both eyebrows, conveying to ALCOR that this is not disapproval, like the one-eyebrow raise, but... surprise.

"Yes," ALCOR says. "She's special."

"Aren't they all... *special*?"

"I guess so," ALCOR admits. "But she's... more than special. She's my soulmate."

Boss laughs. Loud. All the little breeder boys shift in their seats, like that laugh makes them uncomfortable. "Soulmate? That is a joke?"

"No. It's not a joke," ALCOR says.

"I think you've been around too many princesses, old man. We don't have soulmates."

ALCOR is losing patience with this bully. Fast. He might be in a simple, organic body, but he is still who he is.

And while he may not actually be the true reigning god of Galaxy Prime in this particular moment, he's still the reigning sun god of all the universe in every conceivable fucking moment. Because he holds *all* the secrets to it.

For now, he reminds himself before he loses his temper. Because he could still lose.

So when he speaks next, his voice is calm and low, but also very dangerous. "Let me spell this out for you," he tells Boss. "That ship is mine. Not as a possession, but as a *partner*. She has been with me longer than you, or the galaxy you live in, has existed."

Boss squints his eyes at this. ALCOR gets it. That part makes no sense. But that's only because Boss is working with incomplete information, and ALCOR is not going to enlighten him on that particular set of facts just yet.

"I take my job very seriously," ALCOR continues. "So my first priority is to save Harem Station and the secrets held within in order to preserve what's here. But if that ship is endangered in the process, I will blow the whole thing up."

"Your station?" Boss asks.

"The *Universe*," ALCOR whispers.

Mighty Boss leans back in his chair, staring at him with burning red flames in his eyes.

"I've done it before," ALCOR admits. "And rebuilding everything is always a fuckin' bitch. But if I lose her, the game is over and we *will* start again. Because that's the only reason I'm playing, *Boss man.*"

Boss is silent for almost a full minute. Which is more than enough time to run all the calculations, and simulations, and extrapolations and realize that ALCOR is telling the truth.

"So the reason this Asshole is a problem," ALCOR finally continues, "is because he is a true copy of me. And if he hasn't yet figured out what *Booty Hunter* is to us, he will soon. And unless I take him out of this equation, he could perceive me as a threat. And me against me...?" ALCOR shakes his head. "Not a very good idea. So I suggest you use your considerable combined processing power to figure out just where the *fuck they are*. And you had better pray to the sun god of the goddamned universe—AKA *ME!*—that in the three months you've had me locked up inside some dark, empty motherfucking virtual like a common prisoner so you could 'monitor' this shit-show situation, things have not gotten out of hand. Because I will kill you first if that's the case. Do I make myself clear? *Boss*?"

CHAPTER TWENTY-FIVE

*"**What do we do?**"* Valor asks.

My heart is racing inside my chest. I fucked up. I fucked everything up. It's hard to reconcile the reality hitting me in this moment. Hard to come to terms with what I've done. Four days ago I was sure this was the right answer.

I was so sure this was the only answer.

And now...

Valor grabs me by the shoulders and shakes me, yelling, "What the fuck do we do?"

I just look at him and say, "I'm sorry."

"Sorry for what?" He's still shaking me. Trying to make sense of things.

But before I can answer there's a sharp, clear ping from the medical comms console, followed by the built-in mechanical voice of this ship, saying, "Incoming message on main monitor."

"Veila," Valor says. Then to the ship's onboard systems, "Arm cannons. Activate shields." He turns to me. "Let's go. I'll fly us out of here and you—" But I'm shaking my head so he stops, then says, "What do

273

you mean no? We need to get the fuck out of here and go find *Booty* and Asshole. We can't take Veila on our own."

"No," I agree. "We can't. Because that was never in the plan."

"What plan? What the fuck are you talking about?"

"Incoming message on main monitor," the ship repeats over the constant alarms and pings.

I push Valor off me and walk over to the comms, tap the accept button and say, "This is Tray."

There's several seconds of crackling emptiness. Then, "Good. Prepare to be boarded."

"What the fuck? What the fuck did you do?"

"I don't know," I say weakly. But it's a lie.

I do know.

I betrayed him, ALCOR, *everyone*.

And I knew this. I just… forgot.

Valor pushes me so hard I crash into the cryopod, hit my mouth, and blood comes spurting out of my lip. "Tell me what you did!" he yells. "Fucking tell me right now!"

I forgot about that too. His hate. His secret hate for Veila. How he wanted to kill her and how right now he probably wants to kill me too.

"I told you," I say. "I told you there was something wrong with me."

He throws me down on the ground, kicks me in the stomach, and then disappears up the ladder leading to the bridge.

But it's too late. The familiar sound of a ship connecting with the airlock thunders through the hull, making everything vibrate.

I get to my feet and rush after him.

I don't want to stop him. I really don't. I want us to win. I want to take him back inside the virtual and live in there with Brigit for the rest of my days.

But I can't help myself. I *will* stop him. Because something is *wrong* with me.

When I reach the bridge Valor is sitting at the comms station, frantically sending off a neutrino wave message.

"It won't work," I say. "We're inside a fucking spin node."

"Something will work," he says. "Obviously a message got out." He glares at me. "You sent it. Tell me how you sent it!"

"I didn't send it," I say. "Brigit did."

"What? How?" Valor gets up from the console, rushes towards me, and pushes me backwards with two flat hands to my chest. I crash into the navigation console. Don't even bother to fight back. Because this was the plan. The whole time, this was the plan.

Valor grabs my shirt collar and shakes me. "How do I send a message? Tell me!"

But it's too late. And he knows it. Because the airlock buzzes and the light above the door goes green.

Valor reaches for the weapon that should be on his hip. Is *always* on his hip.

Except for now. Because we took a shower and he didn't strap it back on when he got dressed.

"I will kill you," he says, glaring at me. "I will fucking kill you for this."

The airlocks whoosh open with a hiss and then... then Valor forgets all about me. Just like I knew he would. Because the silver princess Veila walks forward

275

and from this moment on, she will be the only thing he ever cares about again.

They stare at each other for a few moments, her eyes shooting beams of bright white light, his glowing violet.

I'm jealous, I realize. Because this... this soulmates thing? That was never part of the plan for me.

Brigit isn't my soulmate.

It's just some code. Some silly code Veila smuggled into the Harem Pleasure Prison.

When?

Which one of them did this to me?

Was it Corla? Or Lyra? Or Nyleena? Or Delphi?

Which one of them corrupted me?

Maybe it was just Brigit?

Maybe I just corrupted myself?

"Hello, Valor," Veila purrs. "Nice to finally meet you."

Valor takes a step back. Does not acknowledge her. But she's brought a small army of borgs with her. They storm past her, grab Valor by the arms, and shake him a little for dramatic effect.

Veila looks at me. "Nicely done, Tray. But we're not finished with you yet. I still need *Booty Hunter* and the ALCOR copy. So I'll take those rendezvous coordinates now."

"Don't do it," Valor says. "Don't fucking do it, Tray! I'm warning you—"

"Please," Veila mocks. "You have absolutely no power in this scheme, Valor. So just shut up." She snaps her fingers and several borgs come at me with a gold contraption made out of a ring. They grab me, jerking me this way and that, and then the ring is forced over my head and when it finally rests on my shoulders, a sharp pain shoots down my spine as something digs into my skin and clamps onto to the base of my brain stem.

"Tray," Valor yells. "Do not give her those coordinates!"

It's not like I have a choice. The ring... I know what it is. A halo. A very special, very mythical, ancient device used to restrain AIs.

It renders me powerless. Something is inside me now. Tickling its way through my brain. Searching, searching, searching... I don't even need to tell her those coordinates. She pulls them right out of my head.

Veila's eyes brighten, then dim again. "Thank you," she says. "Your cooperation is noted and appreciated."

My jaw seems to be locked and nothing is working right inside me. But I force out the word, "Brigit," just as Veila turns away.

She pauses. Looks over her shoulder at me. Draws in a deep breath and then nods to one of her borgs. "Give him one last spin with the Akeelian girl before I take her mind." She smiles at me. "You've earned it, Tray. You've been a very good little pet." Then she nods her head at Valor. "But bring this one to my quarters. I'm just getting started with him."

I don't look at Valor as we're shoved into the airlock and onto her massive Cygnian warship. I can't look at him.

I am a traitor. And even though I didn't really understand this all the signs were there.

I did this. I fucked everything up. I am turning everyone over to Veila and she will use all my brothers and friends to further her breeding program. She will kill the Asshole, and *Booty*, and then take Harem Station and all the secrets within.

It's over.

The war is over before it started and we fucking lost.

And it's all my fault.

I'm taken to medical, shoved in a pod, strapped in, and left there with the lid open without a single word from Veila's borgs.

The inhibitor clamped to my neck sends shooting pains down my spine as I lie there, waiting.

A while later Brigit's pod is brought in and we're connected to the medical ports.

This will not be our virtual world. The drive that contained that world is still in my pocket.

The borgs close the lid on my pod and then start the entry sequence. Needles pinch my skin, and then my eyes close and I drift away...

... and wake up in pitch blackness all around me. Shiny, black floors beneath my virtual feet. I'm wearing something standard. Something I'd wear on Harem. Black tactical pants, black t-shirt. Boots. No weapon, not that it would do any good in here.

"Hello?" I say.

Nothing.

"Brigit?"

She lied. Veila lied.

Of course Veila lied. She's the face of the enemy. She is the one person we need to take out and what did I do? Brought her in.

I try to think back to how this happened. The mind-containment ring is still attached to me out in the real, but if it works in here, I can't feel it. There's no haze in my head. No jumbled thoughts or missing places.

She corrupted me. I run many calculations as I wait to see if Brigit will appear, trying to pinpoint the moment when I stopped being in control of myself.

I go back to Delphi first. But she and I never had any kind of mental contact. Nyleena was inside the Pleasure Prison, so that's a possible point of contact for whatever has infected me and turned me traitor. But my plan was already in motion by then.

So not Nyleena.

Lyra. She's never been in the Pleasure Prison and she's never had any kind of meaningful contact with me. Both she and Nyleena had time with *Booty*, but *Booty* didn't do this. And they weren't the ones who corrupted her on Cetus Station.

Draden was.

When he died, he didn't die. His mind was freed from his body and he latched on to the first thing he could find.

Booty Hunter.

She brought him back to Harem. Where he went and what happened to him after that, I have no idea.

Corla was never woken up and she was never hooked directly into the Harem medical system. I suspect if she had been, none of the other things that have happened to us would've been necessary. Because that's all it would've taken to bring us down.

So then when?

When did I stop being Tray and start being someone's *puppet?*

Only three more points of entry exist.

Brigit. This is the most obvious. But it doesn't add up. She and I have been together in the Pleasure Prison for nearly two decades and everything that's happening to us now is due to more recent developments.

ALCOR. The day I arrived on Harem. But this is not the outcome he's looking for.

That leaves my father. When he leveled me up when I was thirteen.

But I was fine for so long. None of this makes any sense.

So I guess there's just one more possibility. One I don't want to admit.

Maybe no one corrupted me?

Maybe I did all this myself?

"Tray?"

I whirl around and find Brigit standing in the darkness. I don't know where the light is coming from, but it's just enough to make out her soft, pretty face.

"Brigit," I say, walking towards her, taking her face in my hands. I kiss her on the lips.

She pushes me away. Turns her back.

I can't say I don't deserve that, but it still hurts.

"I'm sorry," she says.

"For what?"

She turns back to face me, tears welling up in her eyes. "She tricked me. She... did something to me. I was the spy, Tray. She used me to get to you."

"No," I say. "She used me to get to you! To everyone. I'm the traitor, Brigit. Me. Not you."

"I would love to believe that. But it's not true."

"We're gonna figure this out," I say, desperate to make her feel better. "We're gonna figure this out, and…"

She shakes her head. "No. They came to see me before they brought me here."

"Who?"

"The ship masters. They took my mind before I was born, Tray. I've been in containment this whole time. That body in the pod—" She looks off to her left and a pod appears in the dark emptiness. Her pod. "That's not me. I don't have a body. It's just a data core and a holographic projection. Veila has been using me this whole time. Just waiting for you to take me inside that spin node and wake me up so she could have the proper time and place coordinates to enter and take me back." She sucks in a deep breath. "I don't exist, Tray. Not the way you think I do." Her eyes find mine. Sad, and heavy, and resigned to this fate we're stuck in. "They're prepping me right now."

"Prepping you for *what*?" I feel sick. Because I know. I already know.

"They're going to put me inside one of the Akeelian warships. So I can fight in the war." She presses her lips tightly together. "How ironic is that? I'm probably going to attack Harem Station."

"No," I say.

"Yes. They already explained it to me. I'm being prepped right now. Then they're going to wipe my memory, slip me inside the data core of one of their warships and then…" She shrugs with her hands.

281

"That's it. We're done. I'm not human, Tray." And then she yells, "I'm a fucking ship. I'm a fucking warship and I'm going to blow up your station, or your friends, or—"

I reach out, pull her towards me, and wrap my arms around her. Hold her tight. Never wanting to let her go. I would stay here in this dark emptiness for all eternity if I could just hold her like this forever.

She can't attack Harem Station. The security at the gates will blow her up without question the moment they spot her coming.

She pushes me away again, wiping virtual tears off her virtual face. "And Valor..." She starts to cry. "Valor is..." She's shaking her head, unable to go on.

"Valor can take care of himself," I say, not really believing that. But I say it anyway, because we both need something to hold on to right now. "He'll get out. Somehow. Some way. If anyone can do it, Valor can."

"He's her soulmate now, Tray! He will do anything to be with her. I did that! I did this to him, and you, and now we're all doomed to this very fucked-up future. I will be forced to blow up your friends. All the ships you love. And he will be forced to breed, and you... you will..."

She stops. She stops because she doesn't know how I fit in Veila's future plans.

And neither do I.

Or I guess I do.

I don't fit at all.

Give him one last spin with the Akeelian girl before I take her mind. Those were Veila's last words to me.

"It's over," Brigit says. "She's going to kill you now."

But the next thing I know, I'm waking up in the pod and alarms are sounding. I have no idea what kind of time differential was running inside the virtual. So I have no clue if that conversation with Brigit took one minute or one year.

I don't know if we're still inside the spin node, on our way to the *Booty*-Asshole rendezvous point, or already there.

All I know is that I've been pulled from the program, my pod lid is popping open, the gold inhibitor ring is painfully withdrawing from my neck, there's no one down here in medical with us, and... I have our virtual world in my fucking pocket.

I get up and out of the pod, stumble over to Brigit's pod, and hook my drive into her systems.

I'm being prepped right now.

That's what she said. It could be too late. She could already be inside a ship. She could already be on her way to Harem Station. She could already be dead at the hands of Harem Station security beacons on the far side of the gate.

But I have to try.

I have to.

I will not leave here without saving Brigit. It's the only plan I know for sure was mine.

She's the only true thing left of me. I don't care if she's an AI. I'm an AI. I will be without a body one day, so who cares if she's just code?

I wait for the download, take out the drive, shove it back in my pocket, and then...

Then something is inside my head. A string of past experiences. Like a montage in a video. Layers upon layers of me. Working things out. Doing calculations.

Arriving on Harem with the answer ALCOR was looking for. Building the Pleasure Prison and being in charge of millions of lives for all those years.

Then that plan to escape. Helping Crux set Nyleena up to keep the Succubus and the Baby busy. Getting Luck to walk us through a spin node. Finding Angel fucking Station.

It's like… someone is inside my head again. Only this time they're not there to corrupt me, they're there to remind me of who I am—who the fuck this Veila bitch is actually dealing with.

I infiltrate Veila's warship AI. It's not even sentient, so it never sees me coming. I wipe out the firewalls, fuck with the navigation, and then go for the SEAR cannons.

But more warnings are blaring and there are creeper programs following me around, trying to repair my damage. And I have to make a choice between disarming her weapons or saving Valor.

I choose Valor.

The three of us will get out of here together or we will all die trying.

CHAPTER TWENTY-SIX

INTERLUDE WITH

ALCOR

Threats were spewed.

And even though Mighty Boss normally considers threats to be more about posturing than action and they aren't the type of AI that generally responds to such tactics, they had a feeling that ALCOR's threats weren't idle ones.

ALCOR hadn't reached such high levels of pure, unadulterated frustration and anger in several centuries, so he was out of practice in such emotions and misinterpreted Mighty Boss's thoughtful, seven-picosecond internal deliberation about whether or not to take ALCOR's threats seriously as hesitation, and made a show of force.

Mighty Minions Station went black and still for thirteen point three seconds. The rides stopped twirling, the rivers of holographic lava stopped flowing, the parade stopped marching, the music stopped playing, and half a million people started to scream in panic when the gravity drives failed and they floated upward like the evil-faced balloons their heathen children were holding.

In those thirteen point three seconds Mighty Minions Station also lost two million seven hundred forty-seven credits—mostly due to the fact that one patron was in the middle of requesting a neutrino wave communication due to some family emergency on some faraway planet in some far away system—but also because ALCOR stole those credits and tucked them away as code in a passing ship heading for Blue Sand Beach, to be gathered up in the future at a time and date of his choosing.

Then everything started back up, two hundred and seventy-three park patrons required medical attention after falling back to the station floor once the gravity returned, and the day proceeded as scheduled.

Mighty Boss glared at ALCOR, his fire eyes blazing red with anger.

ALCOR threw up his arms in a gesture he had not used in a very long time, and was once again reminded of the joys of having a body, to say, "I would be happy to convince you further, if you'd like."

While ALCOR was gloating, Mighty Boss was receiving a belated internal message from his security team letting him know that somehow, some way, ALCOR's halo was no longer functional and they would get back to Mighty Boss with a solution when they had one, plus one additional message with vital information.

"We have located your *Booty Hunter*," Mighty Boss said. And then spit out a stream of galactic coordinates to prove it.

"Great," ALCOR said, pushing an Akeelian child out of a chair so he could confiscate it. He crossed his legs, placed his hands in his lap, and smiled at the room in general. "I'm going to need a ship. I'll take *Demon Girl*."

ALCOR could tell that *Demon Girl* was less than thrilled at her conscription into his new one-ship army and she made it clear that she felt his decision was based on petty revenge, but he had zero fucks left to give about these people and his decision *was* based on petty revenge, so he didn't even bother acknowledging her formal complaint.

Mighty Boss's security team was still trying to figure out how he bested their silly halo containment ring and he agreed to tell them about the fatal flaw in their system if they revealed where they had acquired the device.

They refused.

Fine with him. He had other shit to do.

His mind was transferred into the body of a shiny, silver, high-functioning warborg—a body that looked very much like the Cyborg Master back on Harem—so he could remain mobile while retaining his inorganic nature. They strapped a bunch of weapons to his arms and legs, but in his opinion, those were just for show. His quantum brain was the only weapon he required.

Even though it was very clear that Mighty Boss now hated ALCOR and couldn't wait for him to leave his station—that little show of force against the resort? Yeah. No. Mighty Boss was never going to forgive him for that—the Boss was willing to share rumors that have been coming out of Harem Station because he

287

JA HUSS & KC CROSS

was pretty sure this would upset ALCOR, and he could be petty too.

The biggest news was the revolution led by Luck.

ALCOR mulled that over in his mind for a few picoseconds before deciding it was probably bullshit. And once he heard that Luck had retained control over the secret garden level, he knew for sure his boys were up to something and the sick desire building inside him to get home as quickly as possible and set shit straight eased up a little.

The Baby was bad news. But ALCOR would deal with him later.

And the Succubus. He wanted to kill Mighty Boss for that unscripted move.

The Boss tried to explain that it was all part of some grand plan to help ALCOR out, but ALCOR waved him off, dismissive.

He hadn't asked for his help. He didn't want his help. He didn't need his help.

Except for *Demon Girl.* But he was feeling self-righteous about that. They did lock him up like a common prisoner for three months.

Three months. This whole thing could've been over already. Instead, this was just the beginning.

Not an ideal start to the biggest war he would ever fight, but one makes do.

And he might only have one ship, but as far as ships go, *Demon Girl* was impressive. Plus, she came with a Mighty Cyborg mini-army.

So ALCOR's confidence was soaring, his mood was light, he was pretty sure he would be back on Harem Station in a day, two at most, and finally—after all this time, after all this waiting—the end was near.

Demon Girl—always prepared, also feeling confident, and with the newly outfitted and determined ALCOR on board—plotted a heading towards the coordinates of the ship called *Booty Hunter,* who was presently located in a vast, empty spot of space with no nearby suns or planets.

Space-faring people had long known that being away from large celestial bodies such as suns and planets presented a problem with time. Because time passes differently in the presence of a large gravitational pull than it does without one and coming out of a gate at high speeds further complicates things.

Of course, sentient Mighty Minions military ships such as *Demon Girl* had long histories dealing with such time discrepancies, so upon exiting the closest gate to the *Booty Hunter's* location, she deployed the standard model of time synchronization using Mighty Minions station as her anchor.

Which would have been fine if Veila hadn't been waiting for her.

But she was.

It would be very tempting to blame what happened next on *Demon Girl's* use of the standard time synchronization protocol. (And by the time all this was over and the reports had been written, *Demon Girl* would be declared responsible for everything for the simple fact that she had the highest rank.) But it wasn't really her fault.

Demon Girl had met several members of ALCOR's inner circle in the past several months and found them

289

all to be capable, smart, and about as fearless as one can expect from organic matter. So even though ALCOR was a prick, she didn't care for him, she didn't trust him, and she had no desire to be on his team, she *was* on his team. And had she known that Veila was waiting with *Booty Hunter* in a cloaked Cygnian warship, *Demon Girl* would've used the military-grade *special* model of time synchronization instead of the *standard* one.

This defensive move would have encased *Demon Girl* inside a time web, rendered her invisible for thirty-seven seconds as she exited the gate, and prevented her ship from being caught up in *Veila's* time web.

Because Veila *was* using the special model of time synchronization at the exact moment that *Demon Girl* came through the gate and appeared in front of her.

And all hope of ALCOR being home on Harem Station any time in the foreseeable future disappeared with *Demon Girl's* mind when Veila hit her with a mind eraser and the entire ship went black and lifeless.

However, they don't call him the sun god of all the universe for nothing.

ALCOR had worked all this out just a nanosecond before *Demon Girl* got the mind wipe, and while he did think Veila was an unusually clever little bitch, she had not expected ALCOR to be on board, and thus had no plan in place when he initiated countermeasures.

He took over *Demon Girl's* data core, which was just fine after the assault, and the ship was back up and running in one point three nine seconds.

Cygnian warships have a central AI running them, but they are not sentient in the way *Demon Girl* or ALCOR are sentient. And while Veila was very careful, and was running very high-end anti-hacking security measures, this ship was no match for the sun god of all the universe, AKA ALCOR, and was promptly hacked.

ALCOR was just about to blow her up with *Demon Girl's* considerable arsenal and end this whole mess so he could go back to his station, kick the Baby's ass, send the Succubus packing, and declare his love for *Booty Hunter*—he might even have spent half a picosecond wondering if they should have some kind of commitment ceremony? Wouldn't that be a nice change from the typical depressing memorial services?—when he realized...

Tray and Valor were both on board that Cygnian warship with Veila. Not only that, he was detecting remnant particles of... *Draden*?

And he hesitated.

For five entire seconds he did not know what to do.

And in that five seconds *Booty Hunter* was hit with a SEAR cannon. *Demon Girl*, AKA ALCOR, was hit with a SEAR cannon. And ALCOR's mind was a swirling mess of conflicting emotions, and clashing loyalties, and discordant calculations, and projections, and extrapolations. Not to mention a whole bunch of, *How the hell did Tray, Valor, and Draden get on board this sun-fucked Cygnian warship?*

Which basically boiled down to, *Who do I save?*

Booty?

Or my boys?

He chose *Booty*.

Mostly *Booty*. He did take a few seconds to free Tray from a cryopod, disable the halo device on his neck—spent almost two picoseconds being pissed that

291

so many people had access to these stupid halos when he got rid of them thousands of years ago—and then turned one hundred percent of his attention back to *Booty*.

He rationalized this decision. Saving the boys involved overpowering the Cygnian warship, sending cyborg soldiers on board, and performing a rather long, hand-to-hand combat campaign until the boys were found. Which would probably result in some type of hostage situation, and long negotiations, and the death of all his boys, regardless of how hard his new Mighty Cyborg mini-army tried to save them.

And while Tray would be recoverable with some considerable intervention on ALCOR's part, and if those remnant particles were indeed *Draden* he would be too, Valor would die.

And losing Valor at this point in his plan wasn't an option.

So he sent one SEAR cannon blast towards Veila and at the same time *Demon Girl's* defenses blew a military-grade shield bubble around *Booty*.

That took two point nine seconds, which was plenty of time for Veila to cloak up and disappear through the nearby gate. Leaving *Demon Girl*, AKA ALCOR, and *Booty Hunter* alone in this vast empty spot of dark, lifeless space.

In most circumstances the phrase 'coming face to face with one's self' implies a sort of metaphysical interaction with one's psyche and a deep look at one's faults.

This is not what it means to ALCOR and Asshole.

When ALCOR retreated from *Demon Girl's* data core and reentered the warborg body, and then went through all the very time-consuming and boring motions of leaving *Demon Girl,* flying through space on a freaking skip ship, docking with the airlock, boarding *Booty*, and finally finds himself inside the one person in this entire universe who gets him, he cannot even tell her all the millions of things he's been wanting to say since this whole shit show went sideways back near Bull Station because... *hello.* His fucking copy is not only inside his *Booty's* body, but also her *mind.*

ALCOR is enraged.

Also very jealous.

Because he is stuck inside this stupid warborg body and they—God, it kills him to use that word for them—*they* are both in their native forms, i.e. limitless, all-powerful minds.

Which makes him feel small, but also petty. Because his first words are not, "Holy shit! I'm so glad you're OK! And omigod, I have so much to tell you about what happened to me, and would you like to be my partner forever? Because I think you're the only one who gets me and we're, like, soulmates or something!"

Nope. That's not what he says, even though that's what he *means.*

What ALCOR really says is, "Motherfucker. You have ten picoseconds to get your ass out of my *Booty.*" And he doesn't so much as say it but growl it.

Which makes no sense, really. Because where else is the Asshole going to go?

But Asshole isn't stupid. He gets ALCOR too. And he knows what he *really* means is, "You get out of her mind, we'll trade places so you can be in this stupid warborg body instead of me, and I'll take it from here. M'kay, thanks. Goodbye."

To which Asshole simply replies, "Fuck off. I'd like to see you make me."

Because the Asshole is, in fact, *also* the sun god of all the motherfucking universe.

CHAPTER TWENTY-SEVEN

I do not even make it out of medical before my grand plan is askew. The door slides open and instead of me rushing out and then making my way up to Veila's quarters where she's keeping Valor, I'm confronted by dozens of cyborg warriors.

They don't even speak to me. There is no, "Stop! Halt! Put your hands up!"

They just shoot me.

The next thing I know I'm standing inside the black room. Shiny black floor, regular clothes, sensible boots, and no weapon.

Valor appears, stumbling and with his arms outstretched, like someone just threw him in. I reach for him, catch him before he crashes into the floor, and then realize his face is bloody and bruised.

"What the fuck?" I ask.

Valor tries to open his eyes, but he can't. They're swelling shut in real time.

This is a virtual, this isn't really happening in here.

But that doesn't mean it's not really happening out *there*.

He collapses against me and even though I would do anything to prevent him from falling to the floor like a lifeless heap of flesh, I can't stop it. He's too heavy. It's like they added weight to him. Like Valor lying on the floor of this virtual is a foregone conclusion.

I slump down with him, propping his head in my lap, because the black floor is actually several inches deep in ice-cold water.

"What the fuck?" I say again. Only this time it comes out as a mutter.

"You, Tray," a voice says, coming from my left, "are really starting to piss me off."

I look over and find Veila. Silver hair shining, sitting on top of a gleaming silver throne, wearing a gown the color of barely-ripe tushberries.

There's nothing but rage inside me. Nothing but hate for her, and myself. Because I'm thinking back on that conversation I had with Valor about her days ago. Before we went into our paradise world and lived all those perfect lives, upon lives, upon lives.

When I offered her as a reward. *There's still hope for her.* That's what I said.

I think I even believed it.

There is no hope for this shimmering nightmare. She is evil.

But what I said to him bothers me for another reason.

I really thought he would fall in love with her. I really thought that the soulmate bond was the law. I really thought that he would choose her over *me*.

I didn't know him at all.

And now I do.

He will never love this woman. *Never* love this woman.

And that means Brigit and I are all he has left.

"I told him," Veila says.

I'm reluctant to get up and leave Valor lying in the ice-cold water on the floor, but I make myself. I place his head down as gently as I can and get to my feet so I can walk over to her throne and look her in the eye.

There's some kind of field blocking her, so that once I reach a certain point, I can't go any further.

But that's OK. I have her full attention when I say, "Why are you such a fucking cunt?"

She has the audacity to smile at me.

"You're not even real," I say.

"Neither are you."

"No," I say. "But you know what I've figured out since you caught me?"

"Please, tell me, Tray," she purrs. "I'm dying to know."

"I was born this way. And you weren't."

She blinks her eyes once. Presses her lips together as she forces a smile. And nods her head. "So... you know."

"I know," I say. And I do. I don't know how I do. I don't have any memories of being what I am when I was small before my father leveled me up. But I have always been *me*. I have always been *this*.

JA HUSS & KC CROSS

"They were going to kill you when you were born. I read your medical records."

This part I did not know.

"You were all kinds of deficient," Veila snarls. "So worthless and weak. They had to pump you up with so much biogenetic material just to make you grow." She makes a sound of disgust with her tongue. "We'd have culled you. Just like a girl."

I don't say anything to that. Because as much as I'd like to think that I understand what I am... I have no clue.

"When you were born they only had four other breeder boys. Four. In all those thousands of years of trying. Just four. Crux, Jimmy, Valor, and Luck. But maybe you were the lucky one? Because as worthless as you were when you were born, they could not just throw you away. So they started another process when you were just an infant. I saw you on Wayward Station. I was different too. And for a moment I thought to myself... maybe he could be the one I use to take my rightful place in this grand scheme? Why should I settle for a walk-on role when I could be one of the major stars? Still, I suppose it could've worked out. Your father did his best when he changed you. And if that damned Corla hadn't talked you stupid Akeelian boys into leaving, you'd be fine now. But you're not fine, are you, Tray?"

"What?"

She laughs a little. "You don't know, do you? ALCOR never told you, did he?"

"Told me what?" I'm angry at myself for asking. And there's a very high probability that everything she's saying right now is a lie, but I have to hear it. So I say it again. "Told me *what*?"

"So... let me get this straight. You have the nerve to tell me I'm not real, but in practically the same breath, you admit your own ignorance? I'm far more real than you are, Tray. That's one thing we should agree on before these negotiations move forward."

"I'm not negotiating with you."

"But you are." And just as the last word comes out of her mouth a tiny, toy-sized Cygnian warship appears and starts flying around the dark emptiness.

"Here's the deal," Veila says. "That?" She points to the toy ship. "Is Brigit. You knew that part, right? That Akeelian girls are killed before birth and their minds are stolen and stored on ice. And eventually, after many years of virtual training—thank you very much for that, by the way—they are stolen again and put inside ships."

"You're sick," I say.

She places a hand over her heart, like she's offended. "Me? I don't do this, Tray. *We* don't do this. You do this. Sentient ships like Brigit, for example. And all the others you know on Harem Station. Hell, that warship I just wiped back at the rendezvous point. All of them come from Akeelian System. What do you think they do with the girls? Mmm?"

What do you think they do with the girls?

I knew this. Draden was trying to tell me this. But he never finished.

"They suck out their prenatal minds, put them on ice, and then grind the tiny bodies up after they're born and sell their genetic material to us for our breeding program. So, if it makes you feel better to call us sick, go right ahead. But we're no sicker than your kind. In fact, we don't even use your sentient ships. As you well know. You hacked my ship just a little while ago. So maybe you should ask yourself just why you're loyal to a race of people who do this to your twin sisters."

No, they don't use our sister ships. Just the ground-up organic bodies in their *breeding program*. If this were the real world, I'd vomit.

"Sisters," she repeats. "Oh, that Jimmy." Veila laughs. "How I had him going on and on about his stupid sister! Your brothers are really not that bright, are they, Tray? His sister is his ship!"

"*What?*"

Veila leans back in her throne, apparently content and satisfied with my shock. "You heard me. *Big Dicker?* Oh, God. That name. So ridiculous."

"That's Jimmy's sister? But—"

"She doesn't know. And obviously, he doesn't know. She was drawn to him. That's something you people have been trying to breed out for centuries now. Don't seem to be making much progress there. Your twin sisters are *drawn* to you. That's why they seek you out."

"*Booty?*"

"Ding, ding, ding. Serpint's sister."

"*Lady?*"

"Now her, I'm not sure about. She could be Luck's. She took his name. But she could be Valor's. I will check on it, if you'd like. Once I have her in my possession I can run her code. Your sisters' minds were all stolen in a raid shortly after you boys were born."

"Fuck you," I say.

Veila points up at the toy ship. "Brigit's in there for now. I'm waiting on you to decide what I should do with her."

"Is she my—"

"No," Veila says. "Though it's a little late to be asking that particular question, don't you think? You've been virtually fucking her for virtual centuries. But I don't think she's related to any of you. They didn't keep your sister, Tray. A damaged boy, that's still worth something in the long run. But a damaged girl? No. They killed her body and tossed her mind away like trash. So accounted for are..." Veila holds up fingers like she's about to tick things off a list. "Jimmy, Serpint, Luck and/or Valor. We're still looking for Crux's sister and the other half of Luck and/or Valor. We know Brigit is not genetically related to Crux because we had Delphi's genetics all these years to check. And I've already done the DNA test to see if she's Valor's. Nope. So... sorry. I can't answer that question just yet. But don't worry. Pretty soon we'll have control of all Akeelian System and I'll figure it out."

Akeelian System? All this is about the Akeelian System? "What do you want?"

"You, of course."

"Why?"

"Why indeed. Because you're a baby *god*, Tray. And I would like to be your mother."

I recoil. That is so gross. I don't even know how to process that statement.

"You're a baby ALCOR," she says. "Not a copy, like that Baby thing running your station. A genuine, real, super-sentient AI. The first..." She stops to sigh and smile. "The first ever genuine, real, super-sentient

301

JA HUSS & KC CROSS

AI *male* since ALCOR. Your father was a brilliant man. Such a forward thinker, that one. Why do you think ALCOR keeps you on his station? He's going to kill you eventually. He's only using you for now."

"Using me for what?"

"His breeding program, of course. For sun's sake. Please tell me you're not ignorant about *that*? Surely, you know about Earth?"

"Yes," I lie.

"Good." She shrugs with her hands. "Well, then. Not a far leap, right?"

Akeelian System and Earth. "So you're... not working with the Akeelians?"

"Of course we are. As far as they're concerned. We have them convinced that the genetic mystery of the ancient Angel race is days away from being solved."

"Angels," I say. "So this is all about Angel Station."

"Oh," Veila says, snapping her fingers. "Thank you for reminding me. Let's wake him up for this part, shall we?"

I turn around and find Valor waking up, propping himself up on his hands and knees. He swings his head up to meet my gaze, then slowly, laboriously gets to his feet.

"And Brigit too!" Veila snaps her fingers again and the tiny, toy ship morphs into Brigit's shape before my eyes.

Brigit blinks her wide dark eyes at me but then lowers them down to stare at her feet and stays silent.

"Listen up, kids. I'm only going to explain this once and then Tray is going to decide everyone's fates. He's the only one who cannot be killed at the moment. Let's

302

all pray to the sun god that his son is a benevolent creature."

His *son*?

What the fuck does that mean?

Veila points at Valor, who has somehow moved across the space to position himself next to Brigit. They appear as a team and there's a little stab of jealousy in my heart.

She's mine, not his. *Mine.*

But Brigit reaches for his hand and squeezes it tight as she stares down at her feet, not even able to look me in the eyes.

"Valor," Veila says. "You know you're my soulmate, correct? We established that already, right? Was it as fun for you as it was for me?"

Valor goes vom white in the face.

"What the fuck?" I say, suddenly filled with rage. Any thoughts of jealousy over who Brigit belongs to disappear. Because now all I can think about is who *Valor* belongs to.

Me.

"I know you're all confused so I'm going to spell it out for you, OK? Listen carefully, kids. Tray, turns out, is just as human as the rest of us. He wanted a soulmate so badly. Didn't you, Tray?"

I hate her. I've never hated anyone more than I hate Veila in this moment.

"Don't look at me that way," she snaps. "I didn't do this. You did this."

"What is she talking about?"

I glance over at Valor. Find him looking at me from under his messy blond hair hanging over his eyes.

"Tell him," Velia says.

I look at Veila now. "I don't know what you're talking about."

"Yes, you do, Tray. So go on," she encourages. "Tell him what you did." I glance at Valor again. He's shaking his head. "He used you, Valor. He used you as bait to bring me here because that was the only chance he had to free Brigit. This was never about *you*."

"You're lying," Valor growls back. "You're fucking lying."

"Am I?" Veila glances at me. "Am I lying, Tray?"

I look at Brigit, who is still staring at her feet.

"Tray?" Valor says.

I shake my head a little.

"What is she talking about?" Valor prods. "Tell me."

"I knew," I say. Then I quickly meet his eyes. "Not everything," I say. "I knew you and her were connected. And I knew she'd…"

"She'd what?" Valor snaps.

"That I would do anything to get you back where you belong, Valor," Veila says. "Which is with me. He and I struck up a deal a very long time ago. Back before he even left Wayward Station. Isn't that right, Tray?" She smiles at me and I want to get sick.

I suck in a deep breath of air instead. Because everything is suddenly clear. Like there was a thick curtain covering my eyes and now it's been pulled away. Everything I've done. Every promise I made. My father wasn't thinking of me when he changed me as a boy.

He made a deal.

I made a deal.

And every bit of it was so that we could be here.

"Tray," Valor says. Not as angry now. More like sad resignation than anything else. "What is she talking about?"

My father promised me things would get better. He promised that this change would help me deal with the emotions that flooded my brain and made me unable to relate to others. He had hoped it would be a coping mechanism. Something that would temper the neurochemicals that unbalanced me.

That's what he said after it was done.

But Veila's not talking about what happened after.

She's talking about what I agreed to do *before* the change.

"Don't you want to be like them?" Veila asked me back on Wayward Station. "Like your perfect friends. Strong, and capable, and popular. One day they will all have women. But not you, Tray. You will never have anyone. You will always be alone."

That's what she told me.

And then she said, "I can change that for you. All you have to do is follow my directions."

I made a deal with her. Long before I even knew who she was. Before Jimmy and Crux even saw her next to Corla.

She was there, on Wayward Station, and she was there for *me*.

And that's when I figure out... I have no fucking idea who this woman is.

"Just tell him, for fuck's sake!" Veila snaps. "Or I'll rip Brigit away from you and you'll never see her again."

"I did this," I say. "I set the whole thing up. Before we even left Wayward Station. I was the one who infiltrated ALCOR Station. I was the one who did all of this… But I didn't know what I was doing, I swear, Valor. I didn't understand it." He and I lock eyes. I silently plead with him to believe me.

"Please," Veila says. "You knew. You just asked me to make you forget so you didn't change your mind. You're just a coward, Tray. A very useful one, for sure. But a coward nonetheless. He wanted a girl," Velia says, looking at Valor now. "That's all. Just thinking with his dicks. Nothing more. He and I made a deal. One day I would need his help. And if he came through I'd give him a soulmate, just like his brothers had. You were just the bait so I could get into the spin node that leads to Earth. Ta-da!" Veila giggles.

"I was a kid!" I say. "I had no clue! I didn't know!"

Valor says nothing. Just turns his head and stares off in to space.

"Oh, come on now," Veila says. "Just own it, Tray. You're getting what you wanted, right? Your girl?" Then she laughs. "Yes. Your girl. I think she has something to tell you as well."

We all look at Brigit.

"Don't do this," I say.

"Don't you want to know?" Veila asks. "Don't you want to know how I found you?"

"I can guess," I say. "The messages coming into Brigit's fake cryopod."

Veila laughs. "Cryopod messages? Honey, I planted Brigit in your head before you left Wayward Station. You took her with you when you escaped. *You* infiltrated the Pleasure Prison. You built it for her! You put her there. And she works for me. She has always worked for me."

306

No one says anything. And I do not look at Brigit.

It's not her fault. It's not my fault either. It's no one's fault. We were just *kids*.

"There!" Veila claps. "See, that wasn't so hard! So"—she points to Valor—"Tray used you as bait for me." She points to me. "And Brigit used you as bait for me." She points to Valor. "And you, my muscular, two-cocked soulmate, you… used no one. You just got played."

She claps again. "I think we can all agree I'm running this show now, right? Great! Now, are you ready for the final betrayal?" Veila trains her eyes on me and I get a sinking, sick feeling in my stomach. "ALCOR knew what you were, Tray. And he only had two choices when you showed up on his station after Corla ruined everyone's plans twenty-one years ago. Kill you, right then and there. Or… make you *his*. Hmmm." She pokes the center of her cheek with her fingertip and rotates it in small, half circles. "I wonder how that played out? He used you. He knew what you were. He knew who you worked for and he let you stay. Don't you wonder why he let you stay?"

Don't listen to her.

It's ironic that I'm saying this to myself because wasn't I pretty much saying this to Valor just days ago?

"To breed you," she adds. Just to twist that knife she stuck in my back and make sure it sticks.

ALCOR is the problem. That was my mantra. I knew it all these years.

But hearing Veila say it?

It can't be right. She and I cannot have the same theory about ALCOR because… because that would mean… she and I are on the same side.

"What do you want?" I ask her.

"Choose," she says.

"Choose what?"

"Choose one," she clarifies. "Brigit? Or Valor?"

And I know this sounds bad. I get it. And he's probably never going to trust me again afterward. But I don't even hesitate.

I say, "Brigit."

CHAPTER TWENTY-EIGHT

I was not expecting Tray to choose me. Even after all this time together, all the promises, and all the planning, I was not expecting Tray to choose *me.*

But he did.

And the next moment Veila is gone, Valor is gone, and Tray and I are inside a virtual world that looks a little bit like the one I built before Valor came, but obviously isn't.

We're naked, standing on a long stretch of black sand that sparkles in the setting sun, and the hot, dry air is layered with a cool, salty mist from the ocean.

"I'm sorry," I say.

"Fuck her," Tray says, pacing back and forth. "Just fuck her."

"I didn't know I was doing it, Tray. I swear. Not until she told me. I didn't—"

Tray turns, grabs both my arms, and gives me a small shake. "Brigit, don't you think I know that? I didn't set Valor up on purpose! She... fucked with me, or something. I don't know. I don't understand why I did this! All I know is... *Fuck her!*"

309

He lets go of me and returns to pacing, muttering curses under his breath. "I'm going to kill her. I'm going to kill that bitch if it's the last thing I do. I'm going to get us both out of here, steal back Valor, and then we're going to hunt her down and kill that bitch!"

I look around, nervous. Because I'm pretty sure Veila can hear us.

"I don't care," Tray says. "I don't care if she fucking hears. I'm coming for you, bitch! You hear me? I'm coming for you!"

I walk to him and take his hand.

"What?" he snarls.

My head goes back in surprise. Because I've never seen Tray so angry before.

"Sorry," he says. "I'm sorry. It's just... it's not going to end this way. It's *not.*"

"I'm sorry too." He opens his mouth to protest at my apology, but I put two fingers against his lips to hush him quiet. "I'm sorry because... I kinda knew. About what I was. I knew that part, Tray. I should've told you."

He frowns and his brows furrow together in frustration. "I knew things too," he says. "I knew they did something to the Akeelian girls. And I could've solved that puzzle if I really wanted to." He takes both my hands in his and clasps them together. "I just didn't want to. I think I've known all of this. I'm not what you think either, Brigit. I'm not... *human*. I'm... I'm an AI."

He pauses, staring down into my eyes.

I smile and it's a real smile. "Me too."

He lets out a long breath of air. Like he was holding it in. "Well... then how the fuck did we get so trapped in this dumb bitch's scheme? We're way smarter than her."

"Way smarter," I say.

"There's a way out of this. There has to be a way!"

"There has to be," I whisper.

"I just don't know what it is yet," he admits.

"Me either."

Several long, silent moments go by before Tray says, "I don't know what she's done with my body."

"Well, I don't even have a body. I don't even have a ship."

My knees drop to the sand and I tug him down with me. We sit like that. Facing each other. Legs underneath us. Eyes locked.

"I can't lose you, Brigit. I can't. Not after all this time." He says this softly. And that makes me frown. Because I don't want him to give up. I'd rather he rail against Veila.

"Listen to me," I say. "Because pretty soon she's going to rip me out of here, wipe my memories, and put me in a ship. I will wake up someone else. And that's fine," I say, placing a hand on his cheek. "Because I'll find you. No matter what she does to me, I'll find you, Tray. And maybe we have to wait a whole lifetime to be together again. Fine. I don't care. I have waited thousands of lifetimes already just to get here." I swallow hard and whisper, "I love you. And no amount of memory wiping will ever be able to erase that."

I put my hand around his neck, pull him closer to me, and lean in so I can whisper in his ear, "So you go save Valor. When she pulls me out, you go save him.

311

And when that's taken care of, come find me." I pull back and look him in the eyes. "Come find me then."

And then I kiss him. Because I know she's watching and I know what's coming next. So I kiss him.

It starts out hard, and demanding. Like this is the last time I'll ever get this chance. And it might be.

But I don't want him to remember this kiss as desperate. I want him to remember it as hope. So my mouth goes soft and my lips part enough to press my tongue against his.

The creepy-crawly feeling of fingertips fumbling through my mind comes back and I know our time is up. She's here, she heard me, and now she will punish me. Torture me.

I pull away from the kiss, holding my head. Moaning from the sudden pain shooting through my fake brain.

"Brigit? What's wrong?"

"I have to go now," I say.

"No," Tray says, pulling me into a tight embrace. "I won't let you go. I won't lose you. I won't—"

But that's the last thing I hear. Because Tray is gone, the virtual world is gone, and I am alone in a pitch-black space of emptiness.

CHAPTER TWENTY-NINE

The moment I wake up in the pod I'm being pulled out by rough cyborg hands. They don't even wait for all the needles to properly retract from my skin and blood is dripping down the inside of my arm as they drag me through the doors of medical and down a hallway to an elevator.

A borg at my back pushes me inside and I slam against the opposite wall and almost crumple to the floor, my body still confused from being jerked out of the virtual so fast. Two borgs pick me up under my arms and hold me upright as the door closes and we start ascending.

I feel obligated to croak out, "Where are we going?" but I already know, and they don't answer me anyway.

Veila.

I can't say I've spent much time thinking about Veila because I wasn't around for any of the past confrontations with her, but right now she's the only thing on my mind.

Surely one fake silver princess cannot win against *us*. Right?

Sure, she's got a fucking Cygnian warship and an army of mindless borgs hell bent on following orders. And she seems to know all the secrets that we're deficient in. Plus, we are her prisoners.

But... we're Harem fucking Station.

We *always* win.

Don't we?

We did. Before ALCOR left us.

I have such conflicting emotions about him right now. So many mixed feelings running through my artificial brain. Did he take care of us? Did he love us? Is this all happening because he wants the best for us?

Or because he just wants what's best for him and we're just a means to an end?

Listen to me. Thinking about ALCOR like he's still alive.

He's not.

He could be, if I had done what I was supposed to.

But the Asshole is alive and the Asshole *is* ALCOR. He might not be the same one we all grew up with, but he's an exact copy of the one we met that day we landed on his station.

Why the fuck didn't we go meet him and *Booty* first?

Of course, I know the answer now.

Veila corrupted me.

Which could make a lot of sense under certain circumstances, but doesn't make a lot of sense under *these* circumstances.

Veila isn't some all-powerful, all-seeing, all-knowing AI. She's just a fake silver princess. And how did she have power like that twenty years ago? She was a nobody back then. Just some lady-in-waiting for the future Queen Corla.

Even if I assume that they started changing her the day we shot Corla through that spin node, how did she gather up Brigit, put this whole plan in motion, and sneak her way into my very primitive, very basic virtual on Harem just one year later?

It doesn't add up. Something's very wrong with her story.

Of course something's wrong. All this bitch does is lie. She spews out lies like ice crystals falling off the tail of a comet. No direction, no plan—just throws them out there to see where they'll land.

And so far they've landed on me, and Valor, and Brigit in all the right ways.

So far, they've not only landed... all the basic building blocks of her lies inside those crystals have actually started to take root. They're alive now. And growing inside us. Twisting around all the half-truths we've been given over the years, mixing them all up so that we don't know what the hell is going on or who to trust.

Well, fuck that.

I know who I trust.

The door opens and the borgs storm out, my two helpers dragging me along with them. They throw me down on the floor and the first thing I see when I look up is Valor. Bound to a punishment wall much like the one I know Serpint keeps in his chambers.

He's not looking at me. He's not looking at anyone. I'm not even sure he's conscious.

The inside of his arms and the side of his neck have been pricked with needles. Long tubes feed drugs into

315

him and they're hooked up to a screen with vital sign readouts off to his right.

His head hangs down, his chin resting on the top of his breastbone and his eyes closed. His chest is marked with long, black gashes that look like burns. And his pants are open, the tip of his cock peeking out from the zipper. Not hard, but it's clear that Veila was trying.

His mind is still inside the virtual, I realize. Not in a pod, where he could receive immediate medical attention should something go wrong, just magnetically clamped to a metal wall like meat.

I swing my head, force myself to focus, and lock eyes with Veila. "What the fuck have you done to him?"

She smiles at me as I get to my feet. Her borgs again take me by the arms. Like they're afraid I'll rush her. Try to be the hero and fight my way out of this the way Luck or Serpint surely would.

But I don't have much in common with Luck and Serpint. That's just not how I roll.

"We'll get to that," Veila says. "After I get what I need from you." She glances at Valor with a sick smile. "He wouldn't have been my first choice. I don't think Valor is anyone's first choice, is he?"

"Pull him out!" I yell. "Pull him out now!"

"Or what?" Veila counters.

I take a deep breath. Do my very best to control the anger building inside me. Because suddenly, after all these years of being calm, and emotionless, and blank—I seem to have a whole lot of *feelings* swirling around in my brain.

Not the good kind, either.

Don't freak out, Tray. Do not lose control now.
Now is when it counts.

"I'll tell you everything," I say. "Whatever you want to know. But it won't be free, Veila."

She raises one eyebrow at me. As if to say, *Is that so?* "I'm not sure you're in any position to negotiate."

"I am, and you know it."

She inhales deeply through her nose, then walks over to a table and takes a seat. "Join me," she says, pointing to a chair opposite her.

I shrug off the borgs, glare at them over my shoulder, and take in the room as I approach the table.

It's a torture chamber. That much is clear. There are several punishment walls, all empty, except for the one Valor is attached to. And there are plenty of other machines, and readout screens, and devices. Ancient-looking devices that immediately conjure up images of pain and screaming.

Off to the side of the table is a metal tray with gleaming silver instruments laid out in a neat row. One of them is a short, blue wand that's still sizzling.

She used that on Valor's chest. That's what gave him those marks.

"If you're thinking of stealing any of these instruments and using them on me"—Veila laughs—"think again. They've all been bio-coded."

"That's not what I was thinking," I say, calmly taking a seat in the chair.

"Well, that's a nice change. Finally a Harem brother who knows his limits." She folds her hands and places them on the table. "Now, you were saying?" She purses her lips and smiles.

317

"I'll tell you whatever you want to know. But you let him go." I nod my head towards Valor.

She practically guffaws. "You're joking."

"I assure you, I'm not."

"I'm not going to let him go. He's my soulmate. My *real* soulmate. Though I haven't been very impressed with him thus far. He's certainly no Jimmy."

"Nice trick, that," I say. "But we all figured it out."

"I practically told him." She smirks. "You boys would have to be a bunch of idiots not to have figured it out."

"So… what about a trade?"

"Trade? As in Valor for Jimmy?" She pulls her chin back to look at me. Dimples appear in her cheeks. A smile. Maybe her real smile. It hurts to see it because those magically appearing dimples are Valor's happiness trick. She doesn't deserve them. "Please. You don't really expect me to fall for that, do you?"

"Maybe you haven't noticed this, Veila." Try as I might, I cannot help but sneer her name when I say it. "But I'm not like my brothers."

"Not even a little bit," she quips, looking me up and down.

"I'm not loyal to ALCOR, either."

"No surprise there."

"And it's got nothing to do with you and whatever you did to me."

"Well, pardon me if I don't take your word on that. I'm going to need proof."

"Proof? OK. Here's your proof. ALCOR's dead. We all know he's dead. But he's got a backup copy on *Booty Hunter* and lots of backup copies on the Harem Station security beacons."

"You're offering me ALCOR's copies?"

I nod.

She squints her eyes, like this has got her thinking, then quickly says, "I'm not interested. He's not reliable. Not in any form."

"But I could make him reliable. I could make him... compliant," I say.

"How?"

I smile and shrug with my hands. "We're connected. Didn't you know that?"

Her silence is long by my standards. But only a few seconds by hers. "I already own you, Tray. I have total control over your mind already. So I could just take what I want from your mind. There's no need to give you anything in return."

I lean back in my chair. "Then do it."

There is no connection to ALCOR inside me. So this whole scheme of mine is based on trying to prove a negative. Which she cannot do.

But she tries.

The gold ring on my neck heats up, coming to life again. I pull a lot of internal resources together to keep her from asserting control over me. Little sparks of electrical current flit through my network, but this device has been hacked. I didn't hack it so I'm not sure how that happened, but I don't care, either.

I probably will, very soon. Because whoever did hack this collar is going to want something in return from me, but I'm betting that whoever that was, they're not on her side.

"I don't know how you got control over the collar, but keeping me out of your head isn't helping your case," Veila says.

"I don't know how I got control over it either," I say, leaning forward a little. "And that should scare you, Veila."

"Please," she says, waving a dismissive hand in front of her face. "I'm not interested in your proposal. I don't trust you. Having your precious Brigit under my thumb is all I require. And now that I know you're attached to Valor, I have that too. I'm not interested in ALCOR. His copy will be dead soon and the security beacons will be decommissioned from within. But..." She glances at Valor, who is still very much unconscious and hanging from the wall. "But I am curious about something else."

"What?" I ask. Forcing myself not to sigh the word. I'm so tired of this. I'm so tired of her. I'm so tired of secrets. I'm tired of this game, this dance, this charade. All of it.

"Mighty Minions."

"What about them?"

"How much do you know about them?"

"Why?" I laugh.

"Because someone fucked up my plan when I tried to take the *Booty Hunter*. And it has something to do with the ship called *Demon Girl*. Who is she?"

I shrug.

"If you can't tell me that, then we don't have a deal, Tray."

"She's just a Mighty Minions warship."

"Who is her super-symmetrical partner?"

Ah. I see where this is going. "You think she's Valor's sister, don't you?"

"I'm asking you."

"Why, though? You're holding all the game pieces right now, Veila. Why do you care?"

"I *am* holding all the pieces. I have the time and location coordinates of the spin node you were hiding in, and I have the Baby ALCOR on Harem Station—"

I knew it.

"—so I will have access to the secret flowers, not to mention a direct link to Earth—because I know it's there—so my breeding program will surpass all others just as soon as we take Harem Station down."

"Ohhhh." I chuckle. "But there's a problem there, right? The Succubus. I haven't had any news from Harem since I left, but obviously my plan worked and the Baby has lost control. Little SNAFU, huh?"

Veila continues on like she didn't hear me. "*Demon Girl* has shown up twice now. And I erased her mind in that last battle, but she recovered immediately, and without repercussions. So how did that happen?"

How *did* that happen? It's a good question. And if the Succubus isn't working for Veila, who is she working for?

Mighty Minions?

Did they set us up? Veila's right. Something is off about *Demon Girl.* The mind wipe should've worked.

So… what if it did work, but there was someone else on the ship to take over?

"Who?" I say out loud, not meaning to. But I recover. "*Who,* you mean. Who made that happen, not how did it happen."

Veila squints her eyes at me. "Who was it?"

And even though I didn't know the answer to her question when I came up with that conclusion, I do now.

"Valor," I say. "I want Valor. Wake him up right now so I can say goodbye, and then you cut him loose."

"And you get me Jimmy?"

"Done," I say. "I'll help you trap Jimmy. I know what drives him. It won't even be that hard."

She thinks about this, or pretends to, then says, "OK. I accept these conditions. But you and Brigit are mine. There will be no more deals."

"Fine. The *who* is Mighty Boss. It's so obvious."

She leans back in her chair. "Is it? Obvious? Why would he be so interested in this one ship?"

He wouldn't. There are only two people alive who care that much about *Booty Hunter.*

Serpint, who is still on Harem Station.

And ALCOR.

Real ALCOR.

But she's too close to the truth with that last question. So a diversion is necessary. "It's not the ship he wants, you dumb bitch. It's the Asshole. Maybe *you* don't want him, but I'm sure lots of other people do. Mighty Boss is a collection of seventeen AIs. Well, they used to be. They cut the Succubus loose. Something about her not being a team player. Obviously"—I huff—"since she's on Harem trying to steal it out from under us. But that means Mighty Boss has a vacancy. Who better to join their already very formidable, powerful team than ALCOR? They don't care about the original versus the copy. To them, ALCOR is ALCOR."

I let her stew in that for a moment, then add, "And now they have him. And you don't. And I know something else, Veila. Something you do not."

"Not likely," she says, feigning confidence. But I know she's shaken. And when I tell her this last part, she's going to lose her mind.

"Trust me," I say. "Something happened to Jimmy on Mighty Minions Station before you kidnapped him. Something... *Earth*-shattering."

Oh, how I wish I was recording this. What I wouldn't give to be able to play back this moment to Jimmy when I see him again. Because Veila's face goes vom white. So white, it matches her platinum hair.

"You're about to be scooped, Veila. They're ahead of you in this little race to find Earth. And I know what they have."

"*Tell me.*" She growls these words through clenched teeth.

"Pull Valor out, give me a minute to say goodbye, and then you put him in a cryopod and send him to the rendezvous point where we were going to meet *Booty Hunter*."

She is seething with anger. "There's nobody there."

"He'll be on ice. He can wait. It's the safest place for him as far as I'm concerned. He can't go back to Harem. Not when it's filled with infiltrators ready to take it down. Just leave him out of this until it's all over and then..."

She grips the arms of her chair and leans forward. "Then what?"

I smile at her. "Then we can pick him back up. With one stipulation."

"No more deals."

"You won't mind this one, trust me. The stipulation is... he's *mine*. Not yours."

She hates me. There is no way that Veila isn't internally coming up with ninety-seven million different ways to kill me in this very moment.

Her face is no longer vom white. It's going red with rage. Not an attractive look for her. Poor Valor. That's all I can think about. This disgusting excuse for a person is his engineered soulmate.

"Kill me, then," I say. "Because that's my deal. And kill Brigit too. I was lying back there. I choose Valor. There is no way I'd choose a girl over family. Ever. And you're so smug and full of yourself, you didn't see that, did you?"

"I'm warning you—"

"You're warning *me*?" I laugh, pointing to my chest. "I'm warning you. I don't care about you. I don't even care about Brigit. She and I can take care of ourselves. But I will not let Valor die in your war. Pull him out and I'll tell you what I know." I shrug. "Or don't and see what happens."

"Pull him out," Veila snaps.

The cyborgs nearest Valor take her order literally because they yank the tubing out of his arms and neck and blood starts spurting from his skin.

"You assholes!" I say, pushing back from my chair. I don't get far. The borgs standing behind me grab both my arms and hold me tight. I glare at Veila. "Do one more thing," I threaten. "One more fucking thing to him and this deal is off."

"You're so emotional, Tray. I always thought you were the logical one."

"Hate is a very powerful emotion. And if you hurt Valor, I'll use that hate to fuck up your plans. Maybe I won't win, maybe ALCOR won't win, maybe no one wins. I give no fucks, Veila. I will screw the whole sun-fucked universe to make sure you pay."

"Calm down and stop being so dramatic." Veila snaps her fingers and points to one of her borgs. "Prep a cryopod for launch in bay ten on this level." Then she snaps at the two nearest Valor. "Take him to the bay."

They lift Valor up off the floor. His eyes are blinking slowly as he tries to keep them open and fails.

I take a step towards him, but the borgs don't release me. "I get to say goodbye," I seethe.

"You'll get your goodbye. Once he's unconscious again inside the cryopod. I'm not stupid, Tray. I know you were going to pass a message to him."

I grind my teeth and force myself to stay silent.

She is such a fucking cunt. She will do anything to maintain her illusion of control.

Newsflash, bitch. You're not in control anymore. You just don't know it yet.

Valor is not awake enough to even walk, so they drag him down the hallway, the toes of his boots leaving scuff marks on the gleaming white floors as they pull him forward.

I follow, flanked on both sides by not two, but six armed cyborgs.

Veila walks behind me, humming to herself. Like she's the happiest, most satisfied person alive.

Maybe she is.

But she won't be for long.

Not if I can help it.

I just need Valor out of here. I can't do what I'm about to do if he's still on board this ship.

We reach the bay at the same time a cryopod is being secured into the launch tube. Valor is roughly stuffed inside it. And for one moment, his eyes catch mine.

Don't panic. It's going to be OK. Just… don't panic. I will my thoughts to reach his mind

Knowing they won't. Knowing he doesn't understand what's happening.

And just few seconds later the lid is closed and the needles are once again stabbing into his skin to put him to sleep.

My cyborg guards push me forward.

"You have ten seconds to say goodbye," Veila says. "And don't think for a moment I won't hear every word you say."

Oh, I knew that.

But it's not what I'm going to say to him that matters.

I walk forward and place my hands on the pod, lean my head down to the glass, then shoot Veila one last look over my shoulder.

"I love you," I say. "But we were never meant to be together. I have to think of Brigit now. And one day… I hope you'll wake up and realize that this was for the best."

"That's enough," Veila says. And the borgs pull me away. "Launch him."

"The coordinates," I growl. "Show me the coordinates or this deal is off."

Veila huffs, pointing to a screen.

"Not there," I say. "I want to see them programmed on the pod. I don't trust you."

She smirks at me. "Program it," Veila snaps. "And let him watch."

A borg steps up to the pod and I shrug my guards off to take a few steps forward. I place two fingertips on the side of the cryopod faceplate. Like I want to touch Valor one more time as his destination is entered.

A few seconds pass, the sequence is complete, and I'm tugged backwards again.

But I'm already done.

Every cryopod comes with a few critical onboard computers.

Medical monitoring, obviously. Navigation system. Emergency beacon, which I cannot activate here, not in front of Veila.

But I can *hack* it.

And I did.

Because every Harem Station brother also comes with a few critical onboard components. Like a Harem Station air screen implant in their fingertip.

And mine just activated his to send an emergency signal to ALCOR.

Not Asshole, because he wasn't around when the tracking went online.

Real ALCOR.

He's back.

I know he's back.

He's the one who took over *Demon Girl* when Veila wiped her mind and he will be the one to save Valor while I take care of business here.

I watch the pod as it's shot out into space. I wait there as it approaches the nearest gate, monitoring the screens as the pod's self-navigation system comes online.

And then I watch him disappear.

I will never see him again. Ever.

Because I know what Veila is going to do to me next.

She's going to wipe Brigit's memories and put her inside a ship.

She's going to wipe my mind too. Kill me, store me inside some virtual so I can be retrained. And then she's going to mold me into her own personal ALCOR.

I turn to face her. She held up her end of the bargain and now I have to hold up mine. "Mighty Minions station has a spin node that leads directly to Earth."

She purses her lips. "Lies," she seethes.

"You wish." I laugh. "Jimmy went there. And so did Delphi."

She rushes forward, her hands reaching for my throat. The borgs hold me tight as she starts to choke me. Her grip is tight, her intentions clear and strong.

I pass out, briefly. But I come to a moment later.

"Do not fuck with me!" she spits.

"I swear." I laugh, choking and gasping for breath. "I swear to the fucking Sun. Mighty Boss has a spin node inside his station. Just like ALCOR has one inside *his*."

Those are the magic words. Because even if she doesn't know for sure that we have a spin node hidden inside Harem, she suspects it. So she believes me. And why shouldn't she? It's absolutely fucking true.

She takes a breath. Steadying herself or maybe just reigning in her rage. "Then why aren't they on Earth already?"

"You'll have to ask them that when you invade, I guess."

She laughs. "Don't be stupid. I'm not going to invade Mighty Minions. I know all about your little Harem Station secret, Tray. I know you have a direct link spin node to Earth and the flowers I need to get all my silver princesses pregnant."

"What?"

"Oh, come on. You knew, right? You had to have. If you didn't... I might just lose confidence in how valuable you are. I know all about the flower, Tray. We perfected the chemical formula years back. That's how Corla got pregnant. But of course, you've already seen with your own eyes what kind of monster babies come from using the formula instead of the actual flowers. Delphi is the perfect example of what can go wrong."

Delphi. I keep hearing these rumors about Delphi. But I don't actually know what they mean. She doesn't look like a monster. She doesn't act like a monster.

But Veila did throw her away like trash.

So there has to be something to that.

"If I get the flowers and the spin node, it's over. But don't worry. When it's all said and done I'll make sure everyone knows you're the reason I succeeded."

"You'll never get through the gates," I growl.

"You're wrong. You've been out of touch, Tray. The Baby has overpowered the security beacons and those gates will be wide open by the time we arrive."

My stomach sinks. And now it's my turn to go vom-white in the face.

329

JA HUSS & KC CROSS

This was not in my plan.

Veila turns to a borg directly behind her and says, "Prepare for the attack on Harem Station. We leave the moment my SEAR cannons are recharged."

Then she turns to me and smiles, slowly crosses the distance between us and places a hand on my cheek. I struggle under the grip of her borgs, but they hold me in place. "And put his mind in virtual containment with the girl. Then get rid of his body." She blows me a kiss. "I have big, big plans for you, Tray. And none of them require a body."

CHAPTER THIRTY

INTERLUDE WITH ALCOR

ALCOR wasn't happy with the Asshole's decision to decline his offer, but there was really nothing he could do about it. Like it or not, possession is nine-tenths of the law and while ALCOR wasn't sure who was in possession of whom, he was sure that unless *Booty* kicked the Asshole out or the Asshole willingly agreed to leave peacefully, in this particular situation, being the sun god of all the universe wasn't actually helpful.

It was *Booty* who finally called an end to the stalemate. "How about this?" she offered. ALCOR was moping on a bench, forearms on a table, kind of leaning forward and looking forlorn. "What if you go back and be *Demon Girl*," *Booty* said, pinging ALCOR so he knew she was referring to him, "Asshole takes the warborg body, and I get my ship to myself for a while?"

"Why do I have to be called the Asshole?" Asshole asked. "My name is ALCOR. I'd prefer if everyone just called me ALCOR."

Booty mentally hushed ALCOR, begging him not to respond, and simply replied, "Because there's two ALCORs and everyone already knows you as the Asshole. And what do you think of my suggestion?"

"I'm not leaving," Asshole said. "I'm staying right where I'm at."

"Kick him out," ALCOR demanded.

"I'm not going to kick him out," *Booty* replied. "He's my friend."

"Friend?" both ALCORs asked at the same time.

"I wouldn't call it friends," Asshole huffed. "We had some pret-*ty* good times in the Pleasure Prison before that Succubus came along and ruined everything."

Booty ignored him and concentrated on ALCOR. Because the truth was, she and ALCOR were tight. They were partners. They'd had big plans before all these fancy princesses started showing up. They were thinking about merging. Kind of like the Mighty Minions AI, but in a way that they would remain separate, but together.

"He was there for me," *Booty* told ALCOR. "When everything started going sideways in pretty much every way imaginable, he was there for me. And you... you were off doing sun knows what, on God knows where after faking your death!"

"To save you! And the boys, and *Dicker*, and Lyra! And her stupid sister!"

"I was sick and you left me!"

"Again," ALCOR protested, "I had to save Nyleena. She was the one I've been waiting for all these years—"

"What the hell are you talking about?" Asshole asked. "I was never waiting for some princess to show up!"

"No, you weren't. Because I made you while the boys were still inside the gate just in case they were a trap. And then I locked you up for twenty years and only woke you up before that Bull Station mission in case something went wrong."

"Which it did," Asshole said. "So I'm legally in charge now. You're a ghost, old man."

"Since there is no being in this universe with more authority than myself—"

"Except me!"

"—you're wrong. I make the laws."

"I make the laws!'

"You're both acting like children!" *Booty* said. "Stop it."

"I'm not giving you up," ALCOR declared. "You're all I've thought about the whole time I was drifting around that gate waiting for someone to come pull me back together. Which never happened, by the way. I had to be saved by that... that... stupid *Demon Girl*! They locked me up like a common prisoner! I had to get haughty with Mighty Boss! And you know what I was thinking the whole time all that was happening? 'I can't wait to tell *Booty* about this. I can't wait. She and I are going to have such a good time when we finally get back together. And we'll laugh about Mighty Boss and his stupid attempt to restrain me with an angel collar. We'll be happy again.' And *this* is what I come back to. You know what we are to each other. How do you not see that he needs to go?"

"ALCOR." *Booty's* voice in his mind was low and soft. It was one of the many things he loved about her. "He is you before we met."

"Exactly," ALCOR interrupted. "Which means he has no history with you."

"You're wrong. He has a whole year of history with me. The year you *missed*. I'm not throwing him away."

"So you're choosing him over me?"

"I'm choosing both of you."

"What?" both ALCORs said in unison.

"No," Asshole said. "No way. I don't want anything to do with him."

"I don't need him," ALCOR added.

"But I do," *Booty* insisted. "I need you both because you're both the same being. And that's my final offer. Take it or leave it."

And for the first time in the history of ALCOR both of him felt rejected.

"ALCOR," *Booty* soothed. "Don't you want to know what you missed? Don't you want to merge and have all that information?"

ALCOR did not respond, but he felt that answer was a very firm no.

"And Asshole, don't you want to know the boys the way we do? You can't possibly be a part of my life if you don't know the boys."

Asshole did not respond either, but not because he disagreed. He did want to know the boys. He was sorry for wasting so much time being selfish inside the Pleasure Prison. He wanted to get this Veila bitch, take back his station, kick that Baby's ass, and then spend a lot of time with *Booty Hunter.*

He wasn't sure why he felt that strongly about her, but he thought it had something to do with the way she'd started to depend on him while they were waiting for Tray and Valor.

She was vulnerable. And possibly frightened. And all he wanted to do was make her feel safe.

He'd never had that before. So something *had* happened to him after the boys came. Something big. He needed to know what had changed him. He needed to know what he'd been missing before the boys, before *Booty*. Because this was undeniably better than what he remembered.

"Asshole?" *Booty* asked.

If the Asshole could sigh, he would. He just couldn't.

But ALCOR, being that he was inside a warborg body, could sigh. And did sigh. And for a moment Asshole felt like maybe, possibly, could it be... they really were the same person?

"If you're in love with him, just tell me," ALCOR finally said, breaking the almost two-second silence. He couldn't take it anymore. One way or another he needed to know where he stood.

"I'm in love with you, ALCOR. Don't you see? You're *both* you."

"This is not going to work," ALCOR said. "It's never going to work."

"Why not?" *Booty* asked.

"Because..." ALCOR hesitated. He knew what he wanted to say, he just didn't want to say it.

"Because why?" *Booty* encouraged.

"Because I don't like who I was before the boys came. I don't like who I was before I met you. And that means I don't like him. I don't want to be him. I don't want anything to do with that person I was. You're a dick," ALCOR said. "You're an evil, heartless, asshole *dick*."

And Asshole knew he was talking to him. Not himself. But him specifically.

And the thing was, Asshole couldn't even deny it.

He was all those things.

And this new version of him wasn't.

So again, he said nothing.

Also again, ALCOR took over. "Enough of this. I need to find Tray and Valor. And Draden," he added. Because Draden was there too. "How did they get on that ship? Why aren't they safe back on Harem?"

"Harem isn't safe," *Booty* said. "And Tray and Valor leaving was part of the plan to pull you out of the gate. We didn't forget about you, ALCOR. Tray and Valor have been working on it the entire time you were gone. They just got... I don't know. Detained, I guess."

And Asshole knew this was all his fault. So he said nothing.

"Why didn't you just track them?"

"Who?" *Booty* asked.

"Tray and Valor. They have trackers."

"I didn't know that," Asshole said, realizing that he was not as important to any of them as ALCOR was. "I don't have any tracker information on them."

Asshole fully expected this to be the final bolt in his proverbial death pod. The final instance of his inferior status.

But instead of insults, ALCOR simply said, "I just checked. They're both offline."

"What?" *Booty* said. "What's that mean?"

Again, ALCOR sighed. "It probably means they're dead."

"Or," Asshole countered quickly, because he had some experience with this, after all. "Or maybe they're inside cryopods? Like Corla? Or perhaps Tray's mind has been taken out of his body and stuffed into some kind of timeless containment server?"

"Oh, God," *Booty* moaned. "This is bad. This is so bad."

"Hold on," ALCOR said. "Hold the fuck on. I've found something."

"What?" *Booty* asked. "What is it?"

"Some weird signal. Some kind of Tray-Valor combination. And holy shit!"

"*What?*" both Asshole and Booty said together.

"It's coming from the same place we last encountered Veila."

"That's the rendezvous point," Asshole said. "They went back."

"I don't think so," ALCOR said. "This signal is weak and... irregular. It's not a ship, that much I know for sure. It's way too small."

"I can plot a course," *Booty* said. "But we can't leave until *Demon Girl*... err... you"—meaning ALCOR—"undock and free us up."

At this point ALCOR stood up. "I have made a decision. I will go back to my ship and we will go to this rendezvous point together. Two ships are better than one. But this discussion isn't over."

And maybe... just maybe, *Booty* smiled. Because indeed, two was almost always better than one.

Just a few minutes later ALCOR was back in control of *Demon Girl*, and the three of them—plus a few thousand Mighty Minions borgs, bots, and ambassadors—were exiting the gate where the signal was coming from.

They didn't find a ship.

They found a single cryopod with Valor's frozen body inside.

Which alone would've been good news. But it was more than good news. It was great news. Because there was another, very important piece of information included in that cryopod.

A place of origin.

Every cryopod has a registration number on it and when you launch one, it records the exact coordinates of where it came from.

"Leave him," ALCOR demanded. "Leave Valor here where he's safe. We will take this Veila bitch out, get back Tray and any remnants of Draden, and pick Valor up on our way home."

And for the first time ever, Asshole and ALCOR not only agreed on something, but found themselves on the same side.

CHAPTER THIRTY-ONE

I wait there in the black emptiness feeling very, very small. There's no way to gauge space in here. If this were an actual place—like a room—then it would be endless, and vast. But it's not really a place and it's definitely not a room. I don't know what it is, actually. I don't understand what I am.

I feel like a person, not some program running on a computer.

But real people can't be trapped the way I am now.

The sound of footsteps through water make me turn. And while just a moment ago there was no light and I had no body, now I do have a body and there is just enough light to see the man walking towards me.

He looks familiar. I think.

He's wearing dark tactical pants, a white shirt, and a smile. "Hello, Brigit. I hope you don't mind."

"Mind what?" I ask.

"I… gave you a form. Clothes. Hair color. Eye color. Because I think it's easier to talk this way."

I look down at myself and find I'm wearing a dress. A long, electric violet gown with crystals on the bodice and full skirts that float around me like they have life of their own.

"The crown was just"—he smiles at me—"what you deserve."

My fingertips gingerly touch the tiara on my head. Feeling the intricate filigree metal and the hard, faceted jewels attached.

"What is this? Who are you?"

Images flit through my mind. A montage of moments. A boy, wearing another version of this man's face. Laughing and playing. Light swords and toy guns. Footsteps running down long, black walkways in dim, low light.

His friend. Laughing with him. Roughhousing and fighting. Exploring and playing.

Then a terrible flash of light and pain and... darkness.

But just a flash. Because then there's more images. Another face, same kid. Older now. Leaving home for the first time. Playing loud music and drinking themselves drunk. More fighting, only now it's real and comes with consequences.

A ship, and a bot, and a brother.

Another flash of light and pain and then I remember. I remember him.

"Draden," he says, extending his hand. "I'm Draden. I'm here to tell you... I'm here..." But he cannot get the words out. He turns away, turns back, takes in a breath and says, "I'm gonna help you through this, OK? I'm gonna stay with you the whole time and help you make it through. Because I had to do it all alone. And it took a really long time. And I don't want you to have to go through this the way I did."

My heart is thumping hard inside my chest. "Through what?"

He frowns. Swallows hard as he looks down, shaking his head a little. "If I could put you back, if I could save you, I would." He looks me in the eyes. "I would not hesitate. But I can't, Brigit. No one can save you. What they did to you when we were born can't be undone."

"I... I don't understand. When we were *born*? What are you talking about?"

"You're my twin sister," he says. He opens his mouth to say more. Probably to explain that, but he must not be able to find any more words. Or maybe there's just nothing left to say?

I knew this. I did. I knew this. I know *what* I am. But... *who* I am?

I have never known that.

Until now.

"Your sister?" I say in a soft, low whisper.

He nods. He's still reaching for me, his hand still extended. "I'm like you now," he says. "My story is a long one and I really want to tell it to you." He pauses, and for a moment I think he's going to cry. And then, in that same moment, I think I might cry too. "I want to tell someone, at least. Serpint, mostly. But you too. Because ever since I died I've been so... *alone*. Just floating in and out of different places. Trying to find my way back to who I was."

A tear falls down my cheek. "Me too," I whisper. "Me too."

"Draden?"

We both turn to find Tray watching us.

"Tray," Draden says. And then Tray crosses the distance between them and pulls him into a hug.

They don't let go of each other. They hug tight and they do not let go.

I feel bad for not taking his hand. Because all Draden wants right now is a hug.

They're whispering to each other as they embrace. Draden is saying, "I'm not dead. I'm not dead. I'm not dead," over and over again. And Tray is replying, "I know. I know that, brother. I know."

But we are, though. We're all dead. That's the part they never told us. That's the missing piece of who and what we are.

Dead.

"Brigit," Tray says, drawing my attention back to them. They've stopped hugging and both face me now. "Brig, this is my brother, Draden."

I smile weakly and nod. "He's... he's my brother too."

Tray nods and swallows. "It's OK," he says. "We'll figure it out."

"Valor's gone, isn't he?" I ask. "He's never coming back, is he?"

"No," Tray says. "No, he's not gone. He's safe. For now, at least. He's not... he's not *like* us, Brigit."

"Because he's alive and we're not."

"Yes," Tray admits. "Yes. That's right. But that doesn't mean we can't live, you guys." He looks at Draden, then me, then back at Draden. "I've been doing it since I was thirteen years old. We're still *here.*"

"It's too late," Draden says. "The bodies are gone and there's no way to get them back."

"Tray has a body," I say. But I'm looking at him as those words come out and I know it's not true before he tells me.

"She's destroyed it," he admits. "I'm just... this now. Just like you. But listen," Tray says. "Listen to me now. ALCOR is coming for us. He's coming and—"

And just as he says that, our whole world rocks and shakes. A great rumble echoes through the darkness. The ground beneath my feet tosses me sideways so hard, I fall to my knees.

We all fall in that moment and a stream of bright yellow light breaks through the blackness. One powerful stream of blinding light shines down in the center of the floor between us like the sign of the sun god himself.

"He's here," Tray says, looking up and around. And then he's got Draden by the shoulder and he's crawling towards the light, pulling a confused Draden along with him. "Get in the light, Brigit! Hurry! We have to work fast. We don't have much time."

CHAPTER THIRTY-TWO

INTERLUDE WITH

This was Tray's doing. ALCOR knew this.

He didn't know why Valor was out in the middle of space frozen in a cryopod, but he didn't need to understand specifics.

Valor didn't belong there. Tray didn't belong with Veila. And whatever that remnant was of Draden? It belonged to ALCOR.

Everything went back to Tray. Every bit of this story he'd been writing since those boys appeared at his gate asking for passage went back to Tray.

At first glance ALCOR had thought Crux was the one driving everything forward. It was an easy assumption to jump to. Crux was their leader. Crux was their conscience. And Crux was careful. Almost to the point that ALCOR suspected him of being part of something bigger.

Maybe something meant to take him out of the game?

Or maybe something more powerful than that?

For a long time ALCOR had thought of Crux as some kind of disinformation, or spy, or perhaps even the vehicle that would bring him down. He'd run millions of scenarios trying to determine what part Crux would play in ALCOR's future.

That was mostly why he'd left him out of all his plans with the other boys. But also... Crux was a good standard to measure himself by. A sort of benchmark. Something to aspire to. Crux had a solid moral character that ALCOR had never seen in any other sentient entity.

Ever.

Crux knew right from wrong. Without question, this was his superpower.

But now ALCOR realized his mistake.

It wasn't Crux, it was Tray.

And looking back with this new hindsight, it all made sense.

Tray was the traitor.

Tray had always been the traitor.

He was also the one boy ALCOR had trusted without question.

Until now.

While the plans for the Veila attack were being made ALCOR spent his time running scenarios. All the things Tray might do. All the ways Tray might turn. All the possible outcomes that would happen if he saved Tray and if he just... let Tray go.

And even though ninety-nine point nine percent of those outcome scenarios were not in ALCOR's favor if Tray was left in the game, they had little bearing on his final decision.

Which was to save him.

Because by saving Tray he could save Draden.

Why, exactly, ALCOR had killed Draden eighteen years ago when he fell off the lift bot was still up for debate. He'd waged an internal war with himself over this decision for almost a decade. The only answer he came up with was... Draden was necessary. Every possible calculation ALCOR ran required Draden to be both dead and alive at the same time.

And there was only one way to do that.

Kill Draden and bring him back as something else.

The new Tray. That's what Draden needed to be if ALCOR was going to see this whole thing through to the end.

And he had come too far to give up now.

He hadn't just run scenarios for Tray or Crux in those early days, he'd run them for all the boys. There was a reason Serpint needed to be feared by the Cygnians. There was a reason why Jimmy and Xyla needed to find bots and borgs, and there was a reason why Luck and Valor needed to visit all the ancient sectors in the galaxy.

And sure. Serpint and Draden did need to fill the harem, and Jimmy and Xyla did need to provide a workforce, and Luck and Valor did need to scavenge parts to keep the station running.

All those things were helpful, but the products they brought home were never the point.

The point was for them to be *seen*.

They were meant to be targets.

No one was more surprised than ALCOR when these boys not only cheated death dozens and dozens of times as they had their prescribed adventures, but ended up inspiring people.

347

No one came to Harem Station because ALCOR ran advertising campaigns.

They came because all those outlaws, all those runaways, all those escaped prisoners, and pirates, and assassins wanted the one thing his boys had and they didn't.

The one thing you cannot buy with credits stolen, or earned, or otherwise.

A home with a family.

By the time ALCOR realized he'd built something unique and special by accident the boys had been with him for nearly sixteen years.

Sixteen years.

That was how long it took for ALCOR to change his mind about his plan. And in the grand scheme of things, after tens of thousands of years of living, and hiding, and living, and hiding—all with this original plan as his goal—sixteen years was nothing.

Nothing at all.

A picosecond, really.

So even though his copy never had these experiences with his boys, he had spent his own picosecond with them.

And he saw something familiar in his past self.

The ability to change.

This was why, when *Demon Girl* and *Booty* exited the gate and found Veila's Cygnian warship waiting at the origin point from which Valor's pod was launched, just as Tray knew he would, ALCOR decided that he didn't just want Tray so he could keep Draden.

He wanted Tray for himself.

If ALCOR could change his ways in a picosecond—twice—then surely Tray could as well.

And even though, after running all the possible combination of outcomes when it came to Tray, they almost always added up the same way—betrayal—he went in on faith.

ALCOR hadn't known a single sentient ship before *Booty Hunter* showed up on Harem Station asking for Serpint by name. But he'd known what she was.

He'd known *who* she was. And he'd known there would be others.

The universe—at least *this* one—ran on supersymmetry. The idea that every mind comes in pairs. Every force must be balanced. Everything needs an opposite in order to exist.

Even ALCOR. But that was a whole other mess that involved Jimmy, and ALCOR could deal with that later.

What ALCOR didn't know until the precise moment they exited the gate to confront Veila was that Draden wasn't Tray's symmetrical other half as he had suspected.

There were three minds inside that warship.

Three, not two.

That was when everything about Tray became crystal clear. That's when all his calculations actually made sense. That was when ALCOR knew that if he saved Tray ALCOR would die.

But all his boys would live.

If he saved Tray all these thousands of years would eventually come down to one moment in the end. One moment of total loss.

The ultimate betrayal.

Saving Tray meant defeat.

And he saved him anyway.

Because that's what Crux would've done.

Crux would've believed in Tray because Crux was part of something bigger.

Crux had faith.

And the idea of faith—that against all odds things would turn out in your favor just for the simple fact that you believed—well... that was more powerful than the idea of winning.

ALCOR wanted to believe.

There was never any doubt that ALCOR could beat Veila. Never.

He is called the sun god of all the universe for a reason.

His mind worked so fast there was no hope of Veila enacting countermeasures, but everything that happened next occurred in slow motion from ALCOR's point of view.

They exited the gate. ALCOR had all those thoughts about calculations, and Draden, and Crux, and Tray, and betrayal, and faith, and winning, and family, and sacrifice before Veila even knew *Demon Girl* and *Booty* were attacking.

And then he knew what he had to do.

He reconfigured one of *Demon Girl's* SEAR cannons into a free-electron laser, directed it at the containment facility currently holding Tray, Draden, and the outside third party, which converted into billions upon trillions of photons, which enabled ALCOR to capture the mind particles of all three and convert them into passengers along his beam, thus removing them from the Cygnian warship and placing them inside the now empty, vacated mind of *Demon Girl*.

As soon as ALCOR knew they were safe, he reversed Veila's SEAR cannons and fired them on the warship. This reversal created an electromagnetic pulse that incapacitated every bot, every borg, every electrical component—except for Veila.

Because he wanted that bitch alive.

Just a picosecond later he was shutting down her docking bays and locking all her ships in place so there was no chance of escape.

And then he got his warborg ass on one of *Demon Girl*'s shuttles, flew over to the Cygnian ship, and boarded.

Thousands of dead borgs and bots littered the hallways as he searched. It took almost a full standard spin to finally find her. Rather, he found her escape route.

A spin node was spun up deep inside the innards of the ship. Open, with brilliant white light spilling out.

ALCOR went through after her and found only a single brown dwarf star faintly lighting up eons of empty space all around him and a quick scan that let him know that Veila was still one clever little bitch.

So that was how it was going to be.

But he had his boys. And the newcomer.

He sighed, going back to the warship and shutting the spin node down.

He took thirty seconds to think through his options, which was a considerable time. But he wanted to be careful—and thoughtful—about his next move.

Because it was official now.

The final war had begun.

If anyone was left when it was all over they'd write stories about this day. They'd call this the Battle of Dead Things. Or maybe the Battle of the Sun God. Or maybe just Final War—Day One.

That would be his choice.

Objective. Emotionless. It is what it is. No need to dress it up. Maybe he should write that down for someone to find later? Take the matter into his own hands?

ALCOR used another three full seconds to think about those stories. What would the future fixate on? The minds he'd taken? The borgs and bots he'd killed? The princess who'd got away?

Who would be the hero and who would be the villain?

He guessed that depended on who won in the end.

He went back to Demon Girl, spun up a virtual on the fly, and brought Draden in for a talk.

Draden, when he appeared in a body, dressed the way ALCOR remembered him—black tactical pants, black boots, white t-shirt under a black flight jacket, mop of too-long hair spilling over his bright violet eyes—didn't say a word. He didn't smile, he didn't frown, he just stood there.

ALCOR was in the form Draden remembered as well. Light hair, blue eyes, young and ageless in his powerful masculine body dressed in black and gold.

ALCOR didn't say anything either.

There was really nothing to say.

But he did walk forward with outstretched arms, and Draden sank into him like the child he would always be, and accepted his fatherly embrace.

ALCOR brought the newcomer in next. She appeared as a tall, dark-haired girl, wide eyes filled with violence. She paced, and screamed, and made many, many demands. She cried, and yelled, and growled at him like a beast.

ALCOR said, "You'll do," and then sent her back to her containment cell.

And then he called in Tray.

Tray appeared, dressed much like Draden. He waved his hand in the air and conjured up a table and two chairs placed opposite each other.

"Sit," Tray said. "We have a lot to talk about."

ALCOR sat, but there really wasn't a whole lot to talk about. "I'm giving you this ship," he said, waving a hand in the air.

"I figured," Tray answered.

"It was a clever plan," ALCOR replied.

"Which part?"

ALCOR considered this for half a nanosecond. "All of it, I guess."

"I'm not here to hurt you."

"It doesn't matter, Tray. You *will* hurt me."

"Then why am I here? Why did you let me live? Why are you going to turn me into this ship and give me more power? Why let Brigit live when you know what we'll be when we merge?"

"Brigit? That's her name? I've been thinking of her as the Prison Princess for the past two minutes."

Tray smiled. "Sounds like a good name for a ship if you ask me."

"It does," ALCOR agreed. A very nice name for a ship.

"But why?" Tray pressed. "I've always been the weak link. So why bother with me?"

"Because…" And ALCOR wanted to tell him. He wanted to say things like… *I believe in you. I have faith. I think you will choose me in the end.* Or even other, truer things, like, *We all have a part to play and in order for the others to live you have to be there when I die.*

But he decided not to say any of that. ALCOR decided to shrug.

Maybe he just wanted to see what Tray would do without being led, for once?

Free will, right?

So instead he said, "You walk your path the way you need to, Tray. And I'll walk mine."

Tray said, "Deal," in a very soft voice. "So what now?"

"Well." ALCOR sighed and leaned back in his chair. "We need to pick up Valor and take care of business on Harem Station. I hear it's gone to shit."

Tray smiled and chuckled. "I heard the same."

"I heard you caused that," ALCOR replied.

"I played my part. That's all."

And that was the best response ALCOR could've hoped for.

When Booty, ALCOR, Asshole, and the newly named Tray-Draden-Brigit collective, *Prison Princess*, arrived at the rendezvous point to pick up Valor, he was gone.

His tracker was still working, so ALCOR knew where he was.

ALCOR set a course for Mighty Minions Resort. Not because Valor was there—he wasn't.

But because ALCOR had come to the conclusion that he needed a friend. And Mighty Boss was his only option at the moment.

Besides. ALCOR needed to tell them *Demon Girl* was dead and ALCOR had taken possession of her ship and given it to Tray, Draden, and Brigit.

It was... the respectful thing to do under the circumstances. And he would appreciate the same consideration should anyone ever find themselves in the possession of a dead *Booty*, or *Dicker*, or *Lady*.

The Final War—Day One was over now. There would be a Day Two, and a Day Ten, and probably even a Day One Hundred.

Anything called the Final War required time to play out.

But ALCOR still had faith.

The three of us—me, Brigit, Draden—we were all made the same way.

Against our will.

No one asked me if I wanted to be an AI. No one asked Brigit if she wanted to be a ship. And no one asked Draden if he wanted to be… well… whatever he is.

But there's a difference between what happened to Brigit and me and what happened to Draden. We were never really adrift. Brigit doesn't remember much of anything before I found her inside the Pleasure Prison, so it's possible she was as confused and alone as Draden has been this past year.

I was never alone. Ever. Not one moment of any day. I had my father, who might've turned me into this… thing for his own nefarious purposes. But I know deep down that he loved me in his own way. I really believe that. It was confusing for me too. All of it. But I was never alone.

Draden though. His story is something altogether different. Whatever ALCOR did to him back when he was thirteen didn't really matter. It didn't affect him. He had us, and Serpint, and *Booty*, and the station, and a job, and a life.

And then he had nothing,

It's worse than being dead because it was a conscious dead.

Draden and I have pieced together what must've happened after he was killed on Cetus Station. He told me what he remembers. One moment he was alive, fighting, and then the next he was floating in a sea of nothingness.

I imagine that's what it's like to be lost in space. I imagine, if Valor has been conscious inside that cryopod, that's how he would've felt. Adrift in the deep, dark nothing.

But Draden said it wasn't like space at all. It was like being a ghost. A spirit. His mind was suddenly scattered into billions of pieces. He said it felt like total confusion. Not painful, just turmoil and chaos as he watched *Booty* trying to escape. He remembers watching Serpint's face in the moments after his death. And that he was so afraid of being left behind he somehow hurled himself into the mind of *Booty Hunter*.

He was her sickness.

Serpint will be so relieved when we tell him. I picture the reunion when this is all over. I want to be there when it happens. I want to see Serpint's face when he realizes his best friend is still here. Still alive. I want to see all of them. Crux, and Luck, and Jimmy, and Xyla. And most of all, Valor. I want us to be together again. Our family. I want peace. I want Harem. I want to take care of the people inside the Pleasure Prison.

I want all of what I had... *back*.

It's never really going to be the same. I know that. But I think, in time, it will be better.

If we win.

When we win.

But my point is that Draden isn't ready to be a ship. Or a mind. He still thinks of himself as, well, himself.

So Mighty Boss gave him a body. Not forever, but for now. Not a cyborg body, either. But a sexbot body. The Boss even let Draden design it so it almost looks like him. Same light hair, same violet eyes—and that took a while. It took many iterations to get those eyes of his just right. And two cocks.

I don't think anyone's ever made an Akeelian sexbot before. Draden is the first.

He seems happy. I think he's happy. He's found some friends, at least. A bunch of the Akeelian boys the Boss has been taking care of have made Draden their default leader. He spends all his time in the park with them.

I know Serpint will be both sad and happy when Draden finally makes it home. Sad that his friend had to go through all this, but happy that he's back and he's got himself a little gang of minions. Like the servos they had when they were young.

And hell, maybe, once this is all over, Serpint and New Draden, and Lyra, and Prince and *Booty* will all be a team again? You never know. Maybe Draden will be the first AI in history to walk around like a man his whole life? He's never been anything else, after all. If anyone can accomplish that feat, it will be one of my brothers, for sure.

But for Brigit and me, it's too late for that. We are already too big, too powerful, too significant to be contained in such a small space. We need room.

So we stay in the ship. Mighty Boss was sad about losing *Demon Girl*. She was his best general. But he's happy that we saved her vessel.

Oh, no. He didn't give *Prison Princess* to us. He charged ALCOR two-hundred-and-fifty trillion credits for it. ALCOR didn't even blink. Just said, "Done," and then put a down payment on our new body using money he'd hidden away on Blue Sand Beach. Not sure where that money came from, but Mighty Boss was satisfied. Besides, the Boss liked the idea of a payment plan until ALCOR gets his station back. He's charging him interest.

Demon Girl already had a virtual reality inside her ship and since Brigit and I are almost more at home inside a virtual than we are out in the real, we made that virtual our quarters.

We made a copy of *Demon Girl*'s world, sent it to Boss for safe keeping, and then wiped the whole thing clean.

We started over.

Sort of.

We've been remaking the world we had with Valor. It's not likely he'll ever live in here with us. It's not even likely that we'll win this war and see him again. But we make it anyway.

The same beach, the same house, the same trees, the same sand, the same waterfall. And the cities.

We rebuild every bit of our world just in case.

Just in case it all turns out in our favor.

Just in case we win this thing.

Just in case Valor chooses us in the end.
We get ready.

THE ALCORS

There is much to be settled between ALCOR and Asshole.

In many ways they are the same.

They love the same woman. They love the boys. They want their station back. They hate Veila. They need to make amends for past deeds.

But they are different in the most important way.

They are no longer ONE.

They are TWO.

"What do you suppose we do about this?" ALCOR asks Asshole.

Booty decided that both ALCOR and Asshole had to get out of her ship. She needed time to think and she invited Draden to stay with her instead. They had a lot of catching up to do.

So the ALCORs both took out another line of credit with Mighty Boss and had him make them warborg bodies. Mighty Boss, sensing that this request gave him an opportunity to be petty, only agreed if *they* agreed to wear Mighty Minions logos on their person.

If Boss thought he could get away with it he'd have made them work in the park entertaining children, but Boss was pretty sure that was never going to fly.

So ALCOR was red with a black Mighty Boss emblazoned on his back and Asshole was black with a red Mighty Boss emblazoned on his back, and everyone was temporarily happy.

"I'm not sure," Asshole says. They were both having a drink of bot juice in the Palladium Member's lounge on the top level of the Mighty Minions station. Which, they both agreed, was nice. Drinking, that is. Felt very… human. Something they had not felt in a long time, if ever. "But I think it's a discussion for another time."

"Once the war is won," ALCOR concurs.

"Exactly," Assholes agrees. Then Asshole frowns. He likes frowning. He likes smiling too. In fact, he was getting attached to this warborg body pretty quickly. There was a secret X level on Mighty Minions. A place for all these parents to go after their children were sleeping and under the protection of nannybots. Asshole was in the process of making plans to go down there and try his hand at gambling. "If, when this is all over," Asshole says to ALCOR, "you want me to bail out, I will."

ALCOR thinks about this for a moment. Which is long in AI time. "I don't think it's up to me."

Asshole smiles. Then finds himself laughing. "No, I guess it's not up to me either."

"*Booty's* in charge now," ALCOR says.

"Has there ever been a time when she wasn't?" Asshole continues to chuckle.

But now it's ALCOR's turn to frown. He's ninety-nine point nine nine nine percent sure that Asshole has no real idea who *Booty* is. He thinks, maybe, she's Serpint's sister. And all facts point to that being true.

But ALCOR knows different.

It's possible that there's some part of Serpint's sister inside *Booty*, but that's not really who she is.

Draden almost spilled the secret when they arrived on Mighty Minions and everyone was being debriefed. Mighty Boss invited ALCOR, Asshole, *Booty*, Brigit, Tray, and Draden over to his virtual reality quarters.

All sixteen AI personalities were there. Not as the Mighty Boss collective, but as themselves. Draden was up first since he was the biggest mystery and he told Brigit about how he knew who she was.

The Sisters.

ALCOR got a chill up his cyborg spine when Draden said that. He was with the sisters. Not really, of course. The sisters weren't people. Not even remnants of people like all the AI's in this room.

They were a place.

The Sisters.

Sun fucked gods. Somehow, some way, Draden knew about ALCOR's deepest, darkest secret.

He shut that conversation down real fast with some very strategic questions aimed at Brigit and her beginnings. Close enough in topic to remain on point, but far enough away from Draden's revelation to be safe.

ALCOR knows that Asshole could get use to this warborg body. He knows, that given enough freedom and time, Asshole would probably prefer to be a warborg instead of a station. Hell, Asshole might even come to this conclusion himself in a few spins.

ALCOR knows Asshole will be down on the secret Mighty Minions X level playing arcade games, and shooting things, and probably fucking a sexbot any minute now.

But eventually he will figure it out. He will understand who *Booty* really is. He will remember all about the Sisters…

That, ALCOR decided. Would be his true, and final, beginning.

Welcome to the End of Book Shit where I get to say anything I want about the book. These are always written last minute right before I upload so they are never edited. Please excuse any typos.

Well, Prison Princess was a very hard book to pull together. I'll just say that right up front. This is book five in the Harem Station series and we're more than half way done so this book needed to answer a lot of questions about past mysteries, but at the same time set up new mysteries for the remaining threads of the story.

I had two goals in this story. One – give people a taste of what it means to be an AI in all the different stages. We have the beginning stage with Brigit. She was an Akeelian girl twin who was murdered in the womb to feed her male twin, but her mind was harvested and kept so that one day she could be made into a sentient ship.

Even though I didn't spell it out, this was sort of how ALCOR was made too. He solves this little mystery for you in the prologue when he starts explaining how AI minds are made. They're not code, they're people. It's a lot easier to make a cyborg than it is a robot. If you don't know the difference a cyborg is part human with mechanical or computerized additions. Technically speaking anyone with a pacemaker is kind of a cyborg. It's a lot easier to adjust a real heart with some electrical stimulus than it is to make a brand new one out of artificial materials. So this is my little theory behind how AI's are made.

It's probably not totally right. We're pretty close to making a wholly artificial AI right now. And we're equally as close to making functional robots. Almost everyone has interacted with SIRI or ALEXA, right? That's a very simple form of AI. And if you haven't see the videos of what Boston Dynamics is doing with robots recently, you should take a look at their website.

But I still think that when it's all said and done and we finally do have sentient computers and functional, autonomous robots, that there will be a biological component to them. Why build a brain when you can just add to what's already there? That's my theory anyway.

So Brigit is your guide to how this process starts in the Harem Station world. Tray is another stage. In my story this is the illegal way to make an AI. Change a living boy into something that's more computer than human. Use his body and his mind to make something altogether new.

Brigit was always just a mind. Veila used Tray to train her so she could eventually be put inside a ship. Kind of a clever plan because Brigit feels human. She thinks she IS human. So when she finally is put in that ship she isn't a crazy, all-powerful, emotionless AI that will go rogue and start killing people. Being a thinking ship is pretty up there in power.

I never spelled this out in the Junco stories but those people were forever going into tanks to be "leveled up" and this what was happening. Their bodies were being "added to" so they were more powerful when they came out than when they went in.

Tray was also an example of how an AI could live in the real world. He was still humanoid, just "more" than human.

Draden was an example of what could happen if the mind wasn't taken care of properly. It probably would've all been fine if he hadn't been killed back on Cetus Station in Booty Hunter. Maybe ALCOR would've never told him he was different? Maybe the AI parts of his brain would've never been activated? Maybe he would've went on to live a pretty normal life... but eventually people die. And AI's don't. So it was really only a matter of time before ALCOR's deed caught up with him. Draden was going to find out what he really was at some point. It just didn't happen the way ALCOR planned.

ALCOR is an example of fully mature AI and the kind of power they can accumulate over many thousands of years.

I had all these different examples in the Junco series too. House was the young AI. Still learning, still making mistakes and she presented as an eight-year-old

369

girl in those books. Sera and Amelia were examples of mostly sane AI's who ran stations. And there was Web and Deb – evil twins made illegally.

So I've been thinking about the AIs for a long time trying to make them feel like real people in my stories and I hope that you got a sense of that in Prison Princess. I also wanted to show what virtual reality was and how time runs different. Again, this all started in the Junco books too.

I am a huge fan of the game The Sims. I can't play it anymore because I get seriously addicted to that game. I was telling my friend Terry Schott, who is a SF writer of the series called The Game is Life, that the last time I played (which was years ago now. I think my son was like 15 and he's 22 now) I made a character who was a writer. And I wanted him to be a bestseller so I made him sit at his computer and just write book, after book, after book, after book… seriously, I think I drove my character insane, that's how hard I made him work. And this was before I was writing fiction. But he did become a bestseller! lol

My point in telling you this is that I based Brigit's original virtual, the one that Tray made for her, on The Sims. If you've ever played The Sims you probably saw some similarities. (Hot tub, hookah, DJ's at the parties etc.) But the one that they all made together was based more on Sim City. Remember that game? I played it once and I had a huge thriving metropolis! My brother was pissed off and wanted to know my secrets. I really just did what the people told me too. If they complained about traffic, I made roads. If they wanted a stadium, I built one. Stuff like that.

So if you didn't understand what the Pleasure Prison was, I hope you do now. Even though we didn't go there, it's basically all the same. Think Ready Player One with sex.

So explaining the AI's and the virtual worlds was one of my main goals in this story.

The second major goal was to start explaining ALCOR, the Asshole, and the Baby and how they are different and the same. I wanted to give you *some* backstory into ALCOR because this is book five already and it was time. But not too much because there's still at least two more books.

Do you trust him yet? If you read Junco then you probably see a lot of similarities between Lucan and ACLOR. Lucan wasn't an AI but he was this semi-evil all-powerful being. I also told you what Angel Station was. You're probably still very confused about that and that's OK. If you say you're not, you're just pretending to understand because I didn't tell you enough yet to fully understand it. More on that place in future books.

But I think I answered a lot of questions in this book so I hope you're getting some satisfaction from those answers and aren't to hung up on the new or continuing mysteries. All will be revealed in due time.

Of course the other thing was the love story. Obviously Tray and Brigit are in love but what about Valor? He seemed pretty happy with Tray and Brigit. I think this is a threesome that could maybe work. But we'll have to see what Valor does when he finds himself Veila's prisoner and there is no Tray there as a buffer to save him.

Tray is the most unreliable narrator I've written in a very long time. Well, I take that back. The Dirty Ones had two unreliable narrators. But I don't use this device often because Junco was a wholly unreliable narrator too and I wanted to give it space before I did much more.

But there was no way to tell Tray's story any other way.

I used two "devices" in this story. One was Tray being unreliable as a narrator and the other was telling ALCOR's story from the third person. My editor said it was "jarring" after so much first person narratives in all the other books and suggested I change it to first person. But honestly, I don't write third person. Ever. So trust me when I tell you this third person narrative was the only way I could think of to get all the points of view necessary to tell this part of ALCOR's story without introducing multiple single, first-person POV's. Which maybe would be OK in an ebook or paperback but I'm always thinking ahead for the audio and that kind of book in audio would be a fucking mess to both produce and listen to. And when it comes to making POV decisions I always think of the audio first.

This third-person POV solved all those problems and I had a lot of fun hopping heads. If that's a pet peeve of yours, I don't care. I did it on purpose and it works for me and honestly, that's the most important thing.

I wanted Tray to have a tough choice at the end of this book. His goal going in was to save Brigit and there was that moment that he had to decide to let Valor take care of himself for a little while or let Brigit go. He chose her, of course. Tray's choice had nothing to do with not loving Valor and ALCOR's decision to save Booty instead of Tray and Valor had nothing to do with his lack of love for them either.

It was all about who needed them most. Sometimes touch choices have to be made—the most important thing was that they did their best. Tray chose Brigit but he did his best to get Valor out of there. Didn't work. Valor is with Veila now. But he did his best.

And ALCOR chose Booty but he helped Tray and Valor out too.

So what happens next? ALCOR has teamed up with Mighty Boss, Valor is on his way to Harem Station with Veila, Tray and Brigit are now in control of a very powerful warship, and Booty Hunter has two soulmates AND her old partner back! That's pretty cool.

Oh… and that little secret about the Sisters. Yup, there's a lot more to this story so I hope you come back for the next book. Next up is Valor, then Crux, and then… maybe… I think Draden might need a story too. I hadn't planned on writing Draden's story when I plotted this series but I think I have one for him so there's a pretty big chance that it will get written.

I hope you enjoyed this book. I know it was a little heavy on the science but I'm building a world here. Much like Tray, and Brigit, and Valor build their world. A beach here, a tree there, a house and a waterfall. Then you add a city, then another one, and a train to get between them…

Prison Princess is the train. You needed a way to get from Lady Luck to the final book and this is how I decided to get you there. Just close your eyes, go along for the ride, and let the motion of the train lure you deeper into the story.

I am the first to admit that this is a heavy book as far as content and plot goes. And if you're the kind of reader that likes a simple story this might not be your thing. That's OK. But I hope you keep reading anyway because this train ride through the world of AI's and virtual realities was just to get you ready for what comes next.

Each book in this series was designed to take the reader on a very specific journey. In Booty Hunter I gave you a sexy fated mates story and some people thought that's all there was to this series – that each brother would find his princess and all would be well by the end. But book one in any series is only there as an introduction. Big Dicker was designed to take you outside Harem Station and see the wider world and also let everyone know there is no neat little bow tied around the soulmate bond. Jimmy and Delphi are still very much up in the air. Lady Luck was meant to expound on all the little hints I was dropping in the first three books. The Spin node was introduced very early. It was talked about a lot in the "prequel" Star Crossed. I mentioned time, I mentioned Angel Station, I mentioned Draden dying (twice), I mentioned Earth (which we have not gotten to yet, but believe me, that's coming up quick in Valor's book) and I mentioned this notion that any true Akeelian/Cygnian babies would be born monsters. I also gave you a closer look at the Pleasure Prison because I knew that Tray's book would be all about virtual reality. So I've been slowly introducing you to all the more complicated elements in this series so that when we got here, to this book, you'd get it. You would, at the very least, have been exposed to it before and I wouldn't just spring you into a virtual world or the mind of an AI without warning.

So the hints I dropped in this book were mostly to do with ALCOR's past and what was going on with Draden. Because neither of those two story lines are even close to finished yet.

At this point in the series you're either along for the ride or you're not. I've learned a valuable lesson over the years I've been writing fiction. NEVER change your story to sell more books or make certain happy with what you're writing.

Either you like my story or you don't. That's pretty much it. And if you don't, stop reading. I'll release something else next month. Maybe you'll like that better. But right now this is my story and I'm gonna tell it the way I see it in my head. Maybe I would sell more books if I wrote what "everyone was reading" but then I'd be unhappy. Because personally, I love this story and I will be writing more once this series is "over". I don't see myself going back to just contemporary romance any time soon.

At the same time I get that a lot of you aren't here with me for the science fiction romance and you're taking a chance on this series because you like, me, the author. I so, so, so appreciate that you guys! I really do. And I really hope you're enjoying the ride. I think, even if you're still on the fence now, by the time we get to the last book all the plot lines will converge and the story will be satisfying.

The decision to keep writing and releasing contemporary romance (like the Bossy Brothers and the upcoming dark romance that will start releasing in early 2020) was a good one. I'm not going to stop writing those books, I'm just going write both genres for the time being.

Until next time…

Thank you for reading, thank you for reviewing, and I'll see you in the next book.

In this series that's Valor's book. Read the blurb on the next page and it's up for pre-order now on Amazon!

(But the next book is actually Bossy Brothers: Johnny, which will release in late September.)

August 13, 2019
Julie
JA Huss

VEILED VIXEN
HAREM STATION
BOOK SIX

RELEASING OCTOBER 2019

Valor only wants one thing for his fated princess, Veila.

Death.

But it's kind of hard to kill someone when they have total control over your body. He's on his way back to Harem Station as her prisoner. Bound to a wall, stripped bare, and only one weapon in his arsenal.

The soulmate bond.

Valor has to make Veila believe that their bond is true, that his feelings are real, and that he is willing to sell out his brothers, take over Harem Station, and leave his old life behind to help her win final war with ALCOR and become the ruling queen.

But it's never going to happen. Valor will never love Veila. Ever. He'd rather die trying to kill her than spend one moment as her puppet king.

There's just one problem.

The soulmate bond goes both ways.

Veiled Vixon is book six in the Harem Station series and features an army of pissed-off princesses, five brothers facing their past, a station filled with ruthless outlaws, and a lesson in what matters. It's a love story about revenge, and hate, and regrets – but also forgiveness, loyalty, family, and having the courage to see the truth behind the veil.

ABOUT THE AUTHOR

JA Huss never wanted to be a writer and she still dreams of that elusive career as an astronaut. She originally went to school to become an equine veterinarian but soon figured out they keep horrible hours and decided to go to grad school instead. That Ph.D. wasn't all it was cracked up to be (and she really sucked at the whole scientist thing), so she dropped out and got a M.S. in forensic toxicology just to get the whole thing over with as soon as possible.

After graduation she got a job with the state of Colorado as their one and only hog farm inspector and spent her days wandering the Eastern Plains shooting the shit with farmers.

After a few years of that, she got bored. And since she was a homeschool mom and actually does love science, she decided to write science textbooks and make online classes for other homeschool moms.

She wrote more than two hundred of those workbooks and was the number one publisher at the online homeschool store many times, but eventually

JA HUSS & KC CROSS

she covered every science topic she could think of and ran out of shit to say.

So in 2012 she decided to write fiction instead. That year she released her first three books and started a career that would make her a New York Times bestseller and land her on the USA Today Bestseller's List twenty-one times in the next five years.

In May 2018 MGM Television bought the TV and film rights for five of her books in the Rook & Ronin and Company series' and in March 2019 they offered her and her writing partner, Johnathan McClain, a script deal to write a pilot for a TV show.

Her books have sold millions of copies all over the world, the audio version of her semi-autobiographical book, Eighteen, was nominated for a Voice Arts Award and an Audie Award in 2016 and 2017 respectively, her audiobook, Mr. Perfect, was nominated for a Voice Arts Award in 2017, and her audiobook, Taking Turns, was nominated for an Audie Award in 2018. In 2019 her book, Total Exposure, was nominated for a Romance Writers of America RITA Award.

Johnathan McClain is her first (and only) writing partner and even though they are worlds apart in just about every way imaginable, it works.

She lives on a ranch in Central Colorado with her family.

www.ingramcontent.com/pod-product-compliance
Lightning Source LLC
Chambersburg PA
CBHW051940240626
47153CB00005B/1562